# Dirty Little Angel

# Dirty Little Angel

## by

# Erica Hilton

Dirty Little Angel. Copyright © by Melodrama Publishing. All rights reserved. Printed in the United States of America. No part of this book may be used or reproduced in any manner whatsoever without written permission except in the case of brief quotations embodied in critical articles or reviews. For information, address Melodrama Publishing, P.O. Box 522, Bellport, NY 11713.

www.melodramapublishing.com

Library of Congress Control Number: 2007943743
ISBN-13: 978-1934157190
ISBN-10: 1934157198
First Edition: September 2008
10 9 8 7 6 5 4 3 2

# 1

"I get money," blared throughout The Magic Spot, a strip club in West Philly. It was Chaos's theme song every night that she performed. She loved 50 Cent and loved his new hit single with a passion. Every time she got on stage to dance, she requested that the DJ play that song for her opening act.

She twirled herself around the long pole that was positioned from the ceiling to the stage, spinning around in her six-inch wedge heels like a little girl on the playground. She was completely naked, her body gleaming with a mixture of sweat and baby oil as she performed her routine. Her trimmed pubic hairs were in plain view for dozens of men as they ogled over her. Her curvy figure was flawless from head to toe, and her long, side-swept bangs were slightly longer at the crown. It was the perfect hairstyle for her beautiful round face.

Chaos's saucy bedroom eyes stared into the crowd of men as they tossed money at her and fantasized about being in between the sheets with such a beautiful woman. It was clear that she was high and a bit tipsy from the Patrón she'd been sipping on with her girls in the back, but it was her new drink and it was how she got through the night.

Her full, glossy lips curled into a full smile as she cupped her full-sized breasts, which displayed chocolate, erect nipples. Chaos crouched seductively in front of one of her male customers and teased him, her trimmed pussy just inches from his reach. It was apparent that she could easily be the cover girl for *Smooth* or *King* magazines. Her body was just that tight.

She moved closer to the middle-aged man who was at the club almost every night. He wore thick glasses and wasn't stingy with his money. Bobby was known for buying the girls drinks all night and having wandering hands. He loved to touch the ladies and had an octopus-like grip. He clutched one hundred dollars in one-dollar bills in his right hand and was willing to give it all to Chaos.

Chaos took his free hand and slowly moved it between her thighs, close to her goodies. Bobby showed off a broad smile and asked, "Damn, Chaos, why you keep teasing me like this?"

Chaos smiled and moved her pussy closer to his eager reach. Bobby was ready to finger fuck her, but Chaos unexpectedly moved her pussy back a bit and said soothingly, "C'mon Bobby, you know if you wanna play, then you gotta pay."

Bobby flashed a smile and began sprinkling the bills onto her, letting the money rain down on her slowly. Chaos beamed and rubbed the bills all over her chest, giggling as she felt herself becoming aroused. She moved closer to Bobby again and positioned her smooth, meaty thighs around his shoulders, so that her pulsating pussy was up in his face. A few fellows seated next to Bobby peered over with overexcited expressions on their faces—waiting to witness some kind of freakish act.

"Damn, Chaos, I never get tired of you," Bobby proclaimed.

"You better not! You always do me right, Bobby," Chaos replied.

She felt his alcoholic breath blow against her pussy lips and her legs began to quiver as his fingers ran across her thighs. Chaos arched into a backbend, the palms of her hands flat against the stage. She was athletic and well toned, able to contort her body in many different positions that drove niggas crazy.

"You like to eat out, Bobby?" Chaos asked with a smile.

Bobby began to feel her up, yearning for her body to press against his. He had a strong crush on Chaos. He grew erect, wishing Chaos would help take care of his hard dick; but he knew not to get too close or disrespect her, because she was Crown's girl. To get close to Crown's girl, niggas had to pay some serious cash just to sniff the pussy.

Crown was a high-end pimp nigga with a bad temper. He was well known in West Philly, mostly for turning out young chicks to the game and getting rich from what his ladies sold between their legs. He was from South Jamaica, Queens, but got into a beef a few years back with some gangsters and had to leave town in a hurry. Philly had been his home for the past ten years and he had definitely made a reputation for himself.

Crown traveled in style, sporting upscale fashions and blinged out in platinum and diamonds, looking like a blend of Slick Rick and Snoop Dogg. He was tall and stocky with a long perm, a trimmed goatee, and a platinum grill piece that shined like the sun when he smiled.

He definitely had swagger. Crown loved the spotlight and everything about pussy—the look of it, the smell of it, the addiction to it, the feel of it, and especially the money it brought him daily.

Crown had four chicks working for him, each of them having their own traits and diverse bodies. Midnight was his tall, raven beauty from Kentucky. She had the big country booty, big country tits, and a southern slang that drove the men crazy. She was tall and dark-skinned, 5'11" and was the new girl on the scene. She was very passive and somewhat naïve; she was only nineteen and grew up around farmland most of her life.

Then there was Cherish, who was from Philly and had a fierce temper like Crown. Cherish loved the street life. She was 5'6" with a sweet, caramel complexion and a thick, curvaceous body like Beyoncé. Cherish was cute in the face but a thug everywhere else, and she would cut a nigga or a bitch quickly if you fucked with her or her boo, Crown. She loved Crown and everything about him and got jealous quickly when he paid more attention to his other hoes—or any other bitch—when she was around. Cherish's reputation was also fierce, and those who knew about her tried to stay on her good side.

There was Sweet, who had a body like Chaos, but wasn't much of a beauty like the rest of the girls. Sweet had a lazy left eye and tended to wear shades out of insecurity. Her hair was mostly a rich weave that she sewed in herself. The piercings and tattoos that covered sixty percent of her body were somewhat intimidating for some of the men, who sometimes thought that she was a dyke. Sweet's attitude and sexuality made up strongly for what she lacked in the face. Like Crown and Chaos, she was from New York—Bed-Stuy—and moved to Philly to make a better life for herself and to escape the criticism from her family because she was.

Sweet met Crown at a bus stop on Broad Street when he pulled up to her in his bright red convertible Benz and asked if she needed a ride. She was somewhat impressed by the car, but skeptical about taking a ride with a stranger, especially one who was clad in a blue mink coat on a fall day and had two large diamond studded earrings in both ears and a diamond-grill.

Sweet was alone and the coldness in the evening air started to make her tremble. She was dressed in a light jacket and a long skirt and it was a long bus ride to the Gallery mall.

"You'll catch a cold out here in that jacket, beautiful," Crown had said, eyeing Sweet and knowing she was full of potential.

"I'm good," Sweet had replied.

"You sure, luv? I'm in no rush. I like what I see and I'm going wherever you're going. Just give me a few minutes and I promise I got some things that you'd like to hear, believe me. I ain't tryin' to waste your time or mines," Crown had said with confidence and a strong stature.

Sweet smiled. She tried to play hardball with him, but inside, she was as gullible as a little girl during her first kiss. She wanted love. She wanted to be noticed. She wanted security. She hated her job at the clothing store in the Gallery and always dreamed of having a better life.

Crown had been watching her for a month, unbeknownst to her. He first noticed her when he was in the store where she worked to purchase some jeans. He spotted Sweet standing alone and noticed her insecurities. He noticed the lazy eye and saw how she turned her attention away from customers who stared at her for too long. But her body was tight and showed through her beige slacks and white collared work clothing. From that point on, Crown made a mental note to keep an eye on her.

Crown gave Sweet a moment to think about it, and within a moment, she nodded and jumped into the car. Crown smiled, extended his hand out to her, and said, "I'm Crown, beautiful . . . and you are?"

"Kathy," she said, shaking Crown's hand and noticing his impeccable manicure and the encrusted yellow gold diamond ring on his pinky finger.

"Kathy, huh? Typical, but we'll work on that," Crown replied and pulled off.

Kathy a.k.a. Sweet had never been in such a nice ride before and felt like a queen in a noble carriage. She wanted to melt in the plush burgundy leather seats. He had a Chaka. Khan track playing, and she was impressed by his style and taste of music.

She glanced at Crown and noticed how sharp and handsome he looked up close. His smooth, black skin looked polished, and his trimmed goatee highlighted his full lips, his teeth looking white as snow, even under his iced-out mouth grill. His long hair was perfect and straightened out, every strand looking like it was precisely placed.

She felt nervous to speak around him, asking herself, *Why does this nigga want to holla at me?* But Sweet kept her opinions to herself and went along for the ride. She avoided eye contact with him mostly, hating her lazy eye, but Crown made her feel comfortable about herself.

"You're a beautiful woman, Kathy, so stop tryin' to avoid eye contact wit' me. I don't give a fuck about your eye, I care about the woman, and one little flaw doesn't stop me from noticing the rest of you," Crown said with zeal in his voice.

Crown made her smile because no man had ever said that about her before. She knew he was different from most niggas that tried to get at her who only wanted pussy or a blowjob and veered away from having a relationship with her. She was far from being wifey material because they didn't feel comfortable around her. She had too many tattoos (a red devil, numerous flowers and butterflies, and her name in curvy letters) and some of the piercings made her look like a freak. But when it came to her body and her pussy, they jumped on them with the quickness—wham, bang, thank you, bitch—and "I'm good," right afterwards.

Niggas wanted no love from her—just a fuck and a suck. So it fucked with Sweet, and her low self-esteem made her easy and somewhat the talk of the town.

"Can I be honest wit' you, luv?" Crown asked.

"About what?" Sweet asked in a low tone.

"I had noticed you a month before . . . you work at Champions in the Gallery, right?"

"What, you stalking me now?"

"Nah, just needed the right time to get wit' you. I saw you around and when I peeped you at the bus stop, I had to come say hi," he said.

"I'm just shocked that I caught your eye," she replied.

"Why?"

"I don't know, it's just, you're a fine lookin' man."

"And, boo, you gotta stop doubting yourself. Let me tell you somethin'. Power and confidence attracts people to you. To be powerless and feeble repels muthafuckas away from you, so stop acting like you're unattractive, 'cause you ain't. You're beautiful."

She flashed a smile and glanced at him for a moment. "So what you do anyway?" she asked.

"I do me, beautiful. I make my ends."

"How?"

"We can talk about how I get money in the future, but I wanna know about you. Talk to me, beautiful," he said.

Crown called her beautiful to make her sure of herself and make her more comfortable around him. The more she heard the word beautiful come from his lips, the more trust she would put into him. He wanted to tap into her mind first—make love to her soul and change her way of thinking—before he touched her physically. He hated for any of his women to feel negatively about themselves, as negativity brought him less dollars. A positive female was a controlling bitch, and a controlling bitch knew how to regulate a trick for that extra bread. Although he didn't like for his women to have low self-esteem, they needed to be obedient. Crown didn't hesitate to put the smack down!

Crown hated the pimps that drugged their bitches and talked trash to them, bringing down their self-esteem. To him, you couldn't trust a drugged bitch who hated herself, and she was like damaged goods on the streets.

But Crown wasn't scared to put a bitch in place whenever they came out of pocket. He was often violent with his whores to show them that he was in control. He was their daddy. He didn't love his bitches and saw them as currency. In a way, they were like livestock; if you treated your stock right, kept 'em well groomed, fed, and well taken care of they'd never leave home.

Crown was fine, persuasive, a true hustler, and a good fuck. He would lay the pipe game down on his chicks and show them how to fuck a nigga wit' a big dick. He schooled all his hoes on how to suck and fuck a trick off and keep them coming back. You always do a nigga right, but not too right—always have them wanting for more, he would say. And they always gotta pay to play, was his personal motto.

Crown drove across the Vine St. Expressway and slowed down at a red light at Race Street. He continued to talk to Sweet like he cared. He let her talk and he listened, knowing that sometimes a bitch just wanted an outlet. So he played the part, like a concerned boyfriend.

By the time Crown pulled up in front of The Gallery mall on Market Street, he knew much about Sweet—her family, her likes and dislikes, her worries, and her love of travel. He would later use the information she disclosed to his advantage.

Before Sweet stepped out of his car, Crown asked, "So what you lookin' for, beautiful?"

"I just wanna be happy," she said.

"We can see about that, beautiful. I wanna make you happy," Crown replied with a smile.

Sweet smiled back.

"I'll be back around to pick you up when you get off at ten and we'll definitely talk," he said.

Sweet nodded and walked toward the mall, feeling like she'd met the perfect man. That same night, Crown was parked out front, waiting to pick her up and continue their chat. He took her to eat at Ms. Tootsie's, this chic soul food restaurant on South Street. He laid his game down on her heavily and had Sweet feeling like she was the next Ms. Universe.

Within the week, Crown made love to her mind and built her confidence so much, that when they finally had sex, Sweet was totally submissive to him and wanted to please Crown in every way imaginable. When Sweet saw the package he was workin' with, she glowed. Crown had worked his way into her life subtly and slowly starting from her mind, worked his way down to her pussy, pleasing Sweet from head to toe. In the end, he knew he would be her life.

Chaos continued to seduce Bobby with her spicy stage performance. She parted her sweet, juicy pussy lips with the tips of her fingers and played with her clit, arching her back and giving Bobby one hell of a show. Her gentle, manicured fingers ran in and out of her hole like a dick and Bobby couldn't help but gawk at her as he massaged his hardened dick through his pants.

"You ready for me, Bobby?" Chaos asked.

Bobby's heart raced and his hormones raged like a bull in the rodeo. Pussy was the only thing on his mind and Chaos had him in the palm of her hands. Bobby opened his wallet and saw the $300 that he had left from his paycheck. He needed to pay bills with the money, but watching Chaos her play with her pussy was making him think otherwise.

Chaos crawled up to him on her knees and pushed her soft tits into his face. She noticed Crown walk into the joint clad in a long white mink, designer Gucci shades and white wingtip shoes. He looked like a throwback pimp from the seventies. Cherish was by his side in a tight denim mini-skirt and stiletto boots, Sweet was in a micro-mini dress, and Midnight trailed behind them in a catsuit. Crown clutched a cigar between his fingers and scanned the area, looking for his hoes. He took a pull from the cigar and made his way toward the stage where Chaos was working.

Bobby turned and noticed Crown coming his way and got a little nervous. He feared Crown but loved Chaos.

"What's the matter, Bobby? My daddy got you nervous?" Chaos teased.

"Nah, I'm okay," he lied.

Crown towered over Bobby and focused on Chaos. He took another pull from the cigar and asked, "Bitch, you workin' this trick for my fuckin' money?"

"Yes, Daddy," Chaos replied meekly.

Crown looked down at Bobby. "Nigga, you tipping my bitch, right?"

"Yeah, Crown. You know I always got love for Chaos."

"So, nigga, if you got love for her like that, then take her to the back and have her love your ass right back. She'll love you real fuckin' good for that right price. And, nigga, you look like you need some lovin'."

Bobby didn't reply. He looked back at Chaos and watched her crawl up to him on all fours. She moved her lips near his, teasing him like she was about to go in for a kiss and then pecked him on his cheek.

Bobby had never been so hard. He wanted to fuck Chaos with a passion, but he didn't want to come out of the pocket with that $150 she charged for pussy.

Crown watched the show for a short moment, admiring how his bitch took control of a trick like he taught her. He knew it would be a matter of time before Bobby made Crown's pockets a bit richer.

"Nigga, go ahead and get you some fuckin' pussy." It was more of a command than a suggestion. "Stop fuckin' teasing yourself, Bobby. How much you got on you?"

Crown knew that Bobby was intimidated by him, so he used that to his advantage.

Bobby glanced up at Crown and meekly replied, "Crown, I'm just here to observe. I mean, next time . . ."

"Nigga, fuck next time," Crown exclaimed.

"Nigga, you scared of pussy?" Cherish smirked.

"How much you got?" Crown asked again.

"Crown, I mean . . . I ain't got much," Bobby said.

"Nigga, how much you got?"

Bobby knew he was being bullied by Crown for his cash. It wasn't the first time that it happened and it wouldn't be the last. The other patrons in the bar minded their own business; they knew not to get into Crown's business.

"Look, Bobby, either you pay to fuck Chaos or I'm just gonna just straight take it from you," Crown threatened. "I see how you look at her. You know the pussy is good, so go do what you do and don't take too fuckin' long."

"Crown, I would, but I got bills to pay. I can't spend that loot tonight," Bobby tried to reason.

"Then what the fuck you doin' in the club then, touching my fuckin' woman like you ready to fuck? You came to have a good time, right? Then go and have yourself a good time, nigga!" Crown glared at Bobby.

Bobby knew that there was no talking his way out of it. Yes, he so badly wanted to fuck Chaos, but the $300 in his pocket needed to last him until next week. It was money for food, car insurance, and gas money, and without it, he would be fucked until his next paycheck.

Chaos stepped off stage, still nude and grabbed Bobby's hand affectionately. "C'mon Bobby. I'll make it worth your time."

His dick was saying yes, but he knew it was going to hurt his pockets. He also knew it wouldn't be good to go against Crown. Bobby was 5'7", stumpy, and the only street rep he had was getting pulled over for speeding a few months back. He was no match for Crown or the goons that ran the streets under him.

"Nigga, you got a job, so you'll make the money back. I'm doin' you a favor. Go fuck that bitch before I get mad and just end up takin' your shit anyway—and you won't even see the pussy." Crown snarled.

Bobby reached into his wallet and passed Crown $150.

"Nah, Chaos is worth two hundred," Crown said.

"Two?" Bobby was confused.

"Yeah, muthafucka. Two."

Reluctantly, Bobby passed Crown another $50 and followed Chaos into a back room that was sectioned off from the rest of the club.

Crown watched Bobby leave with Chaos. "Stupid muthafucka! Think he could just put his greasy hands all over my bitch, and I ain't gonna have that nigga come out of his pocket? Shit, I'm gonna get my money."

"Crown, why you do that to Bobby? He's cool peoples," Midnight asked.

"Bitch, did I tell you to fuckin' speak?" Crown snapped at Midnight.

Midnight turned her eyes away quickly, regretting that she opened her mouth.

"Shut your fuckin' mouth, then!"

Crown downed a shot of Patrón and talked to a few associates at the bar. He was waiting for Chaos to finish fucking Bobby.

Bobby was saddened by the loss of $200, but staring at a butt-naked Chaos, who looked like the poster child for Black Tail magazine, made him suddenly think that it was worth it. The VIP room was small but comfortable and was only decorated with a torn two-seater leather couch and barren walls. The room reeked of sex from previous customers, and a few open condom wrappers were lying around the wastebasket.

Bobby fell back against the couch and stared up at Chaos. He could feel his erection tearing through his boxers as he watched Chaos rip open a condom and move closer to him.

He unbuckled his pants and asked Chaos, "Why Crown gotta always be fuckin' wit' me? I mean, I do y'all right, pay for it when I can. But he ain't gotta be embarrassing me in front of everyone, like I'm some herb."

Chaos was on her knees, helping Bobby with his jeans and listening to him complain. She personally thought that Bobby was a punk, but he was cool and he was always good to her.

"I mean, damn, Chaos, two hundred? How am I gonna live for the week?" he asked himself aloud.

That wasn't Chaos's problem. She heard him talk, but was far from listening. She pulled out Bobby's erection and stroked him delicately. Bobby let out a tender moan as Chaos's soft grip clutched around his thick piece of meat. He slithered down on the couch a bit and soon forgot about Crown and the money.

"Let me relax you, baby," Chaos crooned, moving her soft grip up and down his thick shaft.

She rolled the condom onto Bobby's dick and positioned herself above his lap. She guided his dick into her slowly, feeling his width stretch her open as she straddled him. Bobby held Chaos tightly against him, her tits pressed against his chest, and grabbed her phat ass for a better thrust. He breathed heavily against her neck.

"Aaaaaahhh, you feel so fuckin' good Chaos," he moaned.

"I know, I know," she replied, making her pussy contract against him.

Bobby moaned and panted louder. "Oh shit!"

# 2

Crown was still at the bar with Cherish and Midnight by his side. He sipped a Kamikaze and waited for Chaos to finish with Bobby. He was left alone by the other patrons as he schooled his hoes by the bar about gettin' that money and eyed potential tricks from a short distance.

"All I know, is that bitch better hurry the fuck up wit' makin' that money. I ain't running a 7-Eleven out this bitch," he complained to no one in particular.

After getting screamed on, Midnight knew to speak only when spoken to, and Cherish didn't give a fuck about the situation. She had her eyes on a potential trick and knew that with Crown's permission, she could come up with some cash for the night for him.

Crown downed his drink and then said to his hoes, "Yo, y'all bitches go do what y'all do and don't fuckin' come back here empty handed. Go make me that muthafuckin' money."

"You know it, Daddy," Cherish said and walked toward the nigga that had been eyeing her for a minute.

Crown turned his attention away from his hoes and said to the bartender, "Yo, let me get another one."

His long white mink was sparkling clean and his jewelry gleamed like the sun itself. His long permed hair rested against his shoulders like he was royalty. He was like a fashionable monument placed in the middle of the bar—an icon for what a pimp should be.

"Yo, Crown, I don't know how you have your chicks in control the way that you do," Angel, the bartender, said with a hint of admiration in his voice. He was always amazed by Crown's way with the ladies and how he controlled them like puppets on a long string.

"Angel, them bitches is like my dogs. Once you train them right, you ain't never gotta worry about them biting the hand that feeds them," Crown boasted.

Angel laughed as he poured Crown's drink. He shook his head and said, "Man, if I could be you for one day."

"Ain't no college degree in pimping, Angel. Trying to be like me would take a lifetime to learn. When God made me, He knew I was only born to be a pimp," Crown said.

"I hear that."

Crown downed his second drink. He noticed YB come into the bar, flanked by his cousin, Rufus.

"Muthafucka," Crown mouthed.

He and YB had an ongoing beef for months because YB was one of the few who didn't fear Crown. YB thought Crown was a weak loudmouth. He hated niggas from New York coming into his hometown and acting like they were running shit.

YB eyed Crown from a short distance and a smirk appeared across his face. He nudged his cousin Rufus and said, "Look at this clown-ass nigga here."

Rufus chuckled and knew it was about to be on. He and his cousin were straight hoods from the west side of Philly. They were into everything from drugs to murder and were two of the most feared men in the city.

YB was a tall figurehead, 6'2" with long braids that reached down his back and striking, smooth dark skin like the night itself. Ladies considered him easy on the eyes, but you could see that he lived a hard life. He hardly smiled and the scar that lined his right cheekbone was an illustration of the harsh life he'd lived since he was five years old.

The only things YB knew were drugs and violence. He earned his respect by hurting and sometimes killing others to survive.

Rufus was the opposite when it came to his looks; he was shorter and stockier than YB. His stomach was big, matching his arms and chest. He sported close-cropped hair and was dark like his cousin, but not as attractive. His lips were black from the weed he smoked constantly, and his eyes were dark and beady as if he were always squinting into the sun.

Both men were clad in Eagles football jerseys, Timberlands, and baggy jeans, but Rufus was the one concealing the .357 tucked in his waistband, snug under his gut. He was the one ready for anything, and seeing Crown in his presence made him more eager to use the gun.

"Crown, I don't need to trouble in here tonight, please," Angel pleaded.

"Nigga, you better check them niggas if you don't want no trouble. Fuck I look like to you?" Crown angrily replied.

Angel shook his head and went about his business. Crown glanced over at YB and shot him a resentful look.

YB paid the nigga no mind and moved through the seedy and dimly lit joint like he owned the place. Rufus was right behind him, being his number two and watching his cousin's back.

YB looked around for Chaos; she was the only bitch he had an eye for, and Crown knew it. YB felt something for her that was unexplainable.

He loved Chaos's demeanor—the way she moved, hustled, and talked.

Even though YB hated niggas from New York, Chaos was something different. He knew she came from the Bronx, but that didn't stop him from having a thing for her. In his mind, Chaos was a down-ass bitch, and he could never figure how Crown got her to do what she did for him.

YB and Chaos met a few months ago, which was around the same time the beef between YB and Crown started. Crown was jealous. He noticed the way Chaos would look at YB, and he felt his bitches should have eyes like that only for him. Crown was furious with Chaos and would beat her just for laying eyes on the nigga.

YB hated a man who beat on women. He was a thug, but he lived by a code that you don't harm women or children. Crown lived by no code, treated his women like products, and made money off their blood, sweat, and tears. YB never respected that type of behavior. He always felt that a true hustler earned his own way through his own sweat and pain. To him, a pimp was a pussy nigga who was scared to get his own hands dirty in the game of life.

YB spotted Sweet, giving a nigga a lap dance in the corner. Crown turned and noticed YB approaching Sweet. His face stiffened and he felt anger and rage growing in his heart.

Sweet had a young nigga in a darkened corner, with her tits pressed against his young face. She grinded on the nigga with fervor and moved her body in tune with a Chris Brown song. She felt his dick hardening through his jeans and wrapped her arms around him, then whispered in his ear, "I can take care of that for you for the right price."

The young nigga smiled. He was tempted by her offer and had had pussy on his mind since he walked into the club. Sweet felt his hands grabbing her ass sternly and knew it was only a matter of time before she enticed him for a private party in the VIP room.

"Sweet, what's good wit' you?" YB asked as he approached from behind.

Sweet turned and a warm smiled curved from her lips. It was always a pleasure to see YB around.

"Hey YB," she greeted with a joyous tune.

"You seen Chaos?" he then asked.

"Yeah, she went to do a VIP in the room," Sweet said.

"Oh word?" YB replied, not really thrilled about it.

"Yeah, she should be back out soon. It's been a while already."

"A'ight."

Sweet's eyes rested on YB longer than they should have, and then she focused her attention back on having the young man fondle her and feeling his hard-on growing bigger.

"You gonna wait around for that bitch, YB?" Rufus asked.

Rufus wasn't too thrilled about his cousin having feelings for one of Crown's hoes. To Rufus, they were all bitches and hoes. They were only good for one thing—being down on their knees or lying on their backs and giving him some pussy.

"Rufus, chill. I'm gonna see what's up," YB said.

"Nigga, fuck that bitch, yo! You got me in here waitin' around for that ho, when we need to be out there gettin' that fuckin' money. And I'm waiting for that bitch-ass nigga Crown to step to me. I'm gonna show that nigga what time it is, fo' real; early, my nigga," Rufus exclaimed.

He tapped the firearm that was tucked snuggly against his gut and continued. "That bitch in the next room, fuckin' a nigga for some bread for that sorry-ass nigga, and you got feelings."

"Chill, Rufus. It's my business, a'ight, nigga?" YB snapped. "You need some pussy or sumthin,' nigga?"

Rufus sucked his teeth. "Nigga, I don't fuckin' pay for pussy. I'll take that shit from these bitches if I want it. Fuckin' bitches don't get none of my fuckin' bread, you hear me, nigga?"

YB knew it was useless to argue with his cousin. Rufus was a thug 24/7, ride-or-die type of nigga and always into some shit. YB, however, knew how to tone it down and not show that thuggish side of him all the time. Unfortunately, he couldn't instill that type of thinking into his cousin.

"Yo, let me buy you a drink, nigga, and calm your attitude," YB said.

"Yeah, spend your money on family, not these chicks, my nigga."

YB shook his head and walked toward the bar. While YB and Rufus approached the bar, Crown left it and went over to Sweet. He was upset with Sweet for the smiles she showed YB. He'd warned his chicks that he didn't want anyone talking to that nigga, and if they were caught doing so, harsh repercussions would follow.

Sweet stood from the man's lap, fixed her G-string, and got ready to take the young man to the VIP room. Crown appeared behind her and grabbed her strongly by her forearm.

"Daddy, what I do?" Sweet asked, panicked.

"Nigga, bounce for a minute. She'll get up wit' you soon," Crown told the young man.

Knowing about Crown's reputation and his violent ways, the young man walked off without hesitation.

Crown yoked Sweet by her throat and pushed her against the wall, knocking over chairs in the procedure. "Bitch, what I told you about that fuckin' nigga, huh? I don't want you fuckin', lookin', or talkin' to him, you fuckin' hear me? Don't get outta pocket again, bitch."

"Daddy, I'm sorry, baby, it won't happen again," Sweet choked out. Tears formed in her frightened eyes.

Crown wanted to hit her, but he knew now was not the time. She still had to go make his money, and her bruised and bloody body would have been bad for business.

He let her go and backed away from her, his eyes shooting daggers of disappointment and rage.

"Go make me my fuckin' money, bitch!" he shouted.

Everyone in the place stared, but it was nothing new to them. Crown was known for attacking and yelling at his hoes in public—it was his way of showing that he was still in control and not to be fucked with.

He already proved his point, and Cherish and Midnight simply observed from a distance. They both were very familiar with Crown's wrath and didn't want that kind of attention on themselves.

Sweet dried her tears and tried to hide her embarrassment by looking for the young man that she was about to fuck in the VIP room. She just wanted to disappear for a moment. Many eyes were still on her, but no one said a word and most just felt sorry for her.

Crown returned to the bar and signaled Angel.

"What you need, boss?" Angel asked.

"Just get me a shot of Hennessy."

"I got you." Angel removed the bottle from a shelf at the back of the bar.

YB eyed Crown with irritation from three barstools down. Pussy nigga, he mouthed.

Crown noticed the nasty look aimed his way and turned to face YB. He didn't fear YB, nor did YB fear Crown. They were like two lions in the joint—kings of their own jungles and feeding off their fierce reputations. There could be only one king of the jungle, though, so it was inevitable that the two would rumble soon.

"Fuck you lookin' at, nigga!" Crown shouted.

"You like hittin' on women, try hitting on me, you bitch-ass nigga," YB retorted.

"Crown, please . . . not here," Angel pleaded. He had worry in his eyes.

"Angel, shut the fuck up!" Crown growled. If looks could kill, YB would be in trouble.

Rufus sneered at Crown, moving his hand near his concealed gun. All YB had to say was jump, and Rufus would have asked, "How high?"

"Fuck y'all West Philly niggas! You think you can come up in here and disrespect my bitches and me?" Crown hissed.

"You ain't shit, nigga! I'll come over there and slap the shit outta you, like you my bitch!" YB yelled.

YB knew he already said too much. He was a man about action, and with Rufus right behind him everyone knew that shots could ring out at any given moment.

It was the calm before the storm. Cherish stood by her man's side and stared at YB and Rufus with the same bitterness as Crown. The quarrel between the two thugs was disrupting business, and wanting to avoid getting shot in the crossfire, a few customers began leaving.

"Yo, what the fuck y'all niggas doin', disrupting my place of business!" Magic shouted.

The owner of the club came from the basement with an irritated scowl across his hard-looking face. Angel had called down to the basement and warned his boss that a situation was brewing between Crown and YB. Magic knew he had to head upstairs promptly and calm them down before they made his seedy underground club hot with gunfire.

"Yo, it ain't nuthin', Magic. Just a li'l dispute," YB said.

"Fuck that, YB. Y'all niggas know better than to come up in here and actin' out in my business. Take that shit to the Westside, nigga," Magic barked.

Magic was an O.G from the days of the Black Mafia. He was in his early fifties, but still portrayed the image of a street thug. He was a young, unbreakable soul trapped in an aging man's body. His presence alone was intimidating, but his reputation was carried through the streets like a cold winter wind.

Magic stared at YB and Crown with dark, menacing eyes. He was tall, still well built, and his aging brown skin was lined with a few wrinkles. His full head of hair was salt and pepper, harmonizing with his thick goatee. He was clad in a black, tight-fitting T-shirt and blue jeans stretched down over a pair of polished, black wingtip shoes. Magic looked good for his age, but his eyes had seen enough bloodshed, prisons, and drugs. When he stared at you for a long time, you almost turned cold from his gaze.

Magic came from an era where heroin was king of the streets. Back in his day, true gangsters sported tailored suits and didn't run their mouths off like a bunch of bitches. His philosophy on the young generation today was that niggas were too soft and weren't about shit except showing off and shooting each other over petty crimes.

"Yo, Magic, no disrespect to your place, but tell that bitch nigga over there to stay the fuck out my business," Crown hissed.

"Fuck you, nigga!" YB retorted.

"Both y'all niggas chill," Magic said with authority in his voice. "Y'all niggas either get your act right or get the fuck out my place."

His statement was short, but well understood. Magic was one of the few men that both thugs respected and knew not to piss off.

Crown looked for his chicks and said, "Y'all bitches get your shit together. We out."

Three of Crown's hoes stopped their action and retreated to the dressing room.

"Chaos still fuckin' that nigga?!" he shouted.

"You know that bitch don't keep time wit' them tricks," Cherish said as she passed Crown and headed for the dressing room.

Crown angrily walked toward the VIP section.

YB wanted to do something, but he suddenly heard Magic calling him over. "YB, let me talk to you for a moment."

YB gave Crown a hard glance and went over to Magic.

"Walk with me downstairs."

YB knew that he would have to see Chaos another time. Magic demanded his time and he knew not to keep Magic waiting.

# 3

Bobby thrust into Chaos's sweet, wet pussy from the back, one leg curled and sinking into the torn leather couch and the other on the floor, giving him support. He gripped Chaos's sweaty hips and focused on busting his nut. Sweat escaped from his brow. He was naked from the waist down, his pants and underwear in a crumpled heap near his leg and the empty condom wrapper.

Chaos backed her phat ass against him like a machine as she clutched the armrest of the couch. She felt Bobby's thick dick digging into her. Bobby stared down at the sexy yet simple tattoo on the small of Chaos's back as he fucked her. The tattoo was barbed wire and roses, colored in black and red.

"Oh shit, your pussy is good, Chaos . . . oh, your pussy is so good . . . oh, your pussy is so good," Bobby chanted.

"Hurry up, Bobby, cum for me," Chaos replied, knowing that he needed to hurry up.

It had been twenty minutes so far, and she knew how Crown was with his time.

Bobby wanted to lick the sweat off Chaos's back. He wanted to be nasty and kiss every inch of her and suck her toes—really show her a good time. The bliss that he felt inside Chaos's body had his body trembling with every thrust. Bobby closed his eyes fucked her fervently, panting and grunting like a wild animal, ignoring everything around him.

The door to the room flew open and Crown marched in with a scowl on his face. Bobby turned around, shocked to see Crown coming toward him.

"You're time is up, muthafucka. You're done," Crown stated.

"Crown, what's up wit' this? I ain't finished," Bobby said, as he jumped out of Chaos's pussy.

Crown grabbed Bobby by his neck and pushed him on the floor. "You're done, nigga! Get the fuck out!"

Bobby looked up at Crown in anger, but was scared to do anything about it. He collected his clothing and scurried out the room.

"Bitch, why you taking forever wit' this nigga? What the fuck I told you? If the nigga don't nut in fifteen minutes, you charge the nigga extra or leave. My time is money, Chaos," he fumed.

"Baby, I know—"

Slap!

Chaos received a hard, right-hand hit across her face. She fell back against the couch, holding her jaw. She wasn't shocked by Crown's abuse; she'd been hit before. He was a bully, and too controlling. She felt sorry for Bobby and embarrassed that Crown interrupted them.

"Bitch, get your fuckin' shit together. We out."

"Yes, Daddy," Chaos replied in an obeying tone.

Crown left the room. Chaos watched him leave and got dressed. She stared at her outfit on the floor, the one Crown just stepped all over with his dirty shoes, and knew that she didn't want to go back out there. But money needed to be made, and she had no other way to live.

Chaos slid back into her stilettos, continued to soothe the side of her face, dusted off her scanty outfit and walked back out into spotlight. She heard someone say, "Damn, Crown got that bitch on lock."

Mocking comments like that made her sour but when a fellow dancer came up to her and said, "Oh, Chaos, YB was just in here lookin' for you." A smile appeared and her thoughts of him made her attitude change.

YB stepped into Magic's office at the end of a long, concrete hallway in the basement. Stepping into Magic's office was like coming through a portal as the décor and atmosphere was much different from the seedy club he owned upstairs.

Magic loved to read, and his entire wall was lined with books that expanded vertically and horizontally against the wall with titles by Robert Greene, Anthony T. Browder, James Patterson, Napoleon Hill, and many more. On one bookshelf alone, he had nothing but bulky books on Pennsylvania law and appeals.

The lavish office also contained a forty-two-inch flat screen TV mounted on the wall, a state-of-the-art sound system, a long, plush leather couch and a polished cherry wood executive desk. A brown tufted leather recliner rested behind it. Magic had taste and he had class. His style of décor represented him, and the chicks loved it.

"Damn, Magic, you be reading all these books?" YB asked, staring at his collection.

Magic closed the door behind him and replied with, "Reading them books helped me avoid the death penalty and also taught me how to file for an appeal. Because of those books, I eventually got my lengthy sentence reduced. Knowledge is power, YB."

"Yeah, whateva…I ain't got no time to have my face in no book.

You know me, Magic. I'm about my business."

"You about your business, huh? Well, your business is fuckin' up my shit upstairs," Magic said with his raspy tone.

"Yo, that nigga Crown . . . he a bitch-ass nigga, Magic. I don't like that nigga."

"He's an asshole, I agree. But that nigga knows how to bring money in for my club. He about his business, too. And besides, I hear you're beefin' with him because you got a soft spot for one of his girls."

"It ain't even like that wit' me, Magic. I mean—"

"What? You're too hard to admit that you like being with a woman? You wanna be an idiot like your cousin, Rufus, and rape chicks and show them no love?"

"Nah, Magic. I ain't like my cousin."

"That's good, nigga, 'cause let me tell you something, YB. Them chicks that work for me upstairs love me, because I show 'em love right back. You show a bitch enough love and she'll go to the end of the earth for you. But you piss 'em off, and you'll see that hell has no fury like a woman scorned."

"I see you, Magic. You the man up in here. I know you done fucked a few of these chicks up in here." YB smiled.

"Little nigga, my business is my business," Magic calmly replied.

"I understand."

Magic walked over to his desk and casually took a seat in his plush recliner. He reached into his drawer and pulled out a long, hand-rolled cigar. He cut it, lit it and inhaled deeply. He thoroughly enjoyed the flavor of a fine Vegas Miami. In a more relaxed mood, he looked over at YB and asked, "How your peoples doing?"

"My mom's good. She asked about you the other day."

"Tell her I said hi."

Magic took another pull from the pricey cigar and studied YB from his chair. He liked YB and he was one of the few niggas coming up in Philly that Magic had love for.

Magic grew up with YB's father, Smoke, and they were crime partners from that era of Superfly and Shaft. They wore Afros and bellbottoms and drove trendy, high-post Cadillac's. Smoke and Magic were infamous for their violence in South Philly, where they did drugs together and ran wild with women, money, and cars.

Smoke schooled Magic in the ways of the streets and the hustle. He took Magic under his wing. Since Smoke had been dead for over twenty years, Magic took interest in YB and, on occasion, looked out for YB's mom when times got hard.

"Y'all little niggas today don't even know the meaning of being a true gangster. Back in my days, nigga, when we did shit, we shut the fuck up about it. Y'all niggas today wanna shoot guns and then toot your own horn for doing so," Magic proclaimed. "Your reputation was everything back then. And your fashion sense too! Fuck you got on, YB?"

"Yo, this jersey cost me $200, Magic," YB said proudly.

"Two hundred for that shit? Muthafucka, you look like a fuckin' clown in it," Magic stated harshly. "You got your hair braided like a bitch, pants off your ass, and you expect a woman to respect that image? A real nigga dresses with style. Coming up, we wore tailored suits, polished shoes, and derbies. Our clothes said something about us, and we were respected because we dressed a certain way. Y'all niggas now look like Ronald McDonald on crack. That ain't how a man is supposed to dress when he's out in the streets." Magic's words shredded YB's image apart.

"Well, times done changed, Magic," YB said in his defense.

Magic chuckled. "For the worse, I see."

YB sucked his teeth.

"I hurt your feelings, nigga?" Magic grinned.

"Nah, I'm good."

"I'm just tryin' to school you YB . . . like your father once did to me"

"I know. I understand."

"You sure, nigga? I keep hearing about you and your cousin in these streets. Your name is ringing out but be careful 'cause soon, you'll have the wolves at your door," Magic cautioned.

"I know how to handle the wolves, Magic. It ain't the first time niggas tried me and I'm still here," YB bragged.

Magic took another pull from his cigar. "The wolves will always be at your door in this game. You just gotta know when and how to tame them."

YB nodded.

"Now, this beef you got with Crown; don't let it happen up in my place again. You beef with him outside this muthafucka and when you do, watch your back, YB. Crown is a dangerous man."

"And what am I, Mickey Mouse?" YB was indignant. "Magic, I know how to handle that nigga."

Magic took another pull from the cigar and eyed YB while still reclined in his chair. "You are your father's son."

YB went back upstairs and was more at ease after his talk with Magic. In his eyes, Magic was like a father to him. Since he was young, Magic had been around, guiding him and taking care of home when shit got rough. When there was beef, Magic supplied the guns and tools so that YB and Rufus could defend themselves. Magic even taught YB how to shoot his first gun.

YB walked back into the club and saw his cousin at the bar, drinking a beer. Neither Crown nor any of his chicks were around. He was disappointed since he had not seen Chaos, but he knew he would run into her again.

He tapped Rufus on his back. "C'mon, nigga, let's go."

Rufus turned to YB and he noticed that the alcohol had begun affecting his cousin already. When Rufus got drunk, his temper and his wild ways were even more extreme. He could easily become a loose cannon ready to blow, and YB knew it was time for them to leave before Rufus did something stupid.

"Let me get another drink, YB," Rufus slurred.

"Nah, nigga, you good. Let's go."

"Yo, one more drink, and then I'll be good," Rufus demanded in an irate tone.

"Nah nigga, let's go," YB said more sternly. He grabbed Rufus by his arm and tried to remove him from the barstool.

Rufus yanked his arm free from YB's grip and shouted, "Nigga, get the fuck off me! Pullin' on me like you my daddy."

YB knew the liquor was talking and cut Rufus some slack regarding his attitude. "Rufus, not here. You're drunk."

"Nigga, I'm good. Fuck Magic and his place," Rufus exclaimed.

Angel and a few other patrons stared, not wanting to intrude, knowing Rufus's heated and deadly temper. They all figured it was best for YB or Magic to handle him.

"Nigga, don't go there. You fucked up right now, so let's be out before I drag your ass out that door, nigga. Don't fuck wit' me right now, Rufus," YB warned.

Rufus let out a drunken chuckle. "Nigga, you family. I ain't got no beef wit' you." His hardened gaze faded and he threw his arm around YB. They both staggered to the exit.

Before they walked out of the club, Rufus asked, "What the fuck Magic wanted to talk to you about, anyway?"

"Just business, my nigga."

"Why that muthafucka don't never wanna talk bizzness wit' me?" Rufus slurred. "He don't like me, YB?"

YB ignored the question and guided his cousin outside. Rufus was the prime example of what Magic thought was wrong with the niggas today—loud, ignorant, and had no kind of class. They were quick to shoot without thinking and then snitch on the next nigga when caught.

# 4

Chaos and Sweet could hear Midnight getting fucked in the next room. Her trick was loud, sounding like a horn from a distance. Sweet smiled and said, "Damn, Midnight is puttin' it on that nigga."

Chaos chuckled.

They were in the second bedroom, both ladies sitting on the queen-sized bed that was covered in hunter green satin sheets and throw pillows in the same color. The room had an elegant look with an area rug covering shimmering parquet floors. The large bedroom windows were draped in long, white blinds and gave the place a homey feeling.

Crown owned a three-bedroom brick house on Sherwood Road, a few blocks south of City Line Avenue. The place came with granite countertops in the master bedroom, kitchen, and around the Jacuzzi area. It had walk-in closets, three bathrooms (one with a sauna), and the living room was furnished with a large leather sectional, plush carpeting, a sixty-inch plasma TV, and a home theater system with ample speakers scattered throughout the place.

The home was designed to make a trick feel comfortable while fucking one of Crown's chicks and to make his chicks feel secure when they were under his wing. Crown knew that his chicks came from less, and he gave them the illusion of having more with the toys (luxury cars, upscale neighborhood, and designer clothing) and comfort he provided for them.

He instilled fear and insecurity into his chicks by always reminding his hoes that they couldn't do better than what he was giving them and that they couldn't run or hide from him. His name rang out in Philly, and whatever happened, he had the power to track down and have a bitch brought back—or killed if he wanted.

Still, Crown always reminded his chicks that they were beautiful and had the potential to earn him top dollar when dealing with a trick. His words and actions were contradictive and conniving.

Crown's right-hand man, Harlem, watched his back and looked out for his chicks. Harlem was ruthless and deadly, and wherever he went, murder and pain were soon to follow.

Harlem was lean and tall like a NBA player. His head was shaved and gleaming, his eyes gray and beady. He looked no older than eighteen even though he was in his late twenties and well experienced with the streets of Philly. Harlem was a product of the notorious project development, Tasker homes, before they were torn down a few years ago.

Crown befriended Harlem a few years ago when they both were in lockup at Philadelphia Riverside Correctional Facility on State Road. With Harlem having Crown's back, nobody fucked with the duo. Harlem had more bodies on him than a cemetery.

Chaos and Sweet continued to talk, trying to ignore the loud sex coming from the next room. Crown had brought the man through and he'd paid $200 for an hour with Midnight. He had fifteen minutes left.

Crown was down in the basement, enjoying his liquor and satellite

TV and keeping tabs on how long Smitty had with Midnight. He held a watch in his hand. He was strict when it came to his women and his time. A few minutes over and niggas had to pay extra. Crown wasn't giving away any pussy for free.

His most profitable ho was Chaos. She was young, nineteen and had been under his wing for almost a year now. Month after month, Chaos's clientele of men—and a few women—seemed to grow. They loved her young, angelic features and her soft, curvy figure. She was known to be a freak in the bedroom who did wonders with her tongue.

With Harlem by his side, Crown would usually scope the bus station and the 30th Street train station for young runaway girls who were looking for something better and would naïvely believe the promises he made to them. Crown lured the young girls in with promises of material things and easy cash to be made. Just as he anticipated, Chaos ate up his lies and promises.

Crown met Chaos when she just arrived in Philly. She came off at the bus station on Market Street with only a tattered book bag in hand and the clothes on her back. She escaped from the Bronx, hoping to make some money for herself and to start a new prosperous life.

When Chaos reached Philly, she only had thirty dollars in her pockets and a number to call. Her cousin Bubbles moved to Philly three years prior and made a fine life for herself since her arrival. She's wanted Chaos to live with her for a while to give her stability, with moving from one foster home to another, and beefing with a few blood chicks from the South Bronx. When gunshots starting ringing out and Chaos's home-girl, Rachael wound up dead on the cold side walk on Third Avenue with a bullet in her head, she decided it was time for a change of scenery and caught the next available bus to Philadelphia.

Bubbles was the closest thing to family Chaos had. When she was five, Chaos's mother signed her over to foster care and she never came back for her. Chaos always felt abandoned, unwanted and never found a place suitable enough for her to call her home.

She was raped by her foster father, abused and teased by the other kids, and was always told that she wouldn't be shit in life but a slut or a ho. And with others knowing her mother's background as a prostitute, they judged Chaos before knowing her and figured the apple didn't fall too far from the tree.

Her mother, Diane, gave birth to Chaos in an abandoned building in Hunts Point on a cold February day. She was sucking the dick of a trick on the third floor for twenty dollars when her water broke and she went into labor.

Diane Mitchell fell back against the dirty and grimy weathered wooden floors, screaming in agony. She clutched her stomach, fell paralyzed to the ground and couldn't get up. All she could do was remain rooted to the ground in her soiled sundress and ragged winter coat and curse her unborn child for fuckin' up business for her.

The trick looked on wide-eyed and was too scared to get involved. He quickly zipped up his jeans, got his shit in order, and ran off, leaving Diane to give birth to her baby alone.

Diane loud cries echoed throughout the empty cold building and fell on nothing but the wind that swept through the rooms.

"Aaaaaahhh ... ouch! Ouch! Ouch ... shit!" she cried out in anguish, as she squirmed around on the ground.

She felt the baby extracting itself painfully from her tearing and bleeding vagina. There was blood underneath her and the wrinkled sundress was ripped by her clenched fists.

For an hour she pushed and pulled her baby out of her. She was still alone with the wind nipping at her skin and exposed, widely spread legs. The rats and creatures scurried around her, smelling blood.

As Diane grunted and panted, one fat rat came to within inches of her face and a second came close to her baby's exposed head that dangled from out her vagina. It scurried around her open legs as if the protruding infant was a snack.

Diane felt helpless as she continued to push her daughter out and tried to defend herself from the nasty rats that wanted to take a bite out of them. She picked up objects within her reach and started throwing them at the rats. They would run off, but not too far, still watching, still waiting. But Diane wouldn't give up without a fight.

She tried to hurry her birth, pushing and grunting, feeling her baby leaving her vagina inch by inch. She felt the cold eating away at her. She cried out and pushed hard, knowing the pain of childbirth would end soon.

She looked over at the rats and had the sick thought of giving them what they came for—her baby. She felt that her life wasn't shit and that her baby would be better off dead and not a bother to her.

But Diane continued to push and fought to get the baby out of her. She arched her back upwards, with her arms outstretched and grabbed the infant by its head and began pulling it out from her as she pushed. She cried out, feeling her pussy widening like the length of a football field.

With the baby's head in her grasp, her body began to tense up and she gritted her teeth and pushed hard. With the strength she had left in her body, she continued to push with every breath she had in her. She soon felt the baby slide out of her and land between her thighs. It was an unsanitary birth, but for Diane, it would do.

She felt the slippery infant with the umbilical cord still attached in her hand and took a deep breath. The painful birth was finally over, and the child's crying was the only thing she heard.

Diane bought the screaming infant close to her and looked around for something sharp to cut the umbilical cord. With the baby crying and resting against her stomach and thigh, she spotted a broken piece of sharp glass. She outstretched her arm and reached for the jagged object, hoping the tool would cut the cord that connected her to the baby.

When the object was in her grip, she grabbed the umbilical cord, took another deep breath and began slicing away at the greasy and slick texture. She cut herself in the process and winced in pain, cursing loudly. Despite her bleeding hand, she managed to free the baby from her and felt relieved that the hard part was finally done.

The infant remained on her stomach and continued to cry. Diane picked up the baby, pushed herself off the floor and moved toward a tattered table, cold, weak and scared. She removed her filthy coat and wrapped the baby in it.

She looked around the floor and spotted a milk crate near the doorway. She picked it up and placed the child inside the crate, neatly wrapped warmly in her coat. Diane shivered and made plans to leave the baby where someone would find her before the rats got to her. She figured after giving birth, the baby wasn't her problem anymore.

Diane looked a mess with blood running down her legs. Her right hand was cut and bleeding. Her sundress was stained and torn and her hair was in disarray. She looked faint and homely—like hell on earth.

Diane stared down at the crying infant and thought of a quick name for the girl. Chaos, she thought, because it was chaos giving birth to the little bitch. The name made her smirk. The baby continued to cry louder and louder, as if she sensed that her mother was going to abandon her.

Diane began moving away from the child, trying to ignore its agonizing cries for a mother's affection.

"You'll be a'ight," she said to the infant.

With that said, she rushed out the door and went flying down the dilapidated stairs, hoping the farther she got away, the better she would feel. But she could still hear the baby crying.

Diane got to the front exit of the building and the cold hit her hard. She shivered and clasped her arms together, trying to rub some warmth into herself. But the cold February night was relentless and almost brought her to her knees.

She walked half a block, but her mind couldn't escape the fact that she left her newborn baby girl alone in the cold with the rats.

That's your baby, go get your baby, her mind kept saying to her. She never done any wrong to you . . . get your baby, because she will be the only thing on this earth that will love you.

Diane could no longer ignore her conscience. She turned around and ran back to the empty building. She fought the cold and the urge to pass out and ran back up to the third floor. The rats were around the milk crate, nibbling at the coat and searching for a way to get at the crying infant.

Diane ran over, shooing the creatures away and knocking a few off the table. She then picked up Chaos in her arms and knew that her baby didn't deserve death.

Her friend Julie lived in a one-bedroom apartment thirty blocks away so she ran with the baby clutched tightly in her arms. With the cold and weakness bearing down on her, she reached Julie's door looking like she had been to hell and back. When Julie opened the door, she exclaimed, "Take my baby!"

Julie quickly took Chaos in her arms and watched Diane pass out in front of her. She immediately dialed 911.

Diane suffered from pneumonia, but she was very fortunate to be alive. Julie cared for Chaos and supported Diane as she dealt with the caseworker at the hospital. Julie had a two-year old child of her own and cared for Chaos as if she were her own child. After making sure

Chaos was a healthy child, things seemed to get back to normal for Diane. Which meant she resumed whoring herself out to tricks. Julie tried to care for Chaos as best as she could with little money and little help from Diane.

For a moment, it seemed like Danielle Chaos Mitchell would have a normal life.

# 5

Chaos and Sweet lingered in the bedroom and talked while they played a game of blackjack. They were best friends and understood each other. They had a lot in common including living in New York and having similar, troubling backgrounds. They both were also very familiar with sex at an early age and had no one to call family, except for each other and Crown.

Sweet lost her virginity to her older cousin when she was only thirteen. They shared stories of loss and pain and sometimes it felt like they were sisters.

Chaos smiled, listening to Midnight and her trick's loud sexual groans coming from the next room. She sat Indian-style across from Sweet in a pair of coochie-cutting shorts and a yellow baby tee. The day been slow for both ladies—little money was made that morning and in the afternoon. Crown was minding his own business down in the basement, but still periodically checking up on Midnight and her trick, so Chaos and Sweet only had a few sporadic moments of peace.

"I win again!" Chaos turned over a queen, bringing her score up to twenty.

"You cheatin' bitch," Sweet said jokingly.

"Just deal again. Shit, we need to be playin' for money, since it's so slow around here today," Chaos said.

"I know, right? But you know how Crown is. He come up in here and see us gambling and all hell might break loose," Sweet admonished.

"Shit, we make enough money for him already. I don't know why he be trippin' sometimes. Shit, yesterday, I fucked like six tricks for that nigga and he still beefin' wit' me about it being slow and needing to get my clientele up. Yo, fo' real, Sweet, I would like to see that nigga on his back turning a trick for once," Chaos joked. "Turn that nigga into my bitch."

Sweet laughed. "I know, right?"

The girls continued their game and made small talk for a few moments. Chaos shuffled the cards again. She looked up at Sweet with a serious look and asked, "Sweet, you ever thought about leaving here?"

"What you mean?"

"I mean, just one night, get your shit and get the fuck away from here."

"And go where, Chaos? Besides here, I ain't got no other home," Sweet replied.

"But we continue to fuck trick after trick and get this nigga rich. What do we get out of it? A nice place to stay, protection, and comfort is what Crown tells us. I could do that myself."

"Chaos, beside that bullshit job I had at the mall, I've been doin' this all my life. I might as well get paid to fuck a nigga. I was tired of giving my pussy away for free," Sweet proclaimed.

"But are you happy here?"

"Are you?" Sweet countered.

"I don't know. I just want somethin' better for me, Sweet. I left New York to get into somethin' of my own and to be with my cousin. But the minute I met Crown he had this way over me. He had me hyped about gettin' money and being a woman and living like a queen. But lately, I've been feeling like I'm a prisoner up in this bitch."

"I understand how you feel that way, Chaos. But I know that before Crown, I didn't have shit for myself. I shared a one-bedroom apartment with five other people and two of them couldn't keep themselves from climbing on top of me night after night. And since it was their place, they felt my pussy was theirs for the taking, too. I got raped by my seventeen-year-old cousin when I was only thirteen, and they looked at me like I was the one that did the family wrong when I accused him of it. So if I gotta fuck and suck a few niggas to live comfortable in this crib, have Crown provide security, and ain't gotta worry about cash in my hand, then this ain't so bad after all. I can deal wit' his abuse. Shit, Chaos, I've dealt wit' worse."

"It's a hard-knock life for us, right?" Chaos said, trying to ease the situation.

Sweet laughed. "Jay-Z ain't got shit on us."

They continued with their game and then suddenly Sweet asked, "You got somethin' goin' on with YB?"

Chaos smiled. "Why you ask?"

"Crown almost went upside my head the other night, just for talkin' to YB while I was workin' a trick. Y'all got somethin' goin' on that I don't know about?"

"Nah, we just cool peoples. I met him a few months ago." Chaos was deliberately being sparse with the details.

"Um-hmm, right. You got somethin' goin' on wit' him, Chaos, be fo' real wit' me. What's up?"

"He just cool peoples, Sweet. I'm fo' real."

"A'ight bitch, you keep your stank business to yourself. But I tell you don't let Crown find out that y'all got a thing for each other and got somethin' goin' on, 'cause you know his temper. And you know he don't like that nigga, either."

"Crown ain't gonna find out shit with me and YB, 'cause there ain't shit to tell about us," Chaos stated.

"You my girl, Chaos, so watch your back. You know they are both dangerous men in this city and I don't wanna hear about you ending up in the morgue because of either one of them niggas," Sweet said sincerely.

"I know, girl. You know I stay watching my back, but there ain't shit goin' on with me and YB," Chaos lied.

Sweet smiled. She looked Chaos in her eyes and felt so much love for her friend.

They continued their game once again and finally heard Smitty, Midnight's sexual escapade come to an end. Her trick came out the room, zipping up his jeans and sweating like a slave picking cotton in a sweltering field. He looked over at Chaos and Sweet seated on the bed and smiled.

"You want next wit' one of us?" Sweet teased.

He smiled back and said, "Nah, I'm good."

He left, looking exhausted. Midnight walked into the room right afterward, sweating profusely as well. She was butt-naked and wiped her face with a towel, looking like she just came from working out in the gym.

"Damn, you put it on the nigga like that? Gave him his money's worth, didn't you, Midnight?" Chaos said.

"It took forever fa' him to come," Midnight drawled in her thick, country accent.

The girls laughed.

"Well, the way that nigga looked after he left here, you know he comin' back for seconds," Sweet stated.

Midnight smiled and sat next to the girls on the bed. "I didn't take too long wit' him, right? I mean, Crown won't be mad wit' me, will he? I kept within my time?" she asked.

"I think you had, like, five more minutes left wit' him," Sweet mentioned.

"Midnight, you need to chill out. You did good, girl, stop worrying so fuckin' much," Chaos told her.

"I know. I try not to worry, but I hate upsetting him. I'm one of the new girl's in this house and I wanna make right. Ya know?"

"You'll be a'ight, Midnight. The way you put it on that nigga in there, you gonna have a lot more customers comin' for you in no time. Your money is definitely gonna be up, and Crown ain't gonna have a reason to beef wit' your ass," Sweet said.

Midnight smiled. "Let me get dressed."

She got up to return to the next room, but when Crown appeared in the doorway wearing a wife-beater, jeans, and his Timbs, the room got quiet. His muscular physique showed through the wife beater and his attitude didn't look too agreeable.

"Y'all bitches talk too fuckin' much," he complained.

He eyed each one of his hoes, noting the concern on their young faces. "Y'all bitches hurry up and get dressed. I'm takin' y'all down to the club to get this money."

He walked away and the ladies didn't hesitate to get dressed. They scurried around the bedroom for their things, knowing it was not good to keep Crown waiting for long.

# 6

The two-story brick building on Brown Street in West Philly, also known as "The Bottom," was hectic with business. Fiends of all shapes and sizes traveled in and out of the dilapidated structure for that dope that had them going senseless and wide-eyed. Devil's Play, black tar heroin that YB and Rufus pushed, was the shit to get high with. It was raw and had the fiends dropping hard and coming back for more. Devil's Play came straight from the Mexicans and was nothing to play with. It was making niggas money around the way.

Evening descended on the hardcore streets of Philly. The corners and streets were as busy as Grand Central Station during rush hour. The hustlers, fiends, locals, and pimps were out in full swing, trying to get that paper or get that high.

YB and Rufus controlled the corners on Brown Street from 38th to 39th Streets. Their operation was a problem for some of the local hustlers around the way. The cousins had a strong connect and a fierce reputation of protecting what was theirs. The wolves came at them plenty of times, but failed to do any damage to their rising drug domain.

YB and Rufus sat in a gleaming Escalade parked across the street from their drug spot, chatting it up. YB took a long pull from a burning spliff and passed it to Rufus. As he exhaled the excess smoke, he looked over at his place of business and watched a few young'uns loitering outside the house.

YB's eyes lingered on one particular dude, Toy-T. He was known to be associated with Crown and his chicks. YB knew Toy-T wasn't a threat to him and his business, but it bothered him to see Toy-T around his soldiers.

"What's on ya mind, YB?" Rufus asked. He took three puffs of the spliff and passed it back to YB.

YB took another drag before saying, "Yo, that's Toy-T over there, right?"

Rufus looked. "Hell yeah, that's that faggot nigga! What the fuck he doin' over here?"

"He ain't nuthin', Rufus, probably just stupid," YB said.

"Man, I should go step to that nigga. That's Crown's fuckin' cousin, and anything that's associated with Crown needs to get put down," Rufus said with irritation.

"The nigga only seventeen, Rufus. Let the young'un be," YB said.

"Let him be? Fuck that shit, YB! You gonna let that nigga step foot on our soil and let the nigga continue to keep breathin'?" Rufus lifted his shirt and pulled the concealed .380 from his waistband.

"Rufus, chill the fuck out! You too hype, nigga. Think for a fuckin' minute. You ready to go and shoot the nigga in front of the spot where we get money and make it hot on the block and bring police. What da fuck you thinking?"

YB stuffed the gun back into his waistband. "Yeah, you right, my nigga. I'm gonna chill."

"Toy-T ain't shit to us. He ain't never cause me any problems. Let the nigga be, a'ight? He probably tryin' to cop."

Rufus nodded. "It's your world, YB."

YB looked at his cousin for a moment and then said, "I don't need to hold your fuckin' hand in this game, right?"

"Nigga, stop tryin' to clown me. We family, but don't clown me, YB," Rufus snapped.

"Nigga, I'm just sayin', think before you react sometimes 'cause your actions could cost a nigga money," YB advised.

"So you the Bill Gates of the game, huh?" Rufus joked.

"I just know how to be subtle sometimes."

"Subtle? What the fuck that mean?"

YB just shook his head in shame for his cousin. "Nigga, pick up a dictionary once in a while. You might learn a thing or two."

"Yeah, whatever, nigga. I learn how to make this fuckin' money and hold down the fuckin' block, ya heard, early, my nigga. A nigga ain't got time to read no mutha-fuckin' dictionary when there is money to be made."

YB sighed, knowing that there was no putting any sense into his cousin's head. He was family, but the nigga could get ignorant and his temper could cost them business.

"Anyway, I gotta make this run to my mom's crib and check and see how she's doin'," YB informed Rufus.

"Yo, tell Aunt Monica I said hi."

"Will do."

"What you doin' tonight, anyway?"

"I might go check Magic down at the club," YB said.

"Again? For what, nigga? You on Magic's dick like that?"

"Yo, why you so fuckin' ignorant, Rufus? The nigga is ol' school; you could learn somethin' from the nigga, if you just knew how to shut up and listen for once."

"Man, fuck Magic! That nigga time in this city done came and gone. Y'all niggas actin' like Magic is the shit now. Fuck he got? A club and his name. He ain't holding these streets down anymore," Rufus shouted.

"What the fuck I'm gonna do wit' you, Rufus?"

"What the fuck I'm gonna do wit' you? You know I always got your back, YB, but Magic—he just talk, my nigga. And a nigga like me, talk wit' this." Rufus lifted his shirt once again to show off the .380. "That's where the respect is."

YB sighed.

Rufus looked at his cousin and then a thought came to him. "Nigga, you sure you goin' down to the club to see Magic? Let me find out that bitch got you open. And I know you ain't even fuck her yet."

"Stay out my business, Rufus," YB warned.

"Nigga, you got all these hood bitches dying to fuck you and make some money for you, and you wanna sniff behind some whore that sells pussy for Crown? What da fuck is wrong wit' you, YB?"

"Nigga, it ain't what you think. And I'm goin' to the club to see Magic, don't get that shit twisted," YB hissed.

"A'ight, just make sure it's about business and not about pussy."

"Whatever. I'm out. Hold it down out here till I get back." YB started the truck.

"Yeah, I will. Just remember I'm the nigga in the trenches wit' you, making sure niggas don't forget who we be and what we're about. My gun talk and fear keeps the wolves away," Rufus said.

YB nodded.

Rufus got out of the car and discreetly removed the .380 from his waistband as he watched YB drive off down the block. When the truck turned the corner, Rufus held the gun close by his side. He calmly walked over to where Toy-T stood with a few of his soldiers. "Yo, Toy-T, let me holla at you for a sec."

Toy-T and the soldiers turned when they heard Rufus. When Rufus got close to Toy-T, he brandished the gun and a few niggas took off running. Before Toy-T could run, Rufus grabbed him by his shirt and brought the butt of the gun across his face. He split Toy-T's forehead open and continued to pistol whip him in the streets.

"Nigga, what da fuck you doin' around here, huh? Stay your ass away from here, muthafucka. You hear me, nigga? You hear early, nigga?" Rufus shouted as he beat the shit out of Toy-T. YB said not to shoot the man, but he didn't say anything about not beating him down to send a message.

Rufus glared at the beaten Toy-T, his hand, and the bloody gun. Toy-T lay sprawled out across the chipped concrete and whimpered like a wounded animal.

"Nigga, when I come back out this bitch, you better be gone, nigga . . . early," Rufus warned.

He spit on Toy-T and walked into the building. Rufus's crew looked at Toy-T and laughed as they shook their heads, knowing Toy-T was lucky. He was still breathing.

YB pulled up in the driveway to his mother's exclusive four-bedroom Colonial home on Overbrook Avenue, in the Wynnefield section of Philly. The neighborhood was upscale and quiet. It had its few local knuckleheads around, but it was nothing like The Bottom.

He wanted his mother, Monica Toma, to live comfortably and relaxed. He loved her and she loved him. When Smoke was killed, YB suddenly became the man of the house at the age of five. With Magic not always around to help out, YB learned at an early age that he could do for himself to help his mother in and around the house.

He started in the streets when he was ten years old. He used to steal from the stores on Market Street with a crew he hung out with.

When he turned twelve, he graduated to selling drugs, shooting, and fighting with the older boys on the streets.

By the time YB was fifteen, he dropped out of school and had a reputation. He was working his own corner and put Rufus on to be his muscle. With the money he made, he no longer needed to rely on Magic for support and asked his mother quit her job, because he felt that he was finally able to take care of her.

Mrs. Toma didn't fully agree with her son's choices, but she didn't judge or criticize him either. He was bringing a lot of money into her home and had her living lavishly with furs, cars, trips, and jewelry, something her husband did before he was killed. It felt no different for the gifts to be coming from her son this time.

YB pulled behind his mom's polished black Mercedes truck. The day was still young and he felt good. He was eating lovely and the block had never been so busy. That heroin he got from the Mexicans made his business soar by twenty percent. He wanted to celebrate his success by taking his mother out.

He walked to the front door and unlocked it. He was dressed in a black Nike velour sweat suit with crisp white Air Force Ones. His braids were freshly done and his smooth, dark skin gleamed like the wax job on the Escalade.

He called for his mother once he entered the house. "Ma? Where you at? Your favorite son is in the house!"

"Boy, you're my only child and the best son in the world," Mrs. Toma replied as she walked into the kitchen, holding a glass of red wine as she kissed her son hello.

She wore a long ivory dress with a V-neck and shirred waist and a pair of matching open-toed Paco Rabanne shoes. She was a beautiful, classy, caramel-toned woman with long, sensuous black hair that flowed down to her shoulders. Her skin was smooth like butter.

Even though Mrs. Toma was in her late forties, some thought she didn't look a day over thirty. She spent her days in spas and working out in the gym to keep her figure slim, toned, and sexy. She styled herself in the best fashions that her son provided. She always had money, whether it came from her husband before his death or from her son—or even Magic. The drug game been good to her, which was reflected in her posh lifestyle.

"You look nice, Ma," YB said.

"Don't I?" Mrs. Toma smiled and did a twirl for her son.

"I know you're not going anywhere, because I'm taking you out to eat."

"Dinner? What's the occasion?"

"No occasion. What, a son can't be good to his mother?"

"You're always good to me, Yvonne. But I was thinking of stayin' in and enjoyin' my wine and listenin' to some Luther Vandross while watching the sun set from my yard."

"Scratch that. You need to get out and I'm not taking no for an answer."

Mrs. Toma smiled again. "Business must be really good for you . . . or did you meet a young lady and you want to surprise me with dinner with her?"

"Nah. Just you and me, like it used to be."

"Okay, Yvonne, give me a minute to freshen up. A mother can't complain or say no to her son wanting to spend time with her. Why am I such a lucky woman?" she teased.

"Because you gave birth to me," YB answered smugly.

Mrs. Toma chuckled. "And I don't regret every minute that you had me in labor, with your big head. You damn sure was worth it."

Mrs. Toma went upstairs while YB went into the kitchen to get himself a quick snack. He was a street nigga for sure but a mama's boy in his heart.

YB took his moms to Tre Scalini, a quaint Italian food restaurant on South 11th Street, where the food was mouthwatering and left you full.

Over veal parmesan and clams, they had a nice talk about family and YB's future. His mom, like every mother, wanted him to meet a girl and give her grandchildren to spoil. However, Mrs. Toma knew that YB was a player and went through women the way babies went through diapers.

She asked about Rufus and how was he playing out on the streets. They both knew that Rufus was a very violent man and his temper was deadly, but he was good to have around in the streets. If there was a problem, Rufus knew how to handle it and, in turn, YB kept his cousin under control.

"His mother was no better," Monica said of her sister, Rufus's mother. "The bitch was my sister but she was a headache most of the time. Now that she's is gone, she left her son around to be even more of a headache," she proclaimed.

YB didn't respond. He just listened to his mother talk and watched her drink wine. He admired her elegance.

Before their meal ended, his mother added a few more words about Rufus. "He could be good for business and he could be bad for business."

YB smiled, knowing that his mother could be just as gangster as any nigga in Philly.

# 7

Magic's club was packed with dozens of strippers and men tipping away their paychecks and getting drunk off beer and liquor. The DJ had Biggie's "Hypnotize" blaring throughout the club and the scantily clad young ladies were milling around. Two strippers were nude onstage shaking what their mama gave them.

Chaos, Cherish, and Sweet performed their duties on the floor while Midnight turned a trick in the VIP section. With Crown not around, Cherish was in charge of the chicks because she was Crown's bottom bitch. She worked a customer near the back, pushing her tits in his face and giving him a hard-on as she ground her pussy against his lap. She still managed to keep her eyes on Crown's other chicks, making sure they were getting that money and not getting into any trouble.

Chaos moved through the club in a see-through pink fishnet dress with rhinestone trim and white stilettos. Her matching pink rhinestone-studded thong was on full display underneath the dress.

Her partner in crime, Sweet, wore a tight, black, stretch dress that stopped mid-thigh and silver pumps. Her big booty and balloon tits had the men in the club gawking and grabbing their dicks, tempted to get freaky with her.

They were getting money, and that was the only thing that mattered in the club for them. Chaos was the main attraction and she walked around the club with a handful of money. Niggas constantly tried grabbing her ass and tits.

Chaos and Sweet were about to do a show for the night. The crowd was waiting for a freak-off show with the hottest bitch in the middle. The two loved doing this type of freak show together and it showed during their shows—the sucking, licking, kissing, and fingering. They didn't mind the crowd watching because when it was just them two on stage, it felt like the lights were off and the club was empty, because they only focused on each other.

There was one part of the night that Chaos looked forward to— being sexually engaged with her friend Sweet and getting paid for it. They didn't worry about Crown, Cherish, or money because after they fucked each other in front of everyone, dozens of niggas wanted to fuck them afterwards.

Cherish strutted toward the stage like the diva she knew she was. The men stared in anticipation, waiting for her outfit to come off and the pussy to come out.

The DJ played some old school Prince. It was what Chaos loved moving to when she was about to get her freak on. A Prince song relaxed her body and mind and got her horny and down for whatever.

She stepped on the stage and moved across the raised platform in her six-inch stilettos. The spotlight was on her for a long moment. She twirled herself around the long, golden pole a few times, swinging herself in the air like a schoolgirl in a playground. She slowly came down to the floor and crawled around the stage on all fours like a cat on the prowl and eyed her customers as if they were her prey.

"Purple Rain" blared in her ear. Chaos grabbed the pole a second time and climbed to the top. She suspended herself upside down, her long legs inches from the ceiling, and contorted her body around the pole like a snake. Still upside down, she slithered down the pole seductively. As she got nearer to the floor, she twirled and spread her legs widely.

Chaos put on one hell of a show. Money was thrown at her and niggas fiended to see more.

For the next ten minutes, Chaos did her thing and then Sweet stepped onstage to join her in the show. She sashayed back and forth, exposing her phat ass, pulling up her dress to her hips and revealing that she had no panties on. Men howled as they spotted her shaved mound and meaty, tattooed thighs.

Sweet couldn't work the pole like Chaos could, but she was good with working the floor, enticing niggas by showing and playing with her pierced clit. She rolled over on her hands and knees and lowered her tits to the floor. With her ass in the air and an arch in her back, Sweet reached beneath her and played with her pussy from the back.

She got love with niggas throwing money at her. Chaos stood by the pole and gave Sweet the floor for a moment. Sweet still wore her shades, but niggas didn't pay much attention to her face. They were mesmerized by her body as her outfit came off, little by little.

The crowd got mad crazy and louder and the stage area more crowded when Chaos stripped butt-naked and walked over to Sweet, who once again turned on her back and was playing with her pussy. Chaos perched over Sweet and slowly lowered her wet and moist pussy against Sweet's mouth. Sweet grabbed Chaos's fat, round ass and began eating her out. Chaos turned into the 69 position and put her face between her friend's legs.

The crowd went berserk. Tens and twenties were thrown on the stage, and pictures were snapped by cell phones. Chaos's legs quivered as Sweet's long tongue swam around in her. She returned the favor by sucking on Sweet's clit and fingering her pussy fervently.

Both ladies drowned out the crowd and noise and enjoyed each other. They twisted into each other, rolling over and sucking on each other's nipples and finger fucking. Then the rabbit came out and they took it to the next level.

Chaos was the first to get it. She lay on her back and waited for Sweet to push the thick, pink, nine-inch dildo into her. Sweet got close to Chaos's throbbing pussy and slowly pushed the plastic dick into her.

Chaos moaned and while Sweet fucked her with the dildo, Chaos played with Sweet's clit, giving niggas one hell of a show. The DJ segued into 50 Cent's "Candy Shop," which seemed to be the appropriate music for the scene.

"Aaaaaahhh . . . ummmm . . . ummm . . . ummm," Chaos moaned loudly.

"Yo, I got next," someone shouted from the crowd.

Cherish walked over to the stage naked, her clothes in hand. She saw how the crowd reacted to the show and she wanted in. She saw that money and knew it needed to be collected. Without permission, she stepped on stage, tossed her clothes to the side, and approached the girls.

The crowd of men roared with more hunger as a third girl was about to intervene. But before Cherish got in, she collected the money that was spread out all over the floor and stuffed it into her purse.

She then jiggled her Beyoncé booty and made it clap. She stood erect in her clear stilettos, her nakedness and thick, curvaceous figure attracting niggas like bees to flowers. They threw more money at her and wanted to see more, and Cherish gave them more. She climbed on the pole and began working it like Chaos did earlier, but she put more of herself into it. She ground her wet pussy against the pole and pressed her tits against it, titty fucking the long pole like it was a piece of dick.

Cherish took her show a step further and grabbed someone's empty beer bottle. She lay on stage, spread her thick thighs apart and slowly pushed the beer bottle into her asshole. She almost had all of it stuffed into her.

Chaos looked over at Cherish and sighed because it was supposed to be their show but Cherish wanted the spotlight and she got it, for that moment.

"Yo, yo, do me like that, luv," a man shouted.

"Oh shit, that bitch is nasty! Yo, that shit is crazy," someone else shouted.

Cherish worked the crowd and did things to the bottle that only few could imagine.

But Chaos was determined to keep doing her thing with Sweet, not letting Cherish steal their audience from them. Chaos sucked on the dildo, deep-throating nine inches of synthetic dick while Sweet ate her out. The crowd's attention was split and money was going everywhere.

Three of the baddest chicks were on stage, naked and freaking each other off and the club was becoming chaotic. Niggas were becoming hard and horny from watching all of the action going on.

Cherish finished fucking herself with the beer bottle and sucked it off. The sight of her full, sweet lips wrapped around the bottle after she pulled it out of her ass made one nigga throw a hundred-dollar bill at her.

"Yo, shorty, we need to talk, fo' real," he called out hungrily.

Cherish looked over at Chaos and Sweet in their kinky position and decided that it was time for her to get in on the action. She moved behind Sweet while she was eating out Chaos. Cherish got down on her knees, spread Sweet's ass cheeks apart and tongued Sweet's wet pussy. Sweet tensed with pleasure as she felt Cherish's tongue digging into her pussy wildly. She grabbed Chaos's legs tightly and continued to suck and lick Chaos's pussy, even as she felt her own orgasm building.

By then, the stage was raining money and niggas were getting rowdy and wild.

# 8

YB walked into Magic's club alone. He heard the racket and saw that the stage was swarmed with niggas holding money in their hands. He knew some bitch was probably doing some freak shit on stage that was making niggas go bananas.

He moved farther into the club and looked around for any familiar faces, but he figured that anyone he knew was probably jammed into the crowd by the stage. For a minute, it looked like the trading floor of the New York Stock Exchange, with everyone crammed together around one particular area, shouting and waving money.

"Hey YB," Angel greeted.

YB gave him a head nod.

The other strippers in the place eyed YB. They knew his pockets were fat with that paper he was getting from the block. They greeted him with smiles and flattery but he showed them little love and looked around for Chaos.

The strippers knew who YB was searching for and had no clue to why YB was on Chaos's shit like that. They scratched their heads and wondered what Chaos had that they didn't. They were jealous and hated on Chaos but knew not to fuck with her because she was Crown's bitch.

"YB, if you're looking to get up with Chaos, you need to go check by the stage and see how that bitch gets down," a stripper named Trendy said snidely.

YB looked at her and smirked. He didn't even waste his breath on her. YB moved toward the stage while Trendy kept her eyes on him. When he was a good distance away, Trendy rolled her eyes and said to no one in particular, "He must like them dirty chicks 'cause that bitch ain't got shit over me."

YB navigated his way through the thick crowd of men and reached the stage. He observed Chaos in a contorted sexual position with Sweet and Cherish. Chaos was still on her back, fucking herself with the pink dildo, while Sweet licked at her pussy and Cherish continued to eat Sweet out from the back. It was a pornographic scene and niggas loved every minute of it.

Chaos turned her head and made eye contact with YB, who just continued to stare at her. He was the only face in the crowd that didn't look too excited about the freak show taking place on stage.

Suddenly, Chaos felt guilty but she didn't know why. YB wasn't her man and they weren't fucking but it felt like she disappointed him somehow. She stopped fucking herself with the dildo for a moment and studied YB before he walked away, fighting his way back through the dense crowd.

Chaos closed her eyes and felt Cherish's tongue in her pussy this time. She couldn't help but moan at the oral pleasure Cherish gave her.

YB returned to the bar and ordered a shot of Patrón. He downed that and ordered another. He waited patiently for Chaos to finish with her pornographic show. It didn't bother him that she was naked in front of dozen of men and getting her pussy eaten out by the next bitch, but it did bother him that she was with Crown. He knew a woman like Chaos deserved better.

YB sat alone and lost in his thoughts. He thought about his life in the streets with Rufus and then thought about Chaos. He reminisced about when they first met.

Eight months earlier, Chaos was turning a trick in a nigga's blue Benz truck on Lancaster Avenue. YB and Rufus were half a block down, doing business on the streets when YB heard Chaos scream. He looked and saw a scuffle going on in the truck, which was parked on the block. Without thinking, he walked over to the Benz.

"YB, where da fuck you goin'? What, you wanna be Captain Save-a-Ho now? That ain't our fuckin' business!" Rufus had exclaimed.

YB ignored his cousin. When he got closer to the truck, he saw a man beating on Chaos while forcing her down on the passenger seat. He flared up. He didn't know Chaos, but he'd seen her around a few times and he always thought that she was a cutie.

Chaos screamed, "Get the fuck off me! Get the fuck off me!"

YB removed a concealed .45 from his waistband and opened the driver's side door. He pulled the nigga forcefully out the car. The man was big, but that didn't intimidate YB.

"Yo, what the fuck, nigga?" the man shouted as he pulled up his jeans. He was getting ready to attack YB but before he could, YB had the gun aimed at his head.

"Yeah, go ahead, nigga, get stupid out here," YB warned.

The man glared at YB and retorted, "Nigga, you know who the fuck I am? Get that shit out my fuckin' face."

The man stepped closer and YB fired a round into his leg, dropping the trick to the concrete. He screamed, clutching his leg, and shouted, "Fuck you, nigga! You're a dead man."

Chaos got out of the car. YB looked at her and asked, "Yo, you a'ight?"

Chaos nodded and pulled down her skirt.

YB looked down at the man he shot and said, "You in the wrong place for that shit, nigga."

"Nigga, I'm Shyfe Lyfe! Fuck y'all niggas!"

Rufus walked over with his 9 mm in his hand. He was ready for anything to pop off. He looked down at Shyfe Lyfe and recognized the nigga from being with them Northside niggas over on Diamond Street.

"Nigga, what da fuck you say?" Rufus shouted.

Shyfe Lyfe looked up at Rufus and kept his gangster composure. "Y'all niggas is dead behind this shit. I'm gonna call my niggas down to this muthafucka and fuck y'all whole shit up! DOA, muthafucka!" Shyfe Lyfe tried to crawl back to his truck to get his gun, but Rufus put two holes into the nigga, stopping him cold.

Chaos was startled but she didn't go anywhere. She just looked at the scene unfolding in front of her.

Rufus looked over at Chaos and said, "Yo, bitch, you good, right? You ain't see shit, right? I ain't gonna be hearing about this, or us, in no news or shit?"

Chaos nodded.

Rufus turned to his cousin. "You got me out here killing niggas over some bitch 'cause your ass wanna be weak over some pussy? Nigga, you better fuck that bitch."

Rufus moved away, stuffing the nine back down in his jeans. YB and Chaos looked at each other for a moment. The way they handled her situation with Shyfe Lyfe was harsh, but she appreciated the help.

"You be a'ight, shorty. You ain't gotta worry about that nigga no more," YB said casually.

Chaos nodded again.

YB walked away.

Chaos sighed, fixed her clothing, and strutted away quickly, leaving Shyfe Lyfe sprawled out dead next to his truck.

When word got out about the shooting and Shyfe Lyfe being killed in the Westside of Philly, it caused some tension and havoc with niggas from the Northside. Niggas from Diamond Street wanted to retaliate for Shyfe Lyfe's death, but no one knew who did it. So, they looked at every nigga from the Westside as a suspect and were ready to murder any one of them. YB and Rufus had a fierce reputation around the way, and if anyone other than Chaos did witness the murder, they were scared to come forward.

Chaos kept her mouth shut, though, and continued with business like it never happened—knowing that YB probably saved her life. Later on, she heard about Shyfe Lyfe's callous reputation with women. He put three ladies in the hospital a year ago and killed another ho six months ago.

It was two months later when YB and Chaos crossed paths again. Chaos was staying over at her cousin Bubbles's crib for the weekend. She was chilling alone when she heard police sirens blaring outside. She looked out the window and saw a police car racing down the block. She knew something had happened being it was West Philly, but it wasn't her business so she stayed inside.

Chaos walked into the kitchen and soon heard a small disturbance near her door, outside in the alleyway. She looked out her window and saw a figure moving through the alley. By the way he moved she knew he was probably the one the cops were chasing.

She opened the door and shouted, "You need help wit' sumthin?"

The guy stumbled over a few trashcans and then turned to see Chaos standing in the doorway. They didn't recognize each other at first, but as YB got closer, he placed her face quickly. He ran to her and Chaos let him into the crib just in time to avoid the cop car racing down the alleyway, its lights blaring, seconds later.

YB took comfort in the kitchen, leaning against the sink to catch his breath. He looked at Chaos and asked, "You always let niggas you don't know into your crib so easily, especially hearing cops outside?"

Chaos smirked. "No 'thank you' and shit? Besides, I remembered you and my friend had my back in case you got stupid."

"Your friend?" He looked down and noticed the .22 in Chaos's hand. YB had to respect her character.

"Thanks for returning the favor," YB said.

"You're welcome."

He hid out in Chaos's cousin's place until later that night when the police activity calmed down. The thing that YB liked about Chaos was that she didn't judge him and never asked YB why the cops were after him.

She fed him and they talked. It was their second meeting and it wouldn't be their last. Throughout the months, YB would run into Chaos either at the club or in the streets. They shared an undercover love for each other, but kept it at that—undercover.

YB switched to Hennessy and watched Janet Jacme get fucked from the back in the porno that played on the mounted flat screen over the bar.

"Can I get a drink too?" Chaos asked, sitting next to YB.

"What you want?"

Chaos called for Angel and ordered a Kamikaze with Grey Goose.

She tried to be discreet about talking with YB, knowing that eyes were always watching.

"You had yourself a good time?" YB said mockingly.

"It be just business wit' me on that stage, nuthin' else," Chaos shot back. She stared straight ahead, not giving YB any eye contact.

"Business ... yeah, right. Why you keep letting that bitch-ass nigga Crown run you like some mule?"

"YB, chill out. Just buy me my drink and relax."

Angel set Chaos's drink in front of her and looked at YB.

"I got it." YB pulled out a wad of bills and passed Angel a twenty. "Keep it."

Angel nodded and walked off.

Chaos took a sip from her drink and then said, "You wanna do a VIP wit' me? We can talk more privately in the back."

"You know I don't pay for pussy," YB said.

Chaos sucked her teeth. "I ain't asking you to pay for it. I'm just sayin', pay for the room and break me off wit' somethin' and we can talk in the back."

"Nah, I'll talk to you right here."

"YB, you gonna get me into trouble. You know I ain't supposed to be talkin' to you in the first place. If Crown comes up in here you know what type of drama it's gon' cause."

"Chaos, why don't you leave that nigga? What he do for you? You the one fuckin' niggas and he gettin' rich off your pussy. The nigga blacks a bitch's eye when they don't earn enough and y'all respect that nigga like he somebody."

"Like what you do out in them streets is any better. You a wicked nigga just like him. You sell drugs. He sells pussy. You got guns. He got guns. And from what I've been hearing about you, you ain't too shy about killing, either."

"I do what I do, but I don't respect that pimp and his ways."

Chaos looked at him. "Niggas that live in glass houses shouldn't throw stones."

"Yeah, whatever."

"Say I leave him, YB. You gonna take care of me? I mean, you stable and all, stackin' that paper. I know you been in the game long enough. You ain't gonna be ashamed to have a ho under your arm? You just saw me onstage doin' what I do. So you ready to call me wifey, despite all that greasy talk you gonna hear about me from other niggas and knowing who I fucked? You ready to let my past be and accept that? 'Cause if you are, then I'm ready."

YB just stared at her. Chaos was beautiful, but she was also damaged goods and had fucked many niggas in Philly.

YB's hesitation let Chaos know he wasn't ready to handle it.

"Exactly," she said.

"Look, Chaos, shit is complicated right now," YB said.

"What the fuck is complicated, YB? If you wanna be wit' me, then be wit' me. I ain't gonna front, I like you a lot, but I can't lose out on anything for some part-time shit. I've been in the game too long to know that every word or promise out a nigga's mouth ain't the truth."

YB had to respect her honesty and her edge. She knew the truth about herself and didn't try to mask it for any nigga.

"You're real, Chaos. I like that."

"Well, when a nigga starts being real wit' me and I know he fo' real by his actions and not his mouth, then I'm gonna really show that nigga somethin' about me. But till then this is me and who I am."

YB nodded.

Chaos took another sip from her drink. She wanted to be with YB and she did want to change in her life, but it was risky. To leave Crown was a dangerous task because Crown's ego and pride could be murderous. To even think about taking take that chance Chaos had to know that YB was for real with her.

"I gotta go make this money. I'll see you around, YB," Chaos said.

She walked away from the bar and YB turned to stare at her backside. It was a lovely sight to see. YB wasn't the only one to take notice. Niggas were studying Chaos's figure and booty like it was an exam.

YB sighed and thought about what Chaos said. She was real and a good woman but the shit she did and the niggas she'd fucked clouded his feelings for her.

Angel walked over to YB and said, "Chaos is good people, YB. She done been through a lot. She's one of the better ones in here. And believe me, I've done seen it all."

YB looked at Angel. "Y'all close?"

"We talk. I'm like a brother to her up in here."

YB nodded.

"But it would be good for her to have someone nice in her life, besides Crown. I mean, I talk to Crown, tell him what he wants to hear, but between you and me, he's an asshole. And I don't know how a woman like Chaos got caught up wit' that nigga."

Angel was gay, but he kept it on the down low because he knew most niggas in the place were homophobic so he played straight for the business. Chaos knew about his love for the dick, though.

"I tell you this, Angel. If Crown step to me again like that and I'm gonna bury that fake pimp nigga," YB said.

Angel smiled. "You need another drink?"

YB nodded.

Angel walked off, leaving YB to ponder about Chaos. YB turned to look for her and saw her mixed in the crowd, talking to some dude in a Giants jersey.

*Dirty Little Angel*

Damn, she do look good, he thought to himself.

Angel set another drink in front YB while he was still looking at Chaos.

Chaos began to give the man a lap dance. The man grabbed her ass then reached up to cup her tits.

As Chaos was being groped by the stranger YB just watched, containing the jealousy that was growing in him. He took a sip from his glass and eyed her action. Chaos looked up at YB and they locked gazes.

Fuck this. YB turned himself away from the view. Chaos shrugged it off and went on to give the nigga his money's worth.

# 9

"Rufus did this shit to you, Toy-T?" Crown growled.

"I ain't do shit to the nigga, Crown! Rufus just walked up to me and started wildin'," Toy-T explained. "He hurt me bad, Crown."

Toy-T received ten stitches across his head and suffered a minor concussion. He was badly bruised had and almost lost the vision in his left eye. Now that he was bandaged up, he wanted revenge on Rufus.

"Don't worry about it, little nigga, we on it," Harlem said in his casual tone. "You'll get your chance to hurt back on that clown-ass nigga."

Toy-T nodded. He couldn't wait to get back at Rufus.

"Yo, let us talk. Go somewhere," Crown ordered Toy-T.

Toy-T walked out the room. Crown walked over to his makeshift bar and poured himself a drink. Harlem stood by closely, waiting for instructions from his boss.

"This nigga and his cousin are goin' to be a problem," Crown said.

"I know how to make problems disappear," Harlem replied with a smug look on his face.

Crown took a sip from his glass and stared off into space. Toy-T was kin to him, and he knew if he didn't handle it, then it would be grounds for future problems for him and his chicks. Crown needed to keep his fierce reputation.

Crown looked at Harlem and said, "Shut them niggas down, Harlem. Make it too hot for them to get money and then you body that nigga, Rufus. He put hands on my cousin so you put hands on that nigga."

Harlem nodded. "What about YB?"

"Nah, I'm gonna handle YB. Muthafucka thinks he's too much of a badass to get got. Well, when you're done with Rufus and his niggas, we gonna make that nigga YB die slow. And if Magic wanna step in for that nigga, well, he can get bodied too."

"I'm on it, my nigga. This is gonna be fun." Harlem was ready to lay his gun game down something serious.

Crown took another sip from his drink. "Yo, when you leave, send that new bitch in here. I wanna have a word with her."

Harlem nodded and walked into the hallway. Denise, the new girl that they picked up from Broad Street last night was seated quietly. Harlem looked her up and down and admired her physique. She had on a short denim skirt that showed her meaty thighs and white and red Nikes. Her long hair was in braids and her skin was so light that she could pass for white. Her tight, black T-shirt highlighted her tits and read, in big, white, bold letters, RIP, FOR THE BITCHES DYING TO BE ME.

Harlem liked the T-shirt. He knew she was going to bring in thousands of dollars for Crown and him.

"Yo, go see Crown right now," Harlem instructed.

Denise nodded and stood. She was about 5'5" and was only seventeen. Crown knew that the younger the chicks were, the better.

Denise entered the room while Harlem smiled at her backside.

He stroked his dick through his jeans and knew he wanted a piece of her light-skinned ass. But Crown would be the first to test the waters, and Harlem didn't mind having sloppy seconds after him. However, he did mind being with a bitch after she done worked the track for a few weeks. By then, the pussy was no good for him—too many niggas had stretched their dicks into the pussy and he wasn't down to fuck a bitch after a trick had hit it.

Harlem went to his truck while Denise moved toward Crown shyly. Crown stood by the bar, nursing his Rum and Coke and watched her approach.

Denise stood quietly in the center of the room. She was a runaway from Delaware, and like so many others, she didn't have a place to stay. Crown promised her a home and a better lifestyle.

"Your name Denise, right?" Crown asked.

She nodded.

"I like you already. You're fuckin' quiet and already speak when you're spoken to. Now if you can get this money for a nigga, we gonna be best friends," Crown said.

Denise nodded again.

Crown continued to stare her down from head to toe. So far, he liked what he saw. She was petite, but firm in the right places. Her skin color was appealing; she definitely could be passed off as a white girl. He had one problem with her, though.

"You need to lose the braids," he said.

She nodded a third time.

"And from now on, I'm gonna call you Casper," he added.

Denise didn't object to the sudden name change. She continued to stand still.

Crown poured himself another drink. "Take your fuckin' clothes off, bitch."

*Dirty Little Angel*

Denise looked up at him. Crown gave her such a hard stare that it let Denise know he was nothing to play with.

"I ain't got all day, bitch. I need to see what you're working with and what needs improving so strip, bitch."

Denise pulled off her tight T-shirt and dropped it to the floor before she kicked off her sneakers and pulled down her skirt. Finally, she stood in front of Crown in her matching pink-and-white bra and panties. She crossed her arms across her chest in a protective gesture.

Crown nodded his head, definitely liking what he saw. She had a flat stomach, nice big breasts, and succulent, defined legs.

"Continue," Crown uttered.

Denise/Casper reached behind her back and unsnapped her bra. She pushed the straps off her shoulders and let her bra fall onto her folded arms. She was shy at first, but hearing Crown say, "It's only you and me. Go ahead, bitch." encouraged her to open up.

Denise let her bra fall to the floor and Crown scrutinized her dark nipples. At last, she pulled down her panties and stood butt-naked.

Her body was something every nigga would crave. She had a thin waistline and big tits with nipples that could melt in a nigga's mouth.

"Turn around," Crown commanded.

Denise turned around slowly, giving Crown a nice, clear view of her nude backside.

"Nice, nice. You'll definitely do for me."

Denise turned to face him again. She stood demurely with her arms to her side; her nakedness was turning Crown on. Her pussy was shaved which was a plus and she had no tattoos. Crown loved that shit about her.

"C'mere."

Denise walked over to Crown. He moved closer to her, drink still in hand. He looked Denise square in her eyes and asked, "You ever suck dick before?"

She nodded.

"Let me see then, bitch."

Denise got down on her knees and Crown lifted up his T-shirt, giving her full access to unbuckle his pants and show him how she did business.

Slowly, Denise unbuckled his pants and pulled down his zipper to remove his hardening dick. Crown sipped his drink while Denise gripped his eight inches in her hand.

"I ain't got all day, bitch. Just suck it."

Denise took Crown into her mouth, inch by inch. She began sucking him off and Crown moaned. Crown had one hand tangled in her hair and the other still holding his liquor. He looked down at Denise's head bobbing back and forth and wanted to take a picture of the bitch sucking dick.

"Let me see you deep-throat the dick," Crown said. He admired her form and grabbed her by the back of her head and forced more dick down her throat.

Denise gagged a little but kept it gangster and continued to suck him off like a pro. Crown moaned again. The fellatio was getting so good that he had to set his glass down and focus on the bitch.

As soon as he was about to cum he told her to get up. Denise stood up, wiping her mouth and knowing she'd sucked Crown off like a pro.

"Yeah, with a mouth like that, you gonna make us plenty of money," Crown said. "I'm gonna have you work the club tonight and then put you on the track tomorrow night. I'm gonna pair you off wit' Cherish and let her show you the ropes on how we get this money, a'ight?"

Denise nodded.

*Dirty Little Angel*

"And what's your name again, bitch?"

"Casper," Denise replied.

"You're home now, Casper, so you ain't got nuthin' to worry about. Anybody fucks wit' you, they fuck wit' me, a'ight? You continue to get this money and you'll live like a queen. I take care of my ladies and I expect y'all to take care of me. You fuck and suck niggas when I tell you to fuck and suck niggas. You don't ever give my pussy away for free, you hear me, bitch?"

She nodded.

Crown continued to school her about the game and when he was done he said, "A'ight, you can get dressed now, bitch. We gotta make this money tonight. You're on probation till I tell you that you ain't on probation anymore."

Casper reached for her clothing and quickly got dressed. Crown downed the rest of his drink and delivered a final warning to Casper: "Don't fuck me over tonight. I'm a nice guy when my money is right."

# 10

Harlem was parked a block down from YB's drug spot on Brown Street. He observed the activity that night, his .45 on his lap. He was dressed in all black and sat patiently behind tinted windows in his burgundy Yukon.

He watched the fiends move up and down the block for their high. A few of Rufus's men served their clientele openly like the shit was legal. Besides the drug movement, the block was quiet.

Harlem took a drag from his Newport and kept an eye out for anything unusual. He looked around for Rufus but saw him nowhere around. It didn't matter whether Rufus was around or not, as his objective was to shut their business down and make the block hot. He was determined to do so.

Harlem glanced at the time and saw that it was fifteen minutes past midnight. It was still early for the fiends, and they were still coming and going from the building. He took one last pull from the smoke, removed a silencer from the glove compartment, and attached it to his gun.

Harlem waited for the right time to strike. When the clutter of fiends and niggas cleared from the building, Harlem stepped out of his truck with the gun in his hand.

He moved coolly down the block in his dark denim jacket and jeans and black Timberlands. He didn't stand out, and with his boyish features and he didn't look intimidating to anyone. Looks could be deceiving and Harlem was a ruthless killer who would spill blood from man, woman, or child. He had dead bodies under his infamous name, and his murderous reputation preceded him. The only talent he had was killing.

Harlem continued to move toward the building. He focused on certain niggas out front, knowing that they were Rufus's soldiers. He gripped the gun behind his back and cautiously moved ahead.

The traffic on the block was sparse and the lighting was dim since only three streetlights were working.

With his first victim trained in his sight, Harlem aimed and fired two into the first soldier.

Poot! Poot!

The gunshots were quiet but still deadly and hit the victim in the back. He dropped in front of his homies, but before anyone could help him or realized what was going on, Harlem dropped another nigga dead, and then he shot a fiend in the neck.

"Oh, shit! Yo, niggas is shooting!" one boy yelled. He tried to run for safety, but Harlem shot him in the back of the head.

By now, everyone out front knew of the danger and saw Harlem coming their way with the gun outstretched in his hand. He was randomly shooting niggas down.

Fiends began to scatter, but some got shot down by the gunfire. A few more of Rufus's soldiers came running out of the house with their guns out, but Harlem quickly shot them down where they stood.

Mayhem spread on the block fast, and soon everybody was running for their lives. Harlem looked around and was back in his truck before the gunfire was heavily returned. His job was done. He made the block hot and money stopped flowing in for YB and Rufus.

His truck peeled around the corner, leaving six dead and many wounded. Police would soon be all over the scene, canvassing and asking questions.

# 11

Crown arrived at the club with Casper around one in the morning. The place was jumping with money flowing and the music blaring.

Magic stood behind the bar trying to help Angel out with the drink orders. His other bartender, Peaches, called out for the night, and he had no one to replace her. Magic was never afraid to step up when needed, so he took matters into his own hands.

Magic turned to see Crown walk in. The pimp was dapper in black slacks, a black silk shirt, polished wingtip shoes, and a black derby. He had on a diamond pinky ring and matching bracelet, and the usual cigar was clutched between his fingers. His long, permed hair fell graciously down to his shoulders underneath the derby. He looked like a gangster and a gentleman.

Casper meekly stood behind Crown in her short denim skirt. Six-inch high heels replaced the Nikes she'd had on earlier, and her tight, sexy top accentuated her breasts. She immediately caught everyone's attention. She was fresh meat in the club. Niggas stared at her tight figure and couldn't wait to get a piece of her.

Magic gave a small smile, noticing the sexy new young thing Crown had with him.

"I see Crown got a new girl tonight," Angel said.

Magic sighed.

Crown looked over at Magic and they locked eyes for a moment. Crown puffed on his cigar before walking over to Magic. Casper was right behind him.

"Damn, shorty is nice," a nigga was heard saying as Casper moved through the crowd.

"I got a fresh bitch for the club, Magic," Crown said.

Magic looked at the young girl. "How old is she?"

"Nigga, she old enough to get plenty of money for me and you. You know the routine, Magic: I'll cut you off a percentage for doin' business up in here. I know the house gotta get paid too."

Magic showed no emotion. He just looked at Casper one more time, studying her young, beautiful features. "Just make sure she know how we do things in here."

Crown nodded. He said to Casper, "We got rules to this shit here, and Cherish will let you know how not to fuck up."

Casper gave her usual nod.

Crown looked around for Cherish and saw her by the stage working a trick. She was butt-naked in white, patent leather wedge heels and had a fistful of money.

Crown walked over to her with Casper following. Cherish smiled at Crown's approach, but her smile disappeared when she saw Casper.

"Who that bitch, Crown?" Cherish asked with some attitude.

"This bitch is family now. I want you to take her under your wing and teach her how we do things. Make sure she learns how to get this money, Cherish."

*Dirty Little Angel*

Cherish sighed loudly.

"Bitch, you got a fuckin' problem?" Crown snapped.

"No, Daddy. I'm cool," Cherish replied in a timid tone.

"A'ight then, bitch, you make sure Casper gets this money in this fuckin' club. Her minimum is five hundred for the night. You understand me, bitch?"

"Yes, Daddy, I understand."

Crown said to Casper, "Bitch, get dressed and work these niggas in here."

Casper nodded again.

"You watch her, Cherish," Crown warned.

Cherish nodded.

As Crown walked away, Cherish asked, "Daddy, can I talk to you?"

Crown turned and took a pull from his cigar. "What, bitch?"

"It's about Chaos," she mentioned.

Crown squinted and irritably replied with, "What about that bitch?"

"She broke one of your rules tonight," Cherish informed.

"What fuckin' rule?"

"I saw her talking to YB by the bar earlier, before you came in," she said to him.

"Where that bitch at now?"

"She went to go do a VIP wit' a trick."

Crown didn't say another word and just walked away. Cherish smiled knowing Chaos was in serious trouble with Crown. She violated Crown by even talking to YB when she was forbidden to do so. Since Cherish was Crown's bottom bitch, she had to make sure she kept her Daddy's house in order.

Crown went to the VIP area to look for Chaos. YB wasn't around,

*Erica Hilton*

but he wasn't concerned about that nigga right now. He had to check one of his hoes.

He waited by the VIP entrance smoking on his cigar. He wanted to have a word with Chaos and it was going to be harsh. His bitches needed to know that you didn't fuck with his money or his time.

"Ah, shit, ah, shit, Chaos," Danny moaned, feeling Chaos's sweet lips wrapped around his short, thick dick.

Danny was one of Chaos's regulars. He was slumped on the couch with his legs spread. Chaos was on her knees between his thighs sucking him off like the professional she was.

Danny had his eyes closed as Chaos to work her magic on him. She jerked him off and played with the tip of his dick until she felt him harden and then he exploded into the condom. Danny let out a deep sigh after his nut, looking spent.

Chaos wiped her mouth and stood. "You good, right?"

"Hells yeah, I'm good. Shit, Chaos, you be doin' me right!"

Chaos got dressed. She covered her perky tits and stuffed the money in her G-string. Her olive-colored skin and long jet black hair was dripping with sweat. Danny stood, pulled up his jeans, and tossed the used condom in a nearby wastebasket.

Chaos smiled at him. "You be good and get at me whenever."

"I sure will," Danny replied.

It was her third trick turned for the night, and so far her night had been good. She had made over $500 already and was working to bring Crown over a thousand before the night ended.

Chaos had YB on her mind when she headed toward the exit from VIP. Her attire for the night was a sexy, black-and-hot-pink micro-mini skirt with a matching halter top. Her pussy was still feeling sticky and sore from the last trick she fucked, but she was definitely taking care of business and making her ends for the night.

She wore a small smile on her face when she walked back into the main part of the club, which was called the Violator room. That smile quickly disappeared when she saw Crown coming her way with a furious gaze across his face.

Chaos stopped in her tracks, but Crown continued to walk briskly in her direction.

"C'mere, you fuckin' bitch!" he yelled.

Chaos stood still in horror. Crown grabbed her by her neck, choking her in front of everyone at the club.

"What the fuck I told you about that nigga, YB? Huh, bitch? You wanna fuckin' disobey me?"

Tears welled in Chaos's eyes as Crown's hand squeezed her neck and she began to gag. He pushed her against the wall and smacked the shit out of her. Chaos spit blood and the party stopped for a moment. Everybody saw the scene Crown was causing, but no one attempted to help in any way.

"Baby, Daddy, it was a mistake. I'm sorry, Daddy," Chaos tried to plead with him.

Crown hit her again. Chaos dropped to the floor and landed on her side. Her lip was busted and dripping blood. She peered up at Crown and begged him to stop, but he kicked her in the stomach. Chaos cringed with pain.

"Magic, please do somethin' to help her," Angel pleaded to Magic.

"This muthafucka!" Magic growled.

He didn't care for Crown or any of his chicks, but he had seen enough and knew that Crown had gone too far. That shit he was pulling on Chaos wasn't allowed to happen in Magic's club.

Magic approached Crown with an angry stare, ready to beat him into the ground if he didn't stop with the bullshit.

"Crown, what the fuck you doing?" Magic shouted.

Crown saw Magic coming his way. His face was twisted with anger and rage, but he stopped beating on Chaos for a moment.

"Magic, this ain't your fuckin' business. This is my bitch here, a'ight?"

"Nigga, she in my club, so it is my business," Magic retorted.

"Magic, just step the fuck off and let me handle my bitches like I always do."

"Not in here, Crown. You're out of line, nigga. You take that shit outside; you know my rules, nigga. Take your bitches and get the fuck out my club!" Magic glared at Crown, making sure he got the point.

Crown returned the glare, but knew he couldn't rise up against Magic in his own spot. Magic kept his composure. He wanted to hit Crown but knew it wasn't worth it. The way the pimp beat Chaos down got no respect from Magic and a few of his peoples in the club. Everyone else knew that Crown was trouble, so they tried to keep their distance from him. They all knew to fear Crown because of his hired gun, Harlem.

Magic didn't fear those young niggas. He wanted their business, but in the end, he knew that niggas like Crown and Rufus would eventually become more trouble than they were worth.

Crown turned his attention back to Chaos. She was still on the floor, crying.

"Bitch, shut the fuck up wit' that crying and get the fuck up," Crown sternly commanded.

He looked for his other chicks and yelled, "Yo, all my bitches in this fuckin' club better be dressed within fifteen fuckin' minutes."

Cherish stopped what she was doing and pulled Casper off a nigga's lap. "C'mon, bitch, let's go."

She dragged Casper to the dressing room. Midnight got down from the stage and rushed toward the dressing room as well, her tits jiggling with each step.

"Where the fuck is Sweet?" Crown asked.

"She's doin' a VIP," Cherish informed him.

Crown sighed.

Chaos got up and stood submissively next to Crown. She had a black eye to match her busted lip.

"Fuck you and your club, Magic! We out this bitch," Crown exclaimed.

"Nigga, don't disrespect me and my place like that ever again," Magic warned.

Crown let out an annoyed sigh and just looked at Magic. "We'll soon be seeing a new day, nigga," Crown shot back.

"Don't try me, nigga. I'm old, but I could still be a wicked muthafucka in your life."

Both men exchanged menacing looks. Crown grabbed Chaos by her arm and dragged her out the door. "Wait till we get home, bitch. You ain't seen shit yet."

Angel watched Chaos leave with a panicked expression. He felt sorry for her but he knew there wasn't shit he could do for her. He wished he had YB's cell phone number. If YB had been around the incident with Chaos and Crown wouldn't have gotten that far. But YB left way before Crown arrived.

When Crown and his chicks left, Magic shouted to the DJ, "Yo, now that the trash is out, turn my music back on."

The DJ started playing Jay-Z to ease the crowd's mood.

# 12

Rufus got the call immediately after his spot was hit by Harlem. He was on Girard Avenue, near the highway, getting a blowjob from some chicken head. Mike-Mike called to let him know that the block got hit hard. Rufus was furious and immediately rushed to Brown Street to see his block swarming with cops and news reporters.

He hurried over to the taped-off the area and saw EMT's wheeling out bodies on stretchers and putting them into the meat wagon.

Rufus looked at that carnage with wild eyes. He had his gun on him and looked for his niggas, so he could find out what really happened. He was ready to let loose and kill anybody who was responsible for his business being shut down. Rufus knew it would be stupid to try to get closer to his building, especially being dirty. Cops were all over the place, combing the area for shell casings, knocking on neighbors' doors, and asking questions. The cops were picking up the dead and nursing the injured.

Mike-Mike approached Rufus with a worried look. "Yo, what the fuck happened here?" Rufus snarled. "Who did this shit, Mike-Mike?"

Mike-Mike replied, "It was Harlem. I saw that nigga creeping up the block with the gun. It had a silencer on it."

"Harlem? You sure it was that nigga?"

Mike-Mike nodded. "I saw that nigga shoot J.J. in the back and then he went off on everyone. I hid behind a car and watched this nigga just go crazy."

Rufus's facial expression said it all. Niggas were going to die tonight.

"Yo, gather up who you can and meet me at Magic's spot," Rufus instructed.

"A'ight." Mike-Mike walked off to do as he was ordered.

Rufus walked back to his truck and made a call to YB, but there was no answer.

"Pick up, nigga . . . pick the fuckin' phone up, YB," Rufus said out loud. When YB's voicemail came on, Rufus tossed the phone across the seat and started the ignition. He checked the ammunition in his gun and then reached into the glove compartment and pulled out a Glock 17. He was ready to murder niggas tonight.

Rufus parked his money-green Denali in front of Magic's club. He didn't care about parking or anything else. His main focus was finding Harlem, Crown, or any one of his chicks and gunning them down where they stood. He stuffed the .380 in his jeans and cocked the Glock before getting out of his truck. He looked up the block and saw a black Lexus speeding toward him. It stopped near his truck and Mike-Mike stepped out of the passenger's side. Three more thuggish-looking niggas got out of the car as well.

Rufus nodded and said, "That's what I'm talkin' about. Let's go serve this nigga early, my niggas."

The thugs approached the club with guns in hands and murder in their eyes. They rushed past security and barged into the club.

There were screams of panic and horror when they brandished their guns for everyone to see. Women started to run and niggas tried to hide behind tables, behind the bar, and in bathrooms. The music stopped abruptly as havoc began to spread throughout Magic's spot.

Magic couldn't believe this shit. It was one thing after another. He walked up to Rufus and his crew and shouted, "Nigga, what the fuck you think you're doing? Are you stupid, running up in my spot with them guns?"

Rufus glared and pointed the Glock at Magic's head. "Where the fuck is Crown?"

"He ain't here," Magic replied coldly.

"Magic, don't fuckin' lie to me. Where the fuck are his chicks then?"

"Rufus, don't be stupid. The nigga ain't here. I kicked him and his chicks out about an hour ago."

Rufus looked around the spot. He searched for any familiar face that belonged to Crown but saw none. He knew that he just missed that nigga and was upset with himself.

"You happy now, nigga?" Magic snapped. "I told you they ain't fuckin' here."

Rufus lowered the gun and said, "You see that nigga Crown or Harlem, you let 'em know they're dead men walking."

"Get the fuck outta here, Rufus!" Magic barked.

Rufus smirked. "This was no disrespect to you, Magic, but if I was you, I'd keep them niggas outta your club."

"Get the fuck outta here," Magic repeated unkindly.

Rufus left, followed by his goons. Magic stood outside his spot and watched them leave. When they were gone he got on his cell phone and dialed YB's number. He left YB a message: "If you value your life, or your cousin's, you call me back ASAP, muthafucka."

# 13

Crown parked his truck in his driveway and was still furious about what went down tonight at Magic's. He had his flock of hoes in the back and was upset that he lost out on making money for the night. He turned off the engine and looked at Cherish, who sat in the passenger seat. "Get these bitches into the house and take Chaos down into my room in the basement."

"Yes, Daddy," Cherish replied.

She got out of the Escalade and ushered the girls out of the car and into the house.

Crown followed, smoking his cigar with a scowl. He had definitely shown his true colors in Magic's club tonight, and he knew that the business relationship he had with Magic was either strained or completely dissolved.

He pushed those thoughts out of his mind because he had other matters to attend to. Chaos needed strict discipline in his house. He entered the house and called for Cherish. She came running like a trained dog.

"What you need, baby?" Cherish asked obediently.

"You put that bitch in the basement?" he asked.

"Yes, Daddy."

"A'ight. You tell them other bitches upstairs not to even think that they got a night off. I'm gonna get a few tricks to come over to make us this money tonight."

Cherish nodded.

"You tell them bitches that they're gonna fuck and suck niggas tonight, early, a'ight?"

"Yes, Daddy."

"Now do what you're told."

Cherish strutted upstairs to get Crown's business in order. When she was out of sight, Crown walked toward the basement stairs, unbuttoning his shirt as he did so.

He descended the stairs and heard Chaos's cries coming from the room she was locked in. He unlocked the door and saw Chaos seated on one of his couches. She was curled up like a ball sobbing. Crown was furious. "Bitch! Did I tell you to fuckin' sit anywhere in this room?" he screamed.

Chaos jumped in fear. Crown yanked her by her top and dragged her from the couch. She fell to the floor on her side and Crown continued to drag her. Chaos screamed and fidgeted as her top ripped. The carpet burned against her exposed thighs.

He dragged her to the center of the room and slapped her hard. Chaos cried out in pain and tried to curl into a fetal position to protect herself.

"Bitch, I'm gonna teach you to fuckin' listen tonight! You need discipline, bitch. What I tell you about even lookin' at that nigga YB? I want you to think about that nigga while I'm beating your ass tonight."

He hit her several times, but mostly on parts of her body that

*Dirty Little Angel*

weren't easily visible like the stomach and back. He was angry that he had already blackened her eye and busted her lip because he knew she still needed to make money for him.

Crown panted heavily over Chaos. He glared down at her and commanded, "Bitch, take all that shit off."

Chaos slowly stood, shaken and weak by the abuse she endured. She undressed in a similar manner due to the pain.

"Bitch, you better hurry the fuck up and get naked before you make me really fuckin' mad up in this bitch," Crown warned her.

Chaos quickly came out of her panties and bra and stood butt naked in front of Crown with tears streaming down her cheeks. She shivered and prepared herself for the worst.

Crown smirked and looked at Chaos like she was a piece of meat. She was definitely a money maker for him with the body she had.

"C'mere, bitch." Crown pulled Chaos toward his special area for bitches who misbehaved.

He handcuffed her to a huge steel pipe and positioned her in the doggy-style position, which left her body open for more abuse. Chaos continued to plead with him and attempted to say that she was sorry, but Crown loved the way she begged for his forgiveness. It made him feel powerful and wanted.

"Bitch, you gonna learn! Oh, you're definitely gonna learn tonight." Crown removed his belt.

Chaos was so scared that she felt faint. Tears continued to flow down her pain-stricken face and her naked body quivered.

Crown gripped the thick leather belt and admired her form and backside for a moment. It was making him hard, but before there could be pleasure he needed to let loose some pain.

He raised the belt and swung down across Chaos's exposed back fast and hard like a bolt of lightning. Chaos screamed loudly. Crown hit her with the belt again and her body flinched. Her tears of anguish continued to flow.

"Bitch, when I tell you to do somethin', you fuckin' do it! It ain't gotta be like this, Chaos. You hear me, bitch?" Crown hit her again.

Her back developed bleeding welts, but Crown didn't stop. He took it a step further and got right behind her, pulled down his slacks and showed her how hard he was. He pushed himself into Chaos and she cried out. Even as Crown fucked her from the back, he continued to strike her with the belt. He loved this form of punishment. It was his sick way of keeping his chicks in control.

Chaos's painfully loud cries echoed throughout the house. It was something that the ladies were used to hearing. They hated to hear anyone cry like that, knowing that it could easily have been one of them—except for Cherish. She smiled when she heard Chaos being beaten and abused by Crown. It made her feel like the queen bee bitch of the house.

Sweet sat at the top of the staircase and cried for her friend. It was painful to hear, but there was nothing she could do. Every cry that Chaos made caused Sweet to cringe with sorrow.

"Bitch, what you doin' out here?" Cherish asked as she crept up behind Sweet.

"I'm just chillin'," Sweet replied.

"Bitch, I know you ain't being nosey. You tryin' to hear Crown's business? You feelin' sorry for your friend?" Cherish mocked.

"I'm just chillin', Cherish."

"Well, go and chill your ass in the bedroom and get ready to make some money for Crown tonight unless you want next downstairs with him. You want me to tell him about you, too? You want me to tell him that you're disobeying him by not gettin' ready because you're tryin' to be nosey, bitch?"

"No, I'm good." Sweet rose from her seat on the stairs.

"You better be good, bitch. Remember, I'm his bottom bitch in this crib, and y'all bitches better not forget that."

"Nah, Cherish, I know. I didn't forget." Sweet looked Cherish in the eyes and could have killed her for telling Crown about Chaos's earlier chat with YB.

Sweet walked into her room and took a deep breath. She thought about what Chaos had said to her before—about being a prisoner to Crown and leaving for something better. Sweet didn't have Chaos's ambition, and she felt that she had nothing left but to turn tricks for Crown. She wasn't the flyest chick on the block and she had only completed the ninth grade. She felt stuck and was scared to leave what she knew best for something that was unknown. She might end up worse off than she was. Sweet wasn't qualified to do shit other than prostitute and didn't have a supportive family to have her back. With Chaos being her best friend and Crown providing her a home and a way of living, she felt that she finally had a family.

Hearing the beating that Chaos received from Crown also made her think otherwise. Was it worth it? Sweet asked herself. She sat on her bed and leaned back against the headboard with a pillow clutched tightly to her chest. Tears of sorrow and pain poured out for her friend.

"It's goin' going to be a'ight, Chaos. We'll get through it, baby girl. I promise. We'll get through this," she said out loud to herself.

The sun shined into the bedrooms of the women after a rough and brutal night of turning tricks and hearing Chaos's pain and suffering.

Chaos lay in bed on her stomach, trying to recuperate from the hour-long beating from the night before. Her back looked as if she had been whipped by her overseer. The many welts that covered her olive skin were caked with blood and she was still emotionally scarred. Crown had beaten her before, but never this severely. He looked like a possessed man during the abuse.

She still cried at times, but with Sweet nursing her, Chaos felt a little more at ease. Sweet nursed her wounds gently by tending to it with a warm, wet cloth and Bactine ointment.

"That muthafucka," Sweet muttered in a low tone, making sure no one else heard. "He ain't have to beat you like this. I mean, all you did was talk to YB briefly. It ain't like you been fuckin' the nigga for free or somethin'."

Sweet continued to gently rub the ointment on Chaos's back. Chaos cringed in pain at contact with some of the wounds.

"You okay, Chaos?"

"I'll be better," she replied.

"I know he don't expect you to work tonight?"

"He put me on house arrest. Said he gonna keep me indoors until he feels he can trust me again."

Sweet looked around to make sure no one was listening in on their conversation. "It was that bitch Cherish that told Crown about you and YB talkin' at the bar."

Chaos let out a deep sigh. She never trusted or liked Cherish because she always made it known to the other women that she was his bottom bitch and she was quick to get a bitch in trouble with Crown just to score some extra points with him. Chaos knew that bitch needed a serious beat down, but now was not the time for Chaos to give it to her.

Sweet said, "Remember what you said before, about leaving here and doin' for ourselves?"

Chaos nodded.

"Well, I've been thinking: maybe you were right. Maybe we need to leave this muthafucka and just do our own thang. I mean, we both know the game, so why we can't pimp ourselves and keep our own fuckin' paper? After seeing what happened to you last night, I think we ain't safe here no more, Chaos. Crown might just end up killing one of us, and you know how his temper is."

Chaos didn't respond, but she definitely was listening. Sweet continued to talk while tending to her sore back. She looked at the time and saw that it on one in the afternoon.

"What you think, Chaos? We need to do sumthin'," Sweet said.

"What about Harlem? You know if we run, he'll send that nigga out after us," Chaos pointed out.

"I know. I've been thinking about him, too. What about your boyfriend, YB? Maybe he can help out with our escape."

"Boyfriend?" Chaos chuckled. It was the first laugh she had since the beating. "I don't know, Sweet. If we were caught, I'd hate to think what Crown would do to us. Look at me, and all I did was just talk to YB."

Chaos was scared. Crown definitely put fear in her heart last night and was making her think twice about crossing him. She also knew that she probably wouldn't last too long being under Crown's wicked wing.

"I care for you, Chaos, and I know that this shit can't go on," Sweet began. "You remember when I told you that I was used to Crown's abuse and that I've dealt wit' worse? I lied. Crown is the worst. I'm just scared of being on my own. I never had nothing in my life, and living here felt like I had somethin', Chaos. Shit, I'm only twenty years old and feel like an ol' hag in this bitch. I need to leave here, Chaos. I need to go."

Chaos turned slowly and looked Sweet in the eye. "What's goin' on wit' you, Sweet? Why you sounding like that for? I mean, you ain't doin' shit wrong. You making your ends fo' sure, so what you so worried about? I'm the one he beat last night."

Sweet took a deep breath. "I'm pregnant, Chaos."

Chaos was shocked. "You're what?"

"I'm pregnant. I missed my friend last month so I snuck and took a home pregnancy test. It tested positive, fo' sure."

"Oh my God, Sweet."

"I know if Crown finds out, he's going to beat this baby outta me. I'm scared. I can't have this baby."

"Sweet, relax. You know who the father is?"

"I don't know. Probably some trick I fucked that got a li'l too carried away and he came in me," Sweet replied dryly.

All of a sudden, Chaos's problem was like a traffic ticket compared to Sweet's. Both ladies knew that if Crown found out, he would be furious. He always told his chicks to strap up and don't get pregnant. If a bitch got pregnant by a trick, then Crown saw that as a loss of business and he reprimanded a bitch harshly for loss of business.

"A'ight, don't panic, Sweet. We're gonna figure somethin' out. You know how far along you are?"

"No. I haven't been to a doctor."

"A'ight. I figure you're probably about a month or two. So that means we got a li'l time before you start showing. This is kept between you and me so we gonna work somethin' out. I got you, girl," Chaos said supportively.

Sweet smiled and replied with, "I don't know what I would have done if he killed you last night. I probably would have gutted that muthafucka fo' real, Chaos. I'd be on some real suicide shit up in his crib."

Chaos smiled. "I got your back and you got mine."

They hugged each other tightly and knew that they had to come up with a plan to leave Crown. It was now or never for them.

# 14

YB woke up on his mother's couch with his cell phone ringing near his ear. He sluggishly reached for his phone, but by the time he picked it up, it had stopped ringing. He sighed and tossed the phone on the floor and fell back against the couch, closing his eyes.

He had a slight hangover from drinking at Magic's spot. It was his first hangover, and he hated how it felt. He thought about Rufus and his constant drinking and thought, How could a nigga go through this on the regular?

Instead of driving to his own place, he crashed on his mother's couch for the night, since she was closer. He knew she wouldn't mind.

YB was still in his clothing and didn't want to get up, but his mother came down the stairs in her soft Turkish terry cloth robe and began opening the blinds to the living room. The bright morning sun beamed onto her son's sleeping face. YB squinted and said, "Ma, why you doin' this to me?"

"You need to get your ass up and off my couch and start your day already."

YB tried to block the sun from his face. His mother opened more blinds, further irritating him. "You want breakfast?"

YB grunted, "Yeah, since you ain't gonna let a nigga sleep."

His mother smiled and walked into the kitchen. YB sat up and took a deep sigh. He looked at the time and saw that it was only fifteen minutes after ten. He sucked his teeth and looked for his phone.

He picked it up and saw that he had ten missed calls and had eight new voice messages.

"YB, what do you want for breakfast?" he heard his mother shout from the kitchen.

"I don't care, Ma, anything is good. You know you can burn whatever in the kitchen. Shit, I'm in the mood for one of your home-cooked meals."

"I'll make you up some blueberry pancakes and bacon."

"A'ight."

YB stood, did a little stretch, and wiped the sleep from his eyes. He looked at his phone once again but decided he would check his messages later. He walked upstairs to the bathroom and took a much-needed piss.

When he was done, he looked at himself in the mirror and liked what he saw. Despite the scar across his face, he knew he was a handsome brother. He thought about what Chaos had said to him last night. YB had respect on the streets and was making some paper. How would look for him to have a woman like Chaos on his arm? Everyone knew what she did and she probably fucked some of the niggas that he had beef with. Then there was Crown and Harlem. He knew them two niggas were nothing to sleep on—but neither were he and Rufus. He knew Chaos was right; was he really serious enough about her to go down that road?

YB knew deep down that he and Chaos had something special brewing. She was the girl for him, but he cursed her for being a ho.

"Probably in another city, or in another life," YB said aloud as he continued to look at himself in the mirror.

"Yvonne, you need to answer your phone, it's ringing down here," his mother shouted from the foot of the stairs.

"A'ight, I'm coming."

YB washed his face, brushed his teeth, and tried to make himself look fresh for the day. After he was done, he went back downstairs and into kitchen.

"Hey, Ma," he greeted, giving her a kiss on the cheek.

"Morning. Here, take this thing. It's been ringing and gettin' on my damn nerves." She handed him his phone.

YB took the phone and saw that Rufus had been calling him.

"Everything okay?" his mother asked.

"Yeah, everything's good."

"A'ight. I know it's your business when you be on them streets doin' what you do but you watch your back out there."

"Always."

His mother continued making breakfast while YB walked out the kitchen to call Rufus back. The phone rang three times before Rufus answered with, "Nigga, where the fuck is you?"

"What the fuck, Rufus? You don't know how to say good morning to a nigga?" YB spat back.

"Man, fuck a good morning! We got hit hard last night."

"What the fuck you talkin' about, nigga?"

"Nigga, I'm sayin' we got a fuckin' problem. Harlem shot up our spot last night, killed six muthafuckas outside of our spot and made it hot wit' police activity and shit."

"We got robbed?"

"Nigga, is you fuckin' listening? Wasn't shit taken, but police all up in our shit, investigating every fuckin' thang," Rufus exclaimed.

"Fuck me! Where are you?"

"Over at the rib shack on Chestnut."

"Nigga, stay right there. I'll be there in a minute."

YB hung up and went back into the house. His mind was racing and he needed to concentrate on how to handle things. He walked into the kitchen where his mom was scrambling eggs and said, "Cancel breakfast, Ma. I gotta take care of some business."

"You need to eat?"

"Not right now. I ain't hungry."

"What happened last night? Who was you on the phone with?"

"Listen, you know I don't want you up in my street shit, Ma. You better off not knowing how shit gets down."

"Yvonne, please be careful. I don't wanna lose you like I lost your father."

"I'm good, Ma. You ain't gonna lose me. I promise you that. I love you." He kissed her on the cheek and rushed out the door.

YB jumped into his truck and sped off. While driving down 54th Street, he decided to check his voice messages. The first few messages were unimportant and came from a few chicks he fucked with and some nigga named Jeff, who needed to see him about a cash transaction he needed done. He heard the one from Rufus and then he was shocked to hear the message that Magic left last night.

What the fuck happened last night? YB asked himself.

He knew that he needed to call Magic back right away. Magic picked up with an annoyed pitch. "Fuck you at, YB?"

"I was over at my mom's crib. What's up wit' you?" YB asked.

"Nigga, what's up wit' me? You need talk to your fuckin' cousin. He and his goons decided to run up into my spot last night with guns out, terrifying my chicks and my customers. He was lookin' for Crown."

"Magic, look, whatever happened—"

"Nigga, shut the fuck up and listen! Now, whatever beef you and that idiot cousin got going on with Crown, don't bring that shit into my club. You fuckin' hear me, YB? He disrespects me like that again and I'll cut off his fuckin' nuts and shove them into his fuckin' mouth!"

"I'm gonna go talk to him, Magic. I'm gonna see what's up, a'ight? I promise you—"

Before YB could finish saying what he had to say, Magic hung up. YB sighed and continued to Chestnut Street to have a serious word with his cousin.

He quickly pulled up behind Rufus's truck and stepped out. YB spotted his cousin posted up on the Rib Shack, downing a forty sitting next to some bitch. YB approached him calmly and when he got close, he shouted, "Rufus, what the fuck you do last night?"

Rufus stared at his cousin "Nigga, where the fuck was you in the first place? I'm out here tryin' to take care of business, and your ass is laid up somewhere."

"Walk wit' me nigga, we need to talk," YB said. "What happened? And why the fuck did you run up in Magic's spot like you were on some Terminator shit?" YB continued with him down the block.

"First off, nigga, Crown and Harlem need to get got. And I know that's where Crown be at sometimes, so if he was there, I ain't give a fuck if it was Magic's place or not. We was gonna light him and his chicks the fuck up early, my nigga. And if Magic would have gotten in the way—oh well, it would have been R.I.P for that O.G."

"Rufus, is you crazy? Nigga, it don't work that way!"

"Then tell me, YB, how the fuck does it work? Huh, nigga? We got fuckin' burnt last night by these bitch-ass niggas and you comin' up in my face beefing over some politics shit? Nigga, this ain't back in the day, this shit is now! The streets are harder and a nigga gotta get got if he fucks wit' us, YB. You hear me, nigga?"

"Nigga, you know what the fuck I'm talkin' about! You ain't had to run up in Magic's spot like that. We could have got at Crown another way."

"YB, I ain't fuckin' hearing you right now. You know how much we lost out on last night? After the shooting, police ran up in our shit, confiscated four keys of H and we lost out on fifty Gs. Nigga, I ain't lettin' this shit blow over! There will be blood spilled for this shit here," Rufus exclaimed.

"Damn! Fuck!" YB cursed.

"Yeah, nigga, think about it. Think about it long and hard on that shit we gotta pay back to the Mexicans. That's fuckin' money out our pockets, nigga. And you think niggas still gonna continue to breathe over this shit, here? Fuck outta here! I'm puttin' a hit out on them niggas, YB. Let 'em know we about to set shit off up in this city!"

YB just looked at his cousin. "What gave Harlem a reason to shoot up our spot in the first place? I know I got beef wit' Crown, but it ain't to the point where the nigga needed to come at us, knowing we gonna retaliate."

"I don't know, nigga. He be hating on the money we gettin', nigga."

YB examined his cousin closely. "What you do to Toy-T after I drove off the other day?"

"Fuck that bitch-ass nigga!" Rufus took another sip from his forty.

"Don't lie to me, Rufus. What you do to that li'l nigga?"

Rufus sucked his teeth and glared at his cousin. "I tapped that nigga on his dumb fuckin' face with the burner, a'ight? You happy, cuz? I sent a nasty message to his dumb fuckin' cousin."

YB was heated. "Rufus, what the fuck did I tell you? Let the nigga be! You should have let him be, nigga. Now your stupidity cost us our fuckin' spot!"

"Yo cuz, watch who the fuck you're talkin' to," Rufus warned. He dropped the beer bottle and stepped to YB.

"Rufus, back the fuck down, 'cause I ain't in the mood right now," YB growled.

"What, nigga?" Rufus was incredulous. "That bitch-ass nigga Harlem done shot up our spot and you comin' at me, beefing? Nigga, you need to take your anger out on that muthafucka, you hear me? Early! I should have murdered that nigga Toy-T!"

YB sighed. Rufus just didn't get it. "Nigga, until I work this shit out wit' Magic, you don't do shit."

"Nigga, what? I know you ain't serious!" Rufus looked at YB as if he'd gone completely crazy.

"Rufus, calm the fuck down."

"Calm the fuck down? Nigga, is you fuckin' serious? I'm 'bout to raise hell up in this bitch and all you care about is that nigga Magic and his spot? You gettin' soft on me, YB, 'cause I know our niggas ain't get put in the ground for nothing and we out money and dope, too! Nigga, I'm gon' do me and let these streets know how I get down in case they fuckin' forgot." Rufus finished his speech with a strong passion.

"Rufus, all I'm asking of you is to think before you react," YB reasoned.

"Nigga, that's the difference between me and you. I ain't scared to get my hands dirty, nigga. I'm always ready to pop off and I always got your back, cuz, but you—you tryin' to be like Magic and Magic is washed the fuck up. Him and his kind don't rock like that around here no more. Times have changed, YB, and you better know what year you in, nigga, before you get got too."

YB frowned. "You threatening me, Rufus?"

*Dirty Little Angel*

"Nigga, I ain't sayin' shit but just tryin' to open your eyes, cuz. To let you know that what I did to Toy-T is nuthin' compared to what I'm gonna do to Crown and Harlem when I see them niggas. Now, you go check Magic and babysit that nigga while I'm gonna be the one holding down business out here, like I always do." Rufus walked toward his truck with his lady following right behind him. Before Rufus got in, he turned to look at YB and said, "I got love for you, my nigga, but this shit here is way past words and trying to make amends. This is what I do best, YB, so respect that shit."

Rufus got into his truck and drove off, leaving YB standing on the sidewalk to think about his words.

# 15

YB went to see Magic that same day. It was one PM when YB walked into the empty club. He wanted to apologize to Magic in person for his cousin's stupid actions.

Unlike Rufus, YB respected Magic and his style. He knew that there was a lot to learn from him and appreciated their conversations. Some people thought that Magic was just a washed-up gangster running a hole-in-the-wall strip club, but YB knew the power, influence, and wisdom that he still had in the streets.

"What you doin' here, nigga?" Magic asked as he carried a box up from the basement.

"I came to talk to you," YB responded.

"Talk about what? I said what I had to say to you over the phone."

"Yo, what my cousin did last night was stupid. I know it. I already talked to him and let him know that he fucked up."

Magic walked behind the bar with the box. He set it on the countertop and began removing bottles of liquor and stocking the shelves.

Magic ignored him but YB continued to talk. "Shit popped off last night. We lost four keys raw and fifty thousand in cash. Harlem killed six people on the block and now the cops all over that shit like crazy. Now I gotta deal wit' these fuckin' Mexicans and their money. And Rufus, I know he's my cousin, but he fucked it up. He beat down Toy-T and niggas came back on us. Now you know I don't like Crown and I'm ready to murder that nigga, but I did listen to you, Magic. I was playing it cool. I was chilling. I've been chillin' wit' my moms and gettin' things right wit' me. But this shit wit' Crown and Harlem—you and I know it's going to escalate to some real ugly and bloody shit. And this is my reputation; these are my streets, Magic."

"Your streets, huh?" Magic replied. He stocked the last bottle and turned to face YB. "You pay taxes for these streets? You went out and paved every fuckin' road from corner to corner, nigga? You got a sign in your name?" he asked rhetorically.

YB just looked at him in confusion. Magic continued. "These ain't your streets, nigga. You're just another ghetto-ass, drug-dealing nigga that will come and go, like they all do. And when you go, those same streets you claimed to be yours and to love is going to have the next nigga on the block talkin' that same shit you talkin'. You think when you're dead and gone—or locked the fuck up—that the city is gonna honor your name with a fuckin' ceremony because you claimed that these are yours streets and you get money? Nigga, please! You're just a fuckin' waste of breath and space in this city.

"And your cousin, I give him a year till he's either in the grave or doin' life. Niggas like that will always act on impulse; they don't fuckin' think. He's stupid and disrespectful and if I don't kill him first, believe me, then someone else will. I know he's family, but family like that will fuck you over, as he already did wit' you. You want my advice, YB? Cut your losses and just step away."

"What?" YB was shocked.

"From what I hear from my sources, you might be under investigation," Magic informed him.

"Investigation? The feds?"

"Nah, just city police. But still, it takes one cracker muthafucka to start prying into your business and get themselves a snitch. You'll quickly see how shit for you will start to unravel. And with a nigga like Rufus, he will only add fuel to the burning fire. Now I don't need the heat on me. I've been quiet for too long now. I'm comfortable with what I have, but y'all young niggas gotta learn when enough is enough. You can't keep goin' wit' this shit forever, YB. Everything comes to a fuckin' end. Everything! You retaliate against Crown and that will open more doors to the investigation that they might have on you."

"So you're telling me to chill and let that cocksucker be?"

"Nigga, I'm telling you to take what you got and walk away! Make it easy on yourself. Leave town for a while."

YB chuckled. "I can't believe I'm hearing this from you! I leave town and look like some scared bitch that's running from his beef. And what niggas gonna think about me then?"

"Why the fuck are y'all niggas so fuckin' hardheaded?" Magic threw up his hands in exasperation. "You know, your father was the same way—arrogant. Yeah, he taught me the game, but sometimes he didn't know how to leave well enough alone. And that same way you're thinking now, it's what got your father killed in this game." Magic sighed. "You can't fight every battle, YB. You can't go up against the world and think you can win. Sometimes, a man must pick his battles and know how to calm his temper. Myself, I learned that the hard way. You know me and your father was feared in these streets." YB nodded. "We took what we wanted and niggas never asked questions. I almost got the death penalty for my violent and wild actions."

Magic paused and then continued. "When I was locked up, I learned how to calm my head and started reading and started listening. I became more focused and in due time, I got my appeal going and learned to recognize many of the loopholes in my case. And when they granted my appeal, I knew that I had a second chance with life; a chance that many niggas behind them prison walls would give their right nut for right now. When I came home in '82, you were still in diapers, fresh out your mama's pussy and your father was still wildin' out in them streets. I still did me, but I did it with more of a level head. But your father, he was like your fuckin' cousin and that cost him his life." Magic shook his head. "After his death, eventually I began to slow it down with the drug game and invested what I could into some small businesses. I opened up this spot, some grocery stores, and a restaurant and been comfortable ever since.

"You need to be comfortable, YB, not greedy. Being greedy in this game will get you twenty-five to life and once you get them numbers, you'll soon be filled with regret. You know what you need, nigga? Some pussy to get into. You still soft on Crown's bitch . . . what the fuck is her name?"

"Chaos."

Magic smiled slightly. "Yeah. What's up wit' the two of you?"

YB shrugged. "I mean, she is what she is, right? Ain't no changing on how she gets down. I peeped her on the stage the other night. I mean, I know it ain't nuthin' new, but I got my reputation to think about."

"Your reputation?" Magic laughed. "I noticed how you look at her and, nigga, you're sweet on her. So what, she fucked a few niggas and turns tricks? That's only a small part of her. And I know you don't want to hear this, but you think your mother was a fuckin' angel when she was with your father? Your mother had a past, boy, just like Chaos. But your father was man enough to know that even though she did what she did on them streets, that with him, she was still all woman. And that's what made your father fall in love with her.

"Chaos is too good of a woman to be tricking for that nigga Crown. Y'all two started something with each other and I advise you to finish it. You think I don't know things? Nigga, I keep my ear to the streets and know what's up. You think I don't know about Rufus trying my name and status on them streets? I'm old, YB, but I ain't soft. And aging doesn't mean I'm stupid. This city is going to hell with all the murders and drugs. I know I shouldn't be the one to talk, especially with my jacket, but wake up, nigga, and see! A lot of niggas are going to fall before year's end. I'm telling you this because I care about you. You're like a son to me. So do what you do, take what you can, get your bitch, and take a timeout from this shit. I'm telling you, it will be in your best interest."

Magic wondered if he should mention that Crown beat on Chaos but quickly decided against it. Chaos was a prostitute and that came with the territory. And he didn't want any trouble in his club.

"I hear you, Magic," YB replied.

"Nigga, just don't be hearing me! Take heed to what I say before it's too late."

YB processed Magic's words, knowing the O.G. was the one person who would never guide him wrong. He thought about his options in the drug game and then his mind wandered to Chaos. YB knew that one way to get back at Crown was to take his bitch away from him. He knew that Chaos was one of Crown's favorite chicks and to be spiteful, YB knew that he would leave town and take Chaos with him. He cared for her but he also wanted to hit Crown where it hurt. He had an idea about how to make that happen.

YB and Magic continued to talk about the streets and then the subject turned to Crown. Both men knew that Crown wouldn't lie down easily when it came to his women, so they put together a plan to get at that nigga. YB promised Magic that he would follow his advice and be careful. YB remembered Magic's words: "You need to be comfortable, YB, not greedy."

YB left Magic's spot with a clear head and a better understanding. He had his mind set on what he had to do.

# 16

Sweet was dressed for the night in a flimsy ruffled skirt set that showed more skin than clothing and clear stilettos. Crown had them going out to make money for him, but Chaos was still on house arrest.

A week had passed since the YB incident and Chaos's beating. Both ladies were keeping Sweet's pregnancy a secret until they felt the time was right. Chaos was healing from her wounds and turning tricks in the bedroom, while the other ladies left at night and returned in the wee hours of the morning.

It was a balmy Saturday evening and Sweet strutted out of the house with the rest of the girls toward the parked Escalade in the driveway. Cherish guided them to the ride like they were a herd.

"C'mon! Y'all bitches hurry the fuck up so we can get to the club and make our Daddy this money," she shouted.

Before Sweet got into the truck, she looked up at the window of Chaos's bedroom and felt some sorrow that she had been confined in the house for over a week as if she was young child.

"Sweet! You deaf, bitch? Get in the fuckin' truck!" Cherish

screamed.

Sweet jumped into the truck and squeezed next to the new girl, Casper. Crown walked out the house with the usual cigar clutched between his fingers. He wore a black Nike velour sweat suit with white trim and fresh new Adidas sneakers. Cherish had braided his hair earlier, and it gave him a thuggish look.

Before Crown got into the truck, he pulled out his cell phone and called Harlem. "Yo, we on our way over to Magic's spot. He said it was cool to come back down and have my chicks work his club. But I want you around the area, just in case shit pops off ugly."

"A'ight. Ain't no thang," Harlem replied.

Crown hung up, got into the truck, and drove off. He left Toy-T in charge to watch over Chaos. He'd advised his cousin, "If that bitch tries to try you, you get ugly on that bitch. Work that ho tonight, Toy-T." Crown took one last pull from the cigar and tossed it out the window.

Toy-T was a young pimp in training and Crown passed his bitch off to him to learn for the night. Toy-T nodded with a cunning smile.

Chaos looked out the bedroom window at the Escalade pulling out the driveway. She let out a tense sigh and sat on the bed. She knew Crown left Toy-T in the house to watch over her and she hated to be alone with him. Toy-T was a pervert and an asshole and she felt very uncomfortable around him. She looked at the time and saw that it was fifteen minutes after ten. She sat around in some black coochie-cutting shorts and a loose T-shirt with her hair pulled back into a long ponytail.

For a moment, Chaos thought about being back home in the Bronx again and thought about what some of her peoples were probably up to. It had been two years since she left and she knew a lot had probably changed. Then her mind drifted to YB. For a long while, she yearned to feel his touch and wondered what it would be like to fuck him. She wanted to be with him physically and she dreamed about YB being her knight and rescue her from the evil dragon—Crown—that had her locked up in the tower. But then Chaos snapped back to reality. She knew that she was far from being a princess and her world was no fairytale. She was only twenty years old, but in the past two years, it felt like she aged thirty years. She had experienced things that no other twenty-year-old girl should see. The nickname that her mother gave her at birth fit her life perfectly; her life was chaos.

Chaos sat back against the bed with tears trickling down her face. Her back was healing a lot and she had managed to stay on Crown's good side for the week, mostly doing what she was told and making money for her pimp even though she was on house arrest.

She sat alone for a half hour thinking to herself and enjoying the solitude. She walked over to the window again and peered out at the quiet, tree-lined street. Even though the place looked like paradise, she knew it was far from it. The house was decorated for a family but only sex, pain, and misery existed there. Crown had tricks coming in and out of the house on the regular and the neighbors ignored his illegal action with the girls. They feared him and knew it was best to keep out of the man's business.

Chaos continued to stare out the window until she heard, "Bitch, you need to hurry up and change."

She turned to see Toy-T staring at her with a lustful smile. He was shirtless, exposing his bird-looking chest. A tattoo of a skeleton and two guns graced the right side of his chest. He was slim, about 5'9", and looked like a punk, but everyone respected him because he was Crown's cousin.

"Bitch, Crown left me in charge of you for the night and we need to have some fun. I called up some of my peoples, so let's get this night poppin'," Toy-T continued.

He remained standing in the doorway, undressing Chaos with his eyes. She was quiet for a moment, feeling her heart racing. "Nigga, can I change in private?" she snapped.

Toy-T smiled. "Nah, bitch, you don't get that privilege. I gotta see what you're workin' with."

Chaos let out an aggravated sigh.

"Bitch, I know you ain't tryin' to catch no attitude up in here! Don't forget where the fuck you at. Now hurry up and get dressed so my niggas can spend some money up in here."

Chaos knew that it was no point in talking to the young, dumb nigga. Even though she was uncomfortable changing clothes in front of him she had no choice. Besides, it wasn't like niggas never saw her naked. She stood and quickly pulled her T-shirt over her head. Her perfectly sized tits came into full view and Toy-T licked his lips. She unbuckled and unzipped her shorts and pulled them down, showing him that she had no panties on.

Toy-T's dick started to harden. Chaos had the body of a goddess with her trimmed mound, thin waistline and phat ass.

"You happy?" Chaos said to him sarcastically.

Toy-T just stared at her, thinking about pussy.

Chaos went over to one of her drawers and removed some clothes. She knew that when turning tricks, it would be easier to put on something that had easy access to the pussy.

She tossed a skimpy denim skirt and a tight white T-shirt onto the bed. She wouldn't be wearing any panties or a bra. Chaos was about to put on the skirt when Toy-T said, "Nah, don't do that yet."

He was rubbing his dick through his jeans and had the look of a horny animal.

"Excuse me?" Chaos replied with a look of bewilderment.

"I'm sayin', let's you and me have some fun first." Toy-T said. He stepped farther into the room and closed the door behind him.

Chaos kept her face blank, knowing what to expect from the young pervert. She stood near her bed and watched Toy-T unzip his jeans.

"I'm supposed to work tonight, not fuck for free," she told him.

"Bitch, you work for me too and what's Crown's is mine," he retorted. He stood in front her and slowly cupped her tits and began groping her ass. "You know I love me an older bitch."

Toy-T was a pussy-craving nigga. Chaos and Sweet were the only chicks he hadn't fucked yet. He got to the new girl Casper because her mind was already brainwashed. Cherish took the initiative in fucking him because he was kin to Crown and Cherish was just a chickenhead like that.

Toy-T had always had his eye on Chaos. She was the only one he had a strong yearning for. Girls came and went over the years and Toy-T ran through most of them. Chaos, for some reason, was hard to get and she was one of Crown's favorites.

"Chill, bitch, and let me get this," he said calmly as he continued to fondle Chaos.

Chaos closed her eyes and even though it wasn't anything new to her, she felt violated. The nigga was only seventeen, wasn't paying for it, and he treated her like she was shit. She felt that she had to go along with Toy-T's lust for her because one bad word to Crown and she would have to endure Crown's violent abuse again. She feared going down into that basement.

Toy-T began sucking on her neck and ran his hand in between her thighs, grabbing her pussy. She was far from wet and his breath stank. It felt like she was with an octopus because the nigga's hands were everywhere. Suddenly, Toy-T pushed her down on the bed, on her back. He chuckled and pulled down his jeans and boxers.

Chaos was somewhat relieved that he wasn't blessed in the jeans like Crown. Toy-T was small. He was already hard and only about five inches and looked like a short #2 pencil.

Toy-T stroked what he tried to call a dick and said, "C'mere. I want you to suck my dick."

Chaos positioned herself in front of him. She tried gripping his tiny erection the best she could and slowly began sucking his dick. Toy-T moaned at the feeling of her thick, glossy lips wrapped around his short dick. He grabbed the back of her head and said, "Damn, I wanted this. You feel so good."

Shortly thereafter, he pushed Chaos back down on the bed and stepped completely out of his jeans. He was about to climb on top of her and do his business but Chaos told him to get a condom. Toy-T was against it.

"I want to feel that pussy raw, yo," Toy-T exclaimed.

"If I get pregnant you know there' gonna be hell to pay with Crown," Chaos said to him.

Toy-T tried to roll on a Magnum but it was baggy. He climbed between Chaos's thick thighs and pushed himself into her with the loose condom. Chaos felt nothing as he fucked her but Toy-T was having the time of his life. He thrust into her while sucking on her nipples and kissing her neck. A minute later, it was all over. He came, pulled out, and fell over on his back. Chaos wanted to laugh but she started to cry. She felt like this nigga treated her like a bathroom and took a huge shit on her. It was one thing to turn tricks in the club and on the streets, but to have kin of Crown fuck her like he owned her took her someplace that she didn't want to be. She hated to admit it to herself, but she was nothing but a sperm catcher and a piece of meat. Crown talked all that shit about everyone being family and her being beautiful and well taken care of, but by the end of the day, it was all bullshit. She was nothing but his property; slavery wasn't over for her yet.

Toy-T got out of bed and put his jeans back on. He looked over at Chaos and said, "Bitch, hurry up and get dressed. I got my niggas Jumbo and Danny coming by to do some business wit' you. Crown said to charge them niggas two hundred a pop."

Toy-T smiled and felt very satisfied. He knew her pussy was good even though it was over quickly. He knew that he was the shit.

Chaos sat up, dried away her tears, and reached for her skirt. She now understood that it was now or never for her and Sweet to finally leave the house. They had come up with a plan to get back at Crown but needed YB's help to make it happen. They needed a nigga like YB who wasn't scared of Crown or Harlem to pull off what they had in mind.

Chaos was finally tired of her life. And now that Sweet was pregnant, it was a do-or-die situation for both ladies.

# 17

Magic's spot was jumping, as usual. The money was flowing and the atmosphere was lively. Everyone seemed to be having a good time. Crown had his chicks getting back to business like nothing ever happened with him or Magic. Magic gave Crown a second chance to do business in his spot and the five-thousand in cash Crown gave to Magic for an apology was more than reconciliation.

Crown stood by the bar drinking cognac and talking to Angel like they were old friends.

"Where's Chaos?" Angel asked. He was definitely worried about her because the last time he saw her, Crown was beating her like there was no tomorrow.

Crown downed the last of his drink and replied, "I put that bitch on house arrest. I had to show that bitch, Angel."

Angel showed a counterfeit smile. "She a'ight, though?"

Crown shot him a puzzled look. "Nigga, she still's able to make me my muthafuckin' money, a'ight? What you so concerned about that ho for, anyway?"

"Nah, I mean, it ain't nuthin', Crown. I just like lookin' at her, that's all. She's cool people."

"Well, don't expect to see the bitch up in here anytime soon. I got Casper takin' her place for the moment. And don't be in my business, Angel. You fuckin' hear me?"

Angel nodded. "I meant no disrespect to you, Crown."

"Yeah, you know better."

Angel swallowed his pride and went back to tending the bar. From a distance, Magic kept his eye on Crown, making sure none of his bullshit was taking place in his club. Magic knew that despite their differences, business was still business.

Crown continued to get his drink on and eyed Casper, who was onstage with Cherish. Both women were butt naked and working the crowd and getting that money. Crown showed a slight smile and nodded his head. Casper was definitely learning the business quickly and bringing him in some serious paper. Niggas were always going to love new pussy, and they were ready to wait on line for it. Casper already had four VIPs waiting for her when she stepped off the stage.

While Crown was at the bar, Sweet was working a trick near the back. She grinded and rubbed up against him, feeling his erection grow through his sweatpants. She made sure to keep an eye out for her Daddy and Cherish; one fuckup from her and Cherish would run to tell Crown about it and Crown would be ready to punish her.

Sweet thought about her pregnancy. She truly didn't know who the father of her baby was, but that was the least of her worries. She knew that within a few weeks she would definitely be showing and that there would be no way to explain it to Crown.

She bent over and clutched a chair in front of her. Her trick slid her thong to the side and inserted two fingers. Even though she was uncomfortable, Sweet allowed him to finger-fuck her. T-Pain's "I'm in Luv Wit' a Stripper" blared in her ears.

All of Crown's girls were working hard for him, and Crown felt content. He glanced at his watch and saw that it was midnight. He wanted to drive by the crib and check on Chaos and Toy-T. He nodded at Cherish and she understood that she was to hold his stable down like always. He took a last swig of cognac and left the club feeling at ease with Cherish in charge of his chicks.

Cherish continued to work the thirsty and lustful crowd of men that crowded the stage. She rolled around on the platform, spreading her thighs and showing off pussy. Casper twirled her naked frame around the long pole, cupping her tits and staring intensely into the crowd that was mesmerized by her performances.

By one-thirty, YB walked into the club and Sweet smiled to herself. She had changed into sexy, knee-high boots with a skimpy ruffle skirt and a string bikini top that barely covered her tits. She knew that she needed to speak to YB, but with Cherish around and other eyes watching, she had to be discreet about it. She had to get word to YB indirectly about Chaos somehow.

YB went straight to the bar, ordered a Corona, and glanced around the place. He looked around for Chaos but saw her nowhere around. He thought about what Magic said to him earlier. The part about him probably being under investigation bothered him. YB knew that if Magic said it, chances were it was probably true. Magic had connects in many places.

Sweet scanned the bar and smiled when she saw Bobby coming out the bathroom. She sashayed through the crowd and kept her eyes on him. He was one of the few true sweethearts in the place and that she could trust.

Bobby noticed Sweet coming his way, her eyes glued to his. He swallowed a hard lump of nervousness and took a sip of beer. He took note of Sweet's attire and couldn't help drooling a bit. Even with the tattoos and piercings the bitch still was sexy in her own, freakish way.

Sweet reached Bobby's side and ran her hand down his chest, letting it rest against his crotch. She squeezed gently, causing Bobby to let a moan of pleasure escape his lips. They had fucked once before; Sweet had pussy so good that it probably could stop a nigga's heart. She wasn't Chaos, but she was her runner-up.

"Hey Bobby," Sweet said in a teasing whisper. "Let me get a VIP wit' you."

"Damn, Sweet, I ain't got but a hundred dollars on me. You know I would love too but a nigga short on that paper."

Sweet glanced at YB and knew that time was not on her side. She turned her attention back to Bobby and said, "I like you Bobby."

"You do?"

"Yeah, so this is what I'm gonna do for you. I'll fuck you for fifty dollars and I'll reimburse you for the room, if you do me this one favor."

Bobby felt excited about fucking her for only fifty dollars. He knew it was the best agreement that he ever had. He smiled and asked, "What you need from me, Sweet?"

"I need for you to pass someone a message for me."

"To who?"

"YB."

"Him? Why?" Bobby asked.

"'Cause I got peoples watching me, and you know that him and Crown got beef. But all you need to do is pass him a note that I'm gonna give to you."

Bobby sighed because he didn't want to get in the middle of YB and Crown's beef, but then he looked over Sweet from head to toe and his dick started to do all the reasoning for him. "So for fifty bucks you got me, right?"

Sweet nodded. "This is really important for me, Bobby."

"A'ight."

Sweet walked over to the bar and asked Angel for a pen to write message to YB:

YB, Chaos is in trouble and we need to talk. Something happened the other night that you need to hear about it. I'll be in the VIP room with Bobby and you know I can't talk to you directly because people is watching me. So please meet me in the room with Bobby so I can put you up on the 411.

She folded the napkin and passed it to Bobby. "Be subtle wit' it, please, Bobby."

"I got you, Sweet. But are you in some kind of trouble?" he asked.

"It's out of your hands, baby. But you do me this solid and I'll be good to you by returning the favor," she coaxed.

Bobby smiled.

Sweet walked off and allowed time for Bobby to walk over to YB who was still lingering at the bar getting his drink on. The last time he'd seen or spoken to his cousin was at the rib shack. YB had a lot on his mind and he planned to get with Magic and talk a bit more. At the moment, though, he wanted to chill for a moment and maybe get up with Chaos if she was around. Seeing that she wasn't working that night frustrated him.

He took another swig from his beer and watched the basketball game playing on the television. Bobby walked slowly toward YB and felt his heart racing because he knew about YB's reputation. Bobby lived a normal life and had always tried to stay away from the gangsters and thugs. It wasn't his character. He loved the women, but hated that some of them came attached to some ruthless dudes.

Bobby stood by YB and, at first, neither man acknowledged the other. YB glanced at Bobby and figured him for a sucker because of the way he dressed and his nervous demeanor. He paid him no mind and continued to watch the Philadelphia 76ers play the Miami Heat.

Bobby took a deep breath, got his wits together, and hurriedly slid the napkin in YB's direction. "Sweet told me to give you this. It's important."

YB looked at Bobby. "Nigga, what?"

"It's for you."

Bobby felt his hands getting clammy. YB glared at Bobby for a short moment but took the note and read it.

"When she give you this?" YB asked.

"Just now."

YB turned to look for Sweet and saw her standing by the VIP entrance. Bobby walked away, relieved that his job was done. He couldn't wait for his reward and walked over to Sweet with a giant smile on his face. Sweet smiled back and said, "We good?"

Bobby nodded. He followed Sweet into the VIP room, paying the bouncer $25 for the use of the room.

YB hesitated and then followed the two down the narrow hallway. He watched Sweet lead Bobby into the last back room. The bouncer had no problem with YB knowing his reputation and how close he was to Magic. He let YB pass through without hassle or payment.

YB moved down the long corridor with the napkin crushed in his fist. He got to the last door and already heard the sounds of sex coming from the room. He pulled back the long, dark curtain that blocked any outside view from the corridor and saw Sweet getting fucked, doggy-style.

Bobby jumped at seeing YB sudden presence in the entryway and slid out of Sweet. Sweet didn't notice and was glad to see that YB showed up.

"Sweet, what the fuck is up?" Bobby asked, as he quickly pulled up his jeans.

"Yo, what's this shit about, Sweet?" YB asked, ignoring Bobby.

Bobby looked on nervously. Sweet turned to Bobby and said, "Give us a quick moment."

"Sweet, are you serious? You promised me this favor," Bobby retorted.

"I know, Bobby; just wait out in the hallway for a moment. This is really important," Sweet said.

Bobby sucked his teeth but knew it was best for him to wait while Sweet and YB talked. Reluctantly, he left the room and gave the two some privacy.

YB looked at Sweet and held up the crumpled napkin message. "What's this shit about?"

"Crown beat on Chaos the other night, real bad. He was mad that that she was talkin' to you by the bar," Sweet said to him.

"He did what?"

"He's out of control, YB. I mean, you should have seen her. He got her on house arrest and we can't continue to live like this wit' him." Sweet took a deep breath. "We need your help, YB. Chaos and I, we came up wit' a plan."

"Like what?"

"We gonna rob him and leave his ass but we need a nigga like you to have our back on this."

YB snorted. "Y'all gonna do what?"

Sweet spoke in low, urgent tones. "Listen, I'm pregnant and I know when Crown finds out, he's gonna kill me. Now, I know what happened with Harlem and your spot but you can get back at him. I know everything about that nigga and you can make up on what you lost by taking from him. I know where he keeps his safe and the combination to that shit."

YB was definitely listening. He had too much hate in his heart for Crown and wanted to hit that nigga where he lived. Taking away two of his main ladies—and robbing him too—would be a definite slap in the face.

"What you need from me? I'll do it to get Chaos free from that nigga."

"We tryin' to set this shit up, but the only way we can talk like this is through Bobby. He's gotta be our middleman. If they see me talkin' directly to you then Crown and his peoples are gonna know what's up. And I can't afford to get my ass beat."

"I'll be back through here all week and we'll set this shit up. I'll put my cousin Rufus on. He's dying to fuck that nigga up," YB said.

Sweet smiled. Their plan had been set in motion and the wheels of their fate were starting to turn.

"Let's do this right," YB urged, unafraid. "You lay me down the information about his spot, like how many rooms and how many chicks or soldiers or anything I can use and we're gonna do this."

Sweet nodded. She knew that she didn't have that much time so she let YB leave. Bobby walked back into the room.

"Damn, it's about time," Bobby said. He unbuckled his jeans and was ready to get back down to business.

Sweet smiled, feeling good about things. She got back into the doggy-style position and waited for Bobby to hit it from the back again.

Let it be a new day for us, she thought to herself as Bobby grabbed her hips and pushed himself into her.

# 18

It was six in the morning and the sun was fresh in the sky, breaking night into day once more. The Escalade pulled into the driveway and the girls stepped out and walked sluggishly into the house. They all had a long night of turning numerous tricks, dancing, and making plenty of money for Crown.

Sweet was the last to walk into the house. Her body was limp and her pussy sore from the penetrations she endured. She accomplished a lot with her talk with YB. She smiled to herself as she walked up the steps and thought about Chaos.

Crown was in the basement, counting the night's earning from his hoes. He smiled when he saw that they grossed over $7,000 for him. He placed the cash in the safe and poured a drink before he sat on of the couches and called for Cherish.

Cherish ran down the basement steps in tight shorts and a small halter top. Her smooth, curvy figure gave Crown a huge hard-on.

"I need to celebrate. Tonight was a good fuckin' night," Crown said, unzipping his pants.

Cherish already knew the routine. She walked over to her pimp, unbuttoning her snug shorts. Crown remained slouched on the couch, fondling his crotch. Cherish squatted between his legs while Crown removed his large member from his jeans and stroked himself.

"It's time for you evaluation, Cherish," Crown said.

Cherish smiled 'cause she was getting ready to work her Daddy something lovely. Out of all the girls Crown had fucked, Cherish was the only bitch that knew how to fuck and suck him right—and Crown was not an easy man to please.

Cherish took over with stroking his big dick, while Crown spread his arms across the couch and watched her. She licked him up and down, curling her tongue around Crown's tip, sliding her full, glossy lips around the width, and swallowed him whole, down to the base. Deep-throating was her thang, and that was one of the reasons why she was Crown's bottom bitch.

"Mmmmmmm, shit. Suck my dick, bitch. Yes, do that shit," Crown moaned.

He grabbed a handful of Cherish's long black hair and forced her head farther down onto his dick. Cherish slid his dick out of her mouth, spit on his nuts, and then sucked them dry. She nibbled and licked on them for a moment and then went back to sucking his dick.

Crown let her do her thang for a long while. Cherish was a professional at giving head. When he was satisfied with the blowjob, he ordered, "Stand up and strip, bitch."

Cherish quickly got naked. Crown completely removed his clothing and sat back down on the couch.

"Now ride me crazy."

Cherish smiled and mounted Crown. She cringed for a moment as Crown's dick felt like a truck parked in her stomach.

"Aaaaaaaahhhhh, shit . . . baby, ooooohhh, you feel fuckin' good," she cried out.

Crown pressed his hands into her chunky ass cheeks and ground his pelvis into her as he sucked hard on her dark, hard nipples. Cherish worked her pussy and thighs into Crown, pleasing her Daddy the best way she knew how. Even though she'd fucked all day, she made sure she fucked her pimp right—grinding and sweating it out and staining his couch with ass, nut, and pussy juices.

While Cherish got wild with Crown downstairs, Sweet walked into the bedroom room. Chaos was asleep with her back facing the doorway. It looked like Chaos had also had a tiring and troubling night.

Sweet moved closer and sat next to her friend on the bed, trying not to disturb her sleep.

Chaos had been put through it earlier. Jumbo and Danny definitely got their money's worth—they both fucked her till they couldn't fuck anymore and left Chaos sore and wilted with exhaustion. Toy-T videotaped the entire episode. After their fun, Toy-T had $500 in his hand and some new footage to show around to his peoples.

Sweet sighed, knowing how rough it had gotten over the weeks for them. Even though she was tired, she couldn't sleep. She lay next to Chaos and waited for her to wake up in the morning. She couldn't wait to tell Chaos the news.

# 19

"So, what this ho talkin' about, YB?" Rufus asked. "She tryin' to set that nigga up?"

"Yeah, my nigga. Sweet definitely got info on how to get at Crown. We need to hit this nigga hard and fast," YB replied.

"You trust this bitch, YB? I mean, how we know she ain't tryin' to set us up and shit?"

"Believe me, cuz. She's sick of this nigga's shit just like the two of us. Sweet is good peoples."

"I'm down for whatever, YB. You know I'm gonna murder that faggot-pimp nigga when I see him. And Harlem, he's next. And wit' what we take from this nigga, it should cover our debt wit' the Mexicans."

Both men sat parked on Market Street under an unlit street light. Rufus took a few pulls from the burning spliff and thought about different ways to murder Crown and Harlem and maybe raping one of his hoes. Thinking about the way Harlem disrespected his block and made them lose out on some serious paper kept Rufus's face in a scowl.

YB was always the smart one. He would be the one to execute the strategy while Rufus had his back. He sat quietly in the passenger seat and thought out every possible angle. He even thought about it being a setup but figured Sweet and Chaos had begun to resent Crown and his abusive ways.

YB learned in his early years that hell had no fury like a woman scorned. When he was eighteen, he was stabbed in the back three times by a jealous ex-girlfriend and was fortunate to live. Another girlfriend crashed YB's Benz on purpose because she kept accusing him of cheating. YB beat the shit out of both of them but he understood that once a woman was upset with a man, she didn't have a limit to the damage that she could cause.

"So, how soon we tryin' to do this?" Rufus asked.

"Real soon, my nigga. Everything is being set in motion right now," YB said.

Rufus nodded and took another drag of the burning weed.

YB thought about Magic's advice. In the end, it probably would be best for him to leave town for a while, especially after their plan to rob and murder Crown. YB turned to his cousin and asked, "Yo, how would you feel if after this shit, I leave town for a while?"

"What the fuck you talkin' about, YB? Where you planning to go?" Rufus asked in annoyance.

"I'm just sayin', I'm gettin' tired and shit is gettin' crazy. All this killing and beefing, I mean, where we gonna see ourselves in five years, my nigga, doin' the same shit we doin' now? Locked up or probably dead," YB proclaimed.

Rufus chuckled. "Nigga, you talkin' crazy. You love this street shit! This is us and how we came up. I can't ever get tired of this shit here. Nigga, Philly is all we fuckin' know. And what got you sparking that dumb fuckin' idea in your head? Magic? Or you thinking of skatin' of wit' that ho bitch, Chaos?" Rufus shook his head. "Nigga, she don't give a fuck about you! That bitch lives on her fuckin' back and you ain't even fuck her yet."

YB sighed, knowing he wasn't going to get through his cousin's thick head. Rufus was only concerned about three things: money, his reputation, and raping women.

"Nigga, what you blowing out your mouth for! What, you a nigga wit' a conscience now? What the fuck I done told about these bitches? You can't love these hoes, nigga. You, you tryin' to leave family now for that bitch and live a fuckin' life like the Huxtables? Nigga, wake the fuck up! You ain't Bill Cosby and that bitch definitely ain't Claire."

"Why the fuck you so ignorant, Rufus?" YB snapped. "You always negative about some shit. I'm always defending you against Magic but you always seem to prove me wrong."

"That nigga Magic talkin' shit about me?" Rufus snarled.

Too late, YB realized that he shouldn't have mentioned Magic's opinion of Rufus. "Nigga, chill. I ain't having this conversation wit' you right now, nigga."

"Yeah, whatever YB. Just like when we were kids, you always tryin' to be the boss of things. Like you always fuckin' know any better. Nigga, let's just get at Crown and Harlem, get this money, and do what we do best: We run our fuckin' block and maintain our fuckin' reputation," Rufus stated.

YB sat back and just kept his mouth shut. Rufus was going to continue to be Rufus; but he was still family and YB always had love for family.

# 20

It was a Thursday night and business at Magic's spot was slow. Sweet was working the stage, making her ends for the night and waiting for YB to come through. For the past four days, they'd been relaying info through Bobby and he got free pussy from Sweet in return. It was risky, knowing how Crown felt about fucking niggas for free but Bobby was doing them a huge favor.

It was routine for Bobby and Sweet to talk at the bar while he bought her drinks. She would tell Bobby what she wanted to relay to YB and Bobby would subtly go over to YB and pass on the message. Sometimes they would meet up in the VIP room to talk.

Chaos was still on house arrest, and that worked out perfectly for their scheme. Somebody had to remain in the house to supervise Chaos and it would either be Toy-T or Crown.

Sweet had to figure out a way to remain home with Chaos while the other girls went out to make Crown's money. She wanted to be there when YB came in with his cousin to rob and kill Crown. The only way she saw that happening was to be on house arrest like Chaos and make money at home. But that meant that she'd have to take a chance on getting her ass beat like Chaos and a beating from Crown might cost her baby's life.

Sweet came up with another plan that she thought would work. She told YB about it and they both knew how to execute it. With Chaos informed about everything that was happening, Friday night was the time to make things happen.

Friday night was business as usual. Crown kept a sharp eye out for his chicks and drank cognac. Tonight he was wearing a brown silk suit with a wide-brimmed hat tilted to the side, carrying the true pimp image.

Sweet walked around in a pair of knee-high leather boots and a G-string. Her bikini top was in her hand. She had just finished fucking a trick in VIP and was ready for a drink. When she got to the bar she glanced at Crown, thinking he was going to say something to her. However, Crown just looked at her, sipped his drink, and then left the bar.

Sweet was extremely nervous as the night progressed. YB wasn't around, but she didn't expect him to be. She knew he was parked somewhere, waiting for everything to take place.

Chaos was at home under Toy-T's watch while the other strippers were working the crowd in Magic's. Harlem was nowhere around and that was the only thing that worried Sweet. He was unpredictable and everyone knew that he was likely to show up at anytime. Sweet knew that she had to chance it. It was now or never.

Bobby stood around minding his business. He knew his role in the scheme was over and he was relieved. They didn't tell him much, but he knew that something heavy was about to go down. He was no gangster and the only things he loved were pussy, beer, and his job. He wanted no extra drama in his life. He knew it was wise to stay away from Sweet that Friday night because she warned him to do just that. Bobby set his eyes set on another stripper and went about his business.

Sweet took a few sips of her drink and scanned the place. Casper was onstage making the crowd go wild. Cherish was working a nigga in the corner who had his hand down her skirt. Midnight walked off toward VIP with a trick, and Crown stood by the front doorway to the club talking to another known pimp in Philly.

Sweet took a deep breath and thought to herself, I got this.

She looked around for the right bitch to fuck with and found Mindy had just come from the changing room. Sweet gripped her drink and walked toward Mindy who was the perfect woman to start a fight with. When they were close to each other, Sweet purposely bumped into Mindy and spilled her drink onto Mindy's cute, skimpy outfit.

"Bitch, watch where the fuck you goin'!" Sweet screamed.

"What, bitch? You bumped into me, you lazy-eyed bitch!" Mindy yelled back.

"What the fuck you say, you dumb clown bitch?" Sweet stepped to Mindy.

"You heard what the fuck I said—watch where the fuck you goin'! But I can't blame you; you probably can't still see shit wit' that one good eye," Mindy shot back.

By now, everyone noticed the scene brewing between the two strippers. Crown cursed loudly and moved through the crowd to grab Sweet and keep her from doing something stupid. He and Magic had an understanding that there would be no more drama with him and his girls in the club. Sweet was breaking that agreement and Crown was upset.

Sweet and Mindy got into a shouting match, throwing fingers and hands into each other's faces. Sweet took the altercation a step further and smashed her partially-filled glass over Mindy's head.

Mindy screamed and stumbled while liquor and blood trickled down her face. Sweet threw some punches and yelled, "Don't you ever disrespect me like that again, bitch!"

The fight didn't last long. Sweet got the best of Mindy before Crown pulled her away from the scene. He grabbed Sweet by the back of her neck and screamed at her.

"That bitch started it, Crown," Sweet pleaded with him.

"I don't give a fuck, bitch! You don't lay a hand on anyone without my approval. You fucked up my money!"

"I'm sorry, Daddy! I'm sorry," Sweet cried.

Crown looked over at Mindy and saw that her face was a bloody mess. "Fuck me! Cherish, get the fuck over here!" Crown called out.

Cherish hurried over. She looked at Sweet and knew she was in a lot of trouble.

"I gotta get this bitch outta here, quickly. You in charge of these bitches till I come back. I want you to have all my bitches clothed and ready when I get back," he instructed.

"I will, Daddy," Cherish said.

"C'mere, bitch!" Crown dragged Sweet by her neck toward the club entrance.

Magic emerged from the basement with a serious scowl on his face. What the fuck happened now?

He soon saw Mindy on the floor, clutching her bloody face and crying. Magic cut through the crowd, picked Mindy up and asked, "Who the fuck did this to you?"

"I'm gonna kill that fuckin' bitch, Magic! I'm gonna kill that bitch," Mindy exclaimed. "Fuck that lazy-eyed bitch! Fuck her!"

Magic looked around for Crown and saw him dragging Sweet out the door still dressed in her thong and boots.

"This muthafucka!" Magic cursed.

Crown pushed Sweet to his truck across the street. He didn't give a fuck about the way she was dressed 'cause he just wanted to leave quickly as possible. Everyone outside the club looked on wide-eyed since Sweet's huge tits and ass were in public view.

"Damn, what the fuck happened up in there?" someone inquired.

Crown pushed Sweet into the truck, jumped in behind her, and drove off hastily. As he peeled off down the street, he glared over at Sweet and punched her in the head.

"You stupid bitch! What the fuck did you do!" he shouted.

He began to hit her again, shoving her head against the passenger's side window until a small crack appeared. Sweet cried out and tried to shield herself from the heavy blows, praying that Crown didn't kill her before they got to the house.

"I'm gonna fuck you up when we get home," he threatened.

"I'm sorry, Daddy. I'm sorry," Sweet sobbed.

"Shut the fuck up, bitch! I told you don't act up, don't fuckin' act up! You cost me money tonight and I'm gonna take it out on your ass, fo' sure!"

Crown raced home with Sweet still cringed in her seat and shaking, tears of pain and hurt streaming down her face.

# 21

YB and Rufus sat patiently in the rust-colored, four-door Lincoln across the street from Crown's place. The block was quiet and the traffic was sparse. The thick trees that lined the street and a few bushes gave them good cover from the bright street lights and any unwanted attention. It was twelve-thirty, and the neighbors on the block were either asleep or out on the town. The stillness in the area made it seem like it would be a peaceful night.

Rufus gripped the deadly Ruger P89 and kept an eye out for Crown's truck. He was hungry for murder and said to his cousin, "When I see this nigga, the first thing I'm gonna do is put a hot one in his eye."

"Relax, nigga," YB cajoled. "We work this as planned, so don't go flying off the handle, nigga. It should be anytime now."

"This bitch better be on point, YB, 'cause I won't hesitate to shoot the bitch if she fucks us," Rufus said, referring to Sweet.

"We do it my way," YB said.

"Just make sure your way is gonna have Crown's chest burning wit' a few hot shells, early, my nigga."

Sweet had given them Crown's address and let them know the

layout of the crib and how many people would be inside. YB and Rufus scoped the place out earlier and noted how many exits were in the house and anything else that might spoil their hit. Both men were dressed in black from head to toe and their car contained a small arsenal of weapons—just in case the gunfire got heavy. There was a MAC-10 in the backseat and a shotgun on the floor. They knew not to underestimate Crown and Harlem and came heavily prepared.

"It feels like old times, YB, staking out a hit. Remember, we used to do this shit when were kids? Robbing muthafuckas and murdering these clown-ass dealers on the block if they tried to come at us on some payback shit."

YB smiled, remembering how he, Rufus, and a few others got down. They were definitely ruthless, making a name for themselves at an early age. The majority of the crew had been in and out of jail since the age of fourteen.

"Well, we ain't goin' after petty drug dealers and wannabe gangsters. This is the real thing, so stay close and be on point," YB said.

"I got your back, cuz. You just make sure you have mine."

YB nodded.

They continued to stare at the block, watching the house and watching traffic pass by. YB had his 9 mm Beretta lying on the dashboard and an extra clip in his pocket. He took a lengthy pull from the burning spliff Rufus had rolled up and sparked while sitting in the car. He let the excess smoke escape from his nostrils.

He passed the weed to his cousin and thought about Chaos being locked up in the house like some child on a harsh punishment. He had plans on leaving town after the hit. He didn't tell his cousin anything else, knowing how stubborn Rufus could become. YB knew that Philly could no longer be the place for him after what they planned on doing tonight.

A new life outside of Philly, shit gotta be crazy, YB thought. He gazed out at the night and reflected heavily on his violent past. He thought about the murders he and his cousin committed. He thought about the tons of drugs they sold throughout West Philly. He thought about the women he fucked and the short time he spent behind bars when he was in his teens. He knew that he was fortunate to be free and alive and then the thought of him being under investigation had him thinking. He knew that he had to be very careful and watch his back.

For YB to walk away from everything he knew and loved would be challenging for him. He had his mother, Magic, and Rufus in Philly. It was a hard choice to make because he only knew how to do two things: sell drugs and murder. He hoped Chaos would be worth it. He finally convinced himself to put her infamous past with Crown behind and move on. He wanted them to live a better life in another state with the money from tonight's heist.

"This shit is takin' forever," Rufus muttered.

YB just sat back in his seat and remained patient. This was a one-shot deal, and if they fucked up, it would be costly.

# 22

Chaos got out of bed and walked to the window in her bra and panties. She peered down the block to see the old Lincoln that YB and Rufus were in. They were waiting for her to give them the signal.

Chaos felt that tonight would be the last night of bullshit she would ever have to endure. She cracked a smile, feeling like YB was that prince on a white horse and she was the lady in the tower, waiting to be rescued.

Is this my fairytale? She asked herself.

She sighed and then turned to see Toy-T standing in the doorway in his wife-beater and jeans. "Bitch, we gonna have some company again tonight. I got Jumbo coming over again to fuck you." He chuckled. "You got that nigga open off your pussy. I know the feeling 'cause your shit is good."

Chaos sighed again and turned her attention back to the window. She wasn't trying to hear Toy-T's mouth tonight.

Toy-T got upset. He wanted to be like Crown so he knew he had to lay the smack down if he wanted respect from a bitch. He walked into the room and shouted, "Bitch, you don't ever turn your back to me when I'm fuckin' talkin' to you!"

He grabbed her arm and spun her around to face him. Toy-T glared at Chaos, but his bark was louder than his bite. "Get dressed, bitch. We got some money to make tonight."

Chaos sighed a third time. She could get away with the attitude with Toy-T, but if he were Crown, her jaw would have been filled with blood.

Toy-T pressed himself against Chaos and rubbed his hands against her butt. "Damn, you're so soft, bitch. I like that. I do, I do," he said in a sleazy tone.

Chaos wanted to pry herself out of his greasy hands. She hated the smell of his breath when he tried to kiss her. Chaos closed her eyes and tried to pull away, but Toy-T wasn't having it. He pressed his crusty lips to hers but became startled by the sound of the Escalade pulling into the driveway. Toy-T released Chaos and rushed downstairs to meet his cousin and to see why he was back from the club so early.

With Toy-T finally gone, Chaos sat on the bed and prayed that tonight went down smoothly. She couldn't take another night of Toy-T's shit and his greasy hands.

# 23

Rufus and YB perked up when they saw Crown's Escalade pull hastily into the driveway. With his eyes fixed on the truck, YB reached for his gun and cocked it back. Both men saw Crown drag the semi-naked Sweet out of the truck. He was so busy assaulting Sweet that he didn't look around to see if there was trouble.

"Look at this bitch nigga here. You think he knows it's comin' to him?" Rufus asked. "I should just go over there right now and fire some hot ones into his face and chest."

"Just chill, Rufus. We need to work this as planned," YB said.

"I'm gonna work it, YB. I'm gonna murder this nigga." Rufus kept his eyes on Crown, watching the man's every move.

Crown pulled Sweet toward the door, causing her to stumble over the steps. He pushed her inside and slammed the door behind him.

YB and Rufus waited for the signal from Chaos.

"That should be four inside, right?" Rufus inquired.

"We'll see," YB replied.

They sat and looked up at Chaos's bedroom window and continued to wait for the signal.

Chaos heard the commotion downstairs. She heard Sweet crying out to Crown saying that she was sorry but her pleas fell on deaf ears. Chaos soon heard the sounds of Crown punching Sweet. She crept out of the bedroom and looked over the banister.

"Bitch, you don't fuckin' think! That's the fuckin' problem wit' you hoes. You cost me money tonight wit' your bullshit!" Crown ranted.

He grabbed Sweet by her long weave and dragged her across the marble floors toward the basement.

"Crown, I'm sorry. Daddy, I'm sorry!" Sweet tried to resist being dragged into the basement. She accidentally scratched Crown on his wrist and he became even more furious. He punched her in the face with his cell phone. Blood trickled from Sweet's lips and her right eye was almost swollen shut.

"Fuck is wrong wit' you, bitch? You gon' fuckin' scratch me, huh? I'm gonna fuck you up downstairs."

"Yo, Crown, everything good?" Toy-T asked. He stared at his cousin and then at the battered and bruised Sweet. "What she do?"

"Mind your fuckin' business, Toy-T. I got this. Where the fuck is Chaos?"

"She's upstairs gettin' ready for business," Toy-T informed him.

Crown had the look of the devil on his face. His eyes were sunken with rage. "You tell that bitch to get my money right tonight or she gonna have the same fate as this bitch."

"A'ight," Toy-T responded.

Chaos was horrified look as she continued to watch from the staircase. She wanted to cry. She wanted to help Sweet. It wasn't too long ago that Chaos found herself in the same situation as Sweet. She knew that once Crown got her down into that basement, the punishment would only get much worse.

Sweet's horrifying cries made her cringe and she decided that it would be best for her to walk back into the bedroom and continue with the plan. Chaos took a deep breath, shed a few tears and then walked over to the window. She once again looked for the Lincoln, glad to see it was still there. She pulled back the blinds and curtains and opened the windows. She walked over to the light switch and flicked it on and off twice.

"There we go," Rufus said when he saw the lights flick off and on.

Both men secured their weapons and then pulled on dark knitted ski caps. They got out the car and walked calmly toward the house, keeping a keen eye out for anything unusual.

Chaos looked out her bedroom window again and saw the men coming and smiled. She held a set of house keys in her hand. Toy-T was unaware that while he had been groping Chaos for his own pleasures, she had picked his pocket and removed his house keys, sliding them quickly into her panties. Chaos used to be a thief and pickpocket back in the Bronx when she ran with an all-girl crew.

Before anyone saw her, Chaos tossed the keys out the window. YB caught them and knew it was on and poppin'. With Toy-T and Crown being the only men in the house, YB and Rufus knew that it was easy picking. They could do almost anything with the element of surprise.

By then, Crown had dragged Sweet kicking and screaming into the basement. Chaos could still hear her pleas for help, and she knew help was definitely on its way. The house had motion sensor lights but no alarm system. YB and Rufus walked to the back door, not wanting the neighbors to become suspicious of two young black men dressed in all black with guns in their hands. They easily opened the lock to the rear and moved inside the darkened kitchen. Once the men were in the living room they could hear vicious screams coming from the basement.

"What the fuck is he doin' to her?" Rufus whispered.

The house was large. YB wondered where Toy-T was and then he thought about Chaos. Soon he saw her coming down the steps dressed in jeans, a denim jacket, and Timberlands.

"Where's everyone?" YB asked in a low voice.

"Crown took Sweet downstairs. But Toy-T, he's in here somewhere," Chaos told them. "Fuck that nigga up, YB. He ain't right."

YB didn't say a word. He and Rufus moved toward the basement and opened the door carefully, ready for any kind of trap. They crept down the rickety wooden steps and heard Sweet screaming which was a plus for them because her screams drowned out their approach.

"Crown, Daddy . . . I'm pregnant wit' your baby! I'm having your baby," Sweet screamed out.

"What the fuck you say, bitch? You're what?" Crown exclaimed.

"I'm having a baby," Sweet cried.

"Bitch!!"

Sweet gave an agonizing wail.

Rufus whispered, "Damn, what the fuck is he doin' to the bitch?"

The basement was a big, open concrete area with one closed-off room. It was the room where Crown had his safe and file cabinets and where he held meetings with his people. It was also the place where he disciplined his chicks.

YB quickly scanned the basement as he neared the door with his gun clutched tightly in his hand. He passed Chaos a loaded .380 and hoped she knew how to use it. Chaos nodded.

Rufus and YB looked at each other for a brief moment, reading each other minds. They'd been in situations like this many times before.

"Fuck this shit!" Rufus exclaimed, violently kicking the door open, shocking Crown.

YB rushed in behind Rufus with his gun aimed at Crown's head. "What the fuck!" Crown screamed.

YB and Rufus quickly took in the scene. Sweet was chained to a long pipe, naked with her arms outstretched. Her back was scarred with burn marks and she was also bleeding. Sweet looked up at YB with her beaten and tear-stained her face. She looked so pitiful and distressed. Crown, who was shirtless and sweating, stood over Sweet with a hot comb in one hand and his thick leather belt in the other. He was burning Sweet with the hot comb and then beating her.

"You sick muthafucka!" YB shouted.

"Fuck y'all niggas," Crown retorted. He threw the hot comb at Rufus and tried to run for it, but Rufus was on his ass quickly. He bashed the Ruger across Crown's face. Crown dropped to the floor, scrambling to get away but Rufus, was all over him. Rufus beat Crown the same way Crown beat his bitches. The Ruger came viciously across Crown's face several times until it was red with blood.

Chaos walked in behind the duo and her eyes were drawn to her friend Sweet. "Oh my God! What the fuck?"

She quickly went to her friend's aid, tears trickling down her face. She took Sweet in her arms but forgot that she was still handcuffed to the pipe. She wanted Sweet free immediately. Chaos filled with rage, pulled her gun from her jeans and rushed over to where Rufus and YB were kicking and pistol whipping Crown brutally.

"You fuckin' bastard," she screamed. "Why you do that to her?!"

Chaos kicked at Crown while he was still on the floor. "Give me the fuckin' combination! Give me the combination!" she screamed. She knew that the combination was written on a slip of paper somewhere in his office in case of an emergency.

"Fuck you and that bitch!" Crown retorted with a smirk on his blood-spattered face.

Chaos hit him again and again. YB pulled her off him and said, "Let us do this!"

"Fuck him! Fuck that bitch-ass nigga! Kill that muthafucka!" Chaos cried.

Crown lay sprawled on his marble floor, looking helpless. His nose was broken and his face was covered in blood. He panted but he still had some sarcasm in him. He looked up at YB and Rufus and stated, "Both y'all niggas is dead. I'm gonna make sure Harlem sees to that, and your families."

"What, muthafucka?" Rufus said, towering over the beaten Crown. He kicked Crown in his mouth and made him spit out two teeth.

Crown cried out in pain, clutching his bloody jaw and squirming over the floor. Rufus laughed. They went through his pockets until he found the key to the cuffs and tossed it to Chaos who quickly uncuffed her battered friend and held her in her arms.

"Where the money at?" Rufus asked.

"Fuck you!" Crown snapped.

Rufus beat him again and then asked again, "Where the fuckin' money at?"

"Fuck you!" Crown repeated, spitting up blood.

YB tore through the room, turning over furniture while Rufus continued to torture Crown. Chaos helped Sweet to the couch and draped a sheet around her nude body. Suddenly, Toy-T burst into the room, firing a .45 wildly.

Boom! Boom! Boom! Boom! Boom! Boom!

"Fuck y'all niggas, man! Fuck y'all!" Toy-T shouted.

YB and Rufus quickly ducked behind furniture and returned the gunfire, unloading on Toy-T heavily. Crown scurried to get his Glock 17 from his hidden spot while Toy-T had their attention. Crown was hurt badly but anger and vengeance kept him conscious enough to reach for his gun.

Chaos pulled Sweet down to the floor and looked up to see Toy-T charging into the room with wild eyes, letting off numerous shots everywhere. She gripped the .380 in her hand and fired off two shots at him. The gunfire was chaotic and soon Toy-T was down with a shot in the head and chest.

Before anyone could exhale, Crown moved forward with the Glock gripped in his fist and aimed it at YB.

Bam! Bam! Bam!

He hit YB square in the chest three times, sending YB crashing against the wall. Chaos's eyes widened with shock when she saw her nigga go down. She jumped up from the floor and rushed to YB, not realizing that Crown had his gun aimed at her head and was about to squeeze the trigger.

Before he could fire a round at her, Rufus stood hurriedly shot Crown multiple times in the chest. Crown's body crashed into a glass table.

"Fuck!" Rufus shouted. He then looked over at his cousin lying on the floor and thought the worst.

"YB, get up! Get up, nigga," Chaos begged.

YB coughed loudly and opened his eyes. "Damn, this shit hurt." He was panting loudly but pulled up his shirt to show that he was wearing a bulletproof vest.

Chaos sighed with relief and hugged him. Their joy was short lived when Rufus said to them, "Yo, I think that bitch is dead."

Chaos looked over at Sweet and saw her friend sprawled on her back. She looked dead.

"Nooooo!" she screamed, rushing over to Sweet.

She picked her up in her arms and noticed the blood and the bullet hole in her neck. "Oh my God, no!"

"Fuck!" YB muttered.

Rufus just shrugged and said, "Yo, let it be. The bitch is gone."

"She was pregnant! She was fuckin' pregnant!" Chaos exclaimed, staring at Rufus.

"Yo, YB, we need to be out soon. So let's just get this nigga's shit and bounce."

YB agreed, knowing that there was nothing that they could do for Sweet. She was dead. Chaos continued to hold her friend's lifeless body in her arms realizing that the two of them had almost been away from Crown. They had come so close only for her life to be snatched away.

YB and Rufus ransacked Crown's entire crib and came up with $75,000 cash, jewelry, and minks. Rufus threw everything into Crown's Escalade and YB had to pull Chaos away from Sweet's body.

"We gotta go," YB said.

Chaos didn't resist. She knew that there was nothing that she could do for Sweet. She stared at Sweet's body on the cold floor for a moment longer and then rushed outside with YB and Rufus.

"I'll take the Lincoln and y'all bounce in the truck," Rufus said.

Chaos quickly got in on the passenger side and YB jumped behind the wheel. He peeled out of the driveway and sped down the block, Rufus right behind him.

Chaos rested her head against the passenger window, still upset and crying over Sweet. She looked lost for a moment. YB drove down City Line Avenue. He knew that in a few hours, cops would be all over the gruesome crime scene that they left behind. Word would soon spread about the home invasion and Crown's death. He knew that the best and only thing for him to do was take the money he had stashed plus the shit that they took from Crown and leave town for a while. It felt like he was running away from his beef, but he heeded Magic's advice. YB knew that he had to live for today so he would live to fight tomorrow.

He glanced at Chaos and said, "We gonna do this. I'm sorry about your friend. She was cool peoples."

Chaos turned to YB, her eyes puffy and red from crying. Her face was still wet with tears. "Just get me the fuck outta Philly," she said a hoarse tone.

YB nodded.

# 24

It didn't take long for word to spread about the shooting at Crown's home. Numerous cop cars with their blaring lights were parked outside Crown's house, alarming the neighbors. Uniformed police combed the area, looking for shell casings and searching for any evidence.

Homicide detectives were inside examining the crime scene and trying to reenact what had happened.

"We got two dead, sir . . . and one in critical condition," a uniform cop informed Detective Lemur, the lead detective.

"Where's my survivor?" Detective Lemur asked, studying the crime scene with hard eyes.

"He was rushed to Thomas Jefferson University hospital with three gunshots to his chest. A male victim, in his mid-thirties and the owner of the house," the cop informed him.

Detective Lemur sighed and took in the scene carefully. "City's going to fucking hell with the murders. A'ight, I want everything bagged and tagged and an I.D on the female victim. I want to know if they have any priors and send a cop to the hospital to see if our guy lives or dies. I want a statement from him as soon as he opens his eyes, if he survives.

To me, this looks like a home invasion gone wrong and our female victim got caught in the crossfire somehow. By the looks of things, our male victim was caught up in a very bad business and it probably came back on him."

Everyone nodded and went about their business. The news reporters were camped outside, waiting to get a statement from the detectives. The neighbors were gathered behind the yellow police tape, talking among themselves and concerned about the shooting. No one witnessed a thing but the cops still asked around and got nothing to go on.

Harlem drove up to Magic's spot with his Glock nearby. It was three in the morning and the girls were still clueless about the shooting. He jumped out his truck and rushed toward the club. After calling Crown for hours and not being able to reach him, Harlem went by the house and saw the carnage. He got out of there quickly and then anonymously called the police.

Harlem moved past security and walked into the club with a serious scowl on his grill. Those who knew of Harlem got really nervous.

"Shit," Angel muttered. His heart raced since he knew of Harlem's fierce and murderous reputation and it was rare to see him in the club. Magic came upstairs and the two cut eyes at each other. Harlem wasn't sure if Magic was involved. If he knew for sure, then he would have murdered Magic where he stood.

Cherish was by the bar, talking to a trick, when she saw Harlem. She quickly walked over to Harlem with a curious look on her face. "Harlem, what's going on?" she asked.

"Go get the rest of the bitches and get dressed. We're leaving," he instructed her.

"What happened?"

Harlem looked at her sternly and said, "They gunned down Crown in his crib, along wit' Toy-T and Sweet. Crown's in the hospital but the others are dead."

"What?" Cherish shrieked.

"I'm gettin' y'all the fuck outta here. Get the rest of the bitches ready."

Cherish wasted no time gathering up Casper and Midnight. By their actions, people in the club knew something had gone down. Everyone stopped what they were doing and had their focus on Harlem and the girls.

Harlem moved toward the exit. He turned to look at Magic, who was not too far behind, and said, "I may be comin' to check you soon, nigga."

Magic was far from intimidated by Harlem. He was wary of the man but knew how to stand his ground. Angel looked at his boss with a nervous stare but Magic looked back and said, "Just get back to work, Angel."

# 25

The very next night YB was on his way to New York. He didn't know what the future held for him and Chaos. Word was out about Crown and Toy-T and he knew a war was brewing. The streets of Philly would be spilled with blood. He wasn't a coward but he knew he had to regroup.

Leaving Philly wasn't that easy for YB. He was leaving a lot behind, but with $75,000 in the truck and a fresh start with Chaos, he knew anything was possible. Some of the money was his saved from his time in the drug game and the rest came from the robbery. He and Rufus split the $75,000 and the cash they got for the furs down the middle. It was a good take for both men, and Rufus had enough to pay the Mexicans for the four keys of raw H.

The conflict surfaced when Rufus realized that YB was leaving for New York with Chaos.

"Yo, you gonna break out on me, just like that? We family, nigga! We built this shit together, you and me, YB. What the fuck I'm gonna do without you, nigga?" Rufus was enraged.

"Nigga, I can't hold your hand forever. I gotta do this, my nigga. I need a time out from this," YB had replied.

Rufus wanted to kill Chaos. She was taking away his cousin, the only cousin he had left in the city.

"Ain't no time out from this, cuz. We in this for life, you hear me, nigga, early! And what it's gonna look like, you leavin' for New York after we done made our move on Crown? It's gonna look like you running, nigga, running from your battles. We never fuckin' ran from anything, you hear me?" Rufus exclaimed.

YB heard his cousin but Rufus didn't understand that it was much more for YB than just running. He never told Rufus that he might be under investigation by the feds or local police and that he was growing tired of the game.

"YB, this is us. This is us, nigga! This is what the fuck we're about, nigga! You can't leave. You and me been runnin' this shit since forever. I got love for you, nigga, and you ready to walk out on your own family?" Rufus's voice was filled with hurt and confusion.

"Rufus, I gotta do what needs to be done and I ain't never walkin' out on you," YB said.

"Wit' that bitch, yeah you are, nigga! You gettin' weak over pussy, nigga. This is how you gonna end this shit? Fuck it then," Rufus ranted. "I'm gonna hold it down like I always do and let muthafuckas know I don't run from no man. You think I fear Harlem? You think I fuckin' need you, nigga?" He poked a finger in YB's chest. "You think I need you? I'll be the nigga to run this town when you're gone. Remember that, nigga. I'll be the nigga doin' it big when your bitch ass is rested up in New York wit' that fuckin' ho. And when you get tired of her, nigga, don't fuckin' come runnin' back to me; don't try to come back to Philly to reclaim the throne. I'll be that nigga runnin' this shit without you. You hear me, YB? You fuckin' hear me, nigga?" Rufus turned away from YB. "Run nigga, run . . . run to be wit' that fuckin' ho and see how fucked up it will be for you. I shoulda shot that bitch dead when I had the chance," Rufus snarled in contempt.

YB was upset with what Rufus said but chose not to let his cousin's ignorance and anger deter him from his plans. He kept his composure. He wanted to beat his cousin's ass but let it be since Rufus was upset. He simply walked away from.

"Run nigga, run . . . fuckin' run nigga, run . . . run nigga, fuckin' run. Go be wit' that fuckin' bitch!"

YB got into his truck and just drove off, knowing that he and Rufus would never be the same again. He was still family but YB knew that they were going separate ways. Rufus wanted to run and control the streets and get money and YB only wanted to get money.

Rufus was the hard part. He knew he had to tell his mother and Magic that he was leaving town and while he didn't want to do it, he knew they would be easier to deal with.

YB pulled up to his mother's house and saw her Benz truck parked in the driveway. He got out of his ride carrying a bulky envelope in his hand. He walked into the house and found his mother in the kitchen making lunch.

"Hey baby," his mother greeted without turning to face her son as she chopped tomatoes.

"Hey, Ma." YB gave his mother a hug from the back and then kissed her on the cheek.

"What was that for?" she asked with a smile on her face.

"I love you, Ma."

She continued to smile while YB handed her the envelope.

"What is this?" she asked, drying her hands on a dishtowel and opening the envelope.

"I want you to take a long vacation somewhere and there's $15,000 to help you get started," he suggested.

"Vacation?"

"Yeah just leave town for a while and enjoy yourself."

"Why?"

YB stared at his mother. By the look he gave her, Mrs. Toma already knew that something was up. "What's going on, Yvonne? What happened? Is everything okay?" she asked with concern.

"Some shit popped off the other night wit' me and Rufus," he began to explain.

"Shit like what?"

"Three people are dead and one of the dead was a heavy hitter here in Philly. I know his peoples are gonna come at me and Rufus. I can handle myself, but you . . . I can't have anything happening to you, Ma," YB held his mother's wrist gently as he looked into her eyes.

"Shit, Yvonne," Mrs. Toma cursed.

"I need you to take a long vacation. I need you to be safe while I'm gone."

"Gone? Where are you off to?"

"Somewhere far from here and I don't wanna tell you where. But I promise I'll call you when I get there."

"I already been through this shit with your father and Magic. I know how to handle myself, Yvonne. I can look after myself."

"I know, but I would feel much better if you left town for a minute, at least until everything blows over."

Monica stared at the bulky envelope in her hand and let out a deep sigh. She looked back at her son and joked, "Mexico is good this time of the year."

YB smiled and felt better that his mother was taking his advice. With his mother taken care of, he went to see Magic at the club.

*Dirty Little Angel*

When YB walked in Magic was behind the counter, tallying the sales receipts from the bar. The place was quiet and empty and Magic seemed to be at peace for once.

"What you want, nigga?" Magic asked.

"I'm out for a minute," YB replied.

"You had anything to do with that home invasion at Crown's place the other night?" Magic stared at YB.

YB stared back. "Yeah. You know we did, Magic."

"Streets is hot right now, nigga. Harlem came into my place the night it happened and scooped up the girls and then issued me with a warning," Magic stated. "I figured y'all had set some shit up the way Sweet beat down one of my girls on the same night and Crown dragged her out of here in a hurry. Then I heard the news a few hours later."

"I'm sorry about that."

"What you sorry for, nigga? Crown had it coming eventually, but I'm just sad that it had to be you. But you just watch your back out there. Harlem is still loose and he's a dangerous man to bump heads with."

"Yeah, I know. And I'm taking your advice and skatin' off for a minute and taking Chaos wit' me."

Magic nodded. "You be safe, nigga. Start over with something better for yourself."

YB nodded. It was a complicated moment for both men. They had love for each other and to depart was something YB didn't want to do.

"I don't need to know where you're going, just leave. And don't worry about me, young'un. I survived over fifty years on these streets; I think I know how to handle myself." Magic smiled.

YB smiled back. He gave Magic dap and embraced him. "I always got love for you, Magic," he whispered.

"Go and do you. I know your father would be proud of you. You're his seed so carry his name out there with some fuckin' respect, YB."

YB nodded and walked out the door to make preparations for his trip to New York.

YB crossed the George Washington Bridge around midnight. The shine from the city's skyline was new to him and he was somewhat stunned at how beautiful the city looked.

Chaos was still asleep with her head resting against the passenger window. YB had "What We Do" track by Philadelphia Freeway playing and navigated his way through the thick traffic, heading toward the Cross Bronx Expressway. He was so new to the city that the curves and turns, the bridges, and the dense traffic at such a late hour had his mind spinning. He knew once he got on the Cross Bronx Expressway that he needed to wake up Chaos for further directions. This was her town, her place of birth, and she knew more about the Bronx than he would ever know.

After about a half hour of being stuck in traffic, YB finally got onto the Cross Bronx Expressway, carefully following the signs for route.

"Chaos, wake up. Wake up, baby," YB said as he nudged her gently.

Chaos twisted and turned for a short moment and then opened her eyes to New York—the Bronx, exactly. She smiled and peered out at the city. It had been so long for her that she somewhat felt intimidated. The farther YB drove into the Bronx, though, the more familiar she became with the city again.

She told YB to get off at Jerome Avenue and they headed north.

"We need to find somewhere to stay for the night. I gotta rest," YB stated. He was tired. Since the night of the shooting, he hadn't had any sleep. He had been running around Philly trying to get his shit right

*Dirty Little Angel*

before leaving.

"A'ight, just find a motel to stay at," Chaos said.

Within fifteen minutes they checked in at Howard Johnson on Boston Road. The place was low-key and definitely far away from Philly. With the money packed away in a small duffel bag, the two settled into the quiet room.

The room only had one bed and cable TV. YB tossed the bag on the bed and went to the window where he observed the busy Bronx streets from the fourth floor window. He removed his gun and tossed it onto the bed next to the duffel bag.

"I need a shower," Chaos said, undressing.

YB turned to watch her strip naked and walk into the bathroom. He admired her tight shape and felt bad for Chaos. Like him, she had a hard life.

YB poured the money from the duffel bag onto the bed. He had enough money to live on and to invest into something outside of Philly. He even thought about establishing himself in the drug trade in New York, but without Rufus as his right hand, it would be hard for him. He needed muscle and the Bronx was very unfamiliar to him.

The motel room was quiet except for the shower running in the bathroom. YB was deep in thought. He let out a grave sigh and asked himself, What the fuck do I do now?

# 26

Chaos let the hot shower cascade down her body. She kept her head down and let her tears mix in with the steamy water. She was grateful to be out of Philly but Sweet was supposed to be with her. Sweet wasn't supposed to be dead.

She tried to wash the pain, the hurt, and the transgressions she suffered from her skin—scrubbing and scraping every inch of her body with a wet, soapy washcloth. She thought about the tricks that she fucked and sucked. She thought about the beatings that she endured from the hands of Crown. She thought about Toy-T raping her and videotaping her sexual acts with his friends. Her life was a living hell. She cried under the flowing shower, hoping YB didn't hear her.

The bathroom was saturated with hot steam. The mist blocked any reflection in the mirrors and a thick haze lingered in every corner of the bathroom, making it look like a sauna. Chaos wanted the water hotter because she felt so dirty.

The bathroom door opened and YB walked in quietly. He heard Chaos sobbing through the door. He walked toward the shower, removed his boxers, and got in the shower.

Chaos was caught off guard by his sudden appearance and quickly dried her tears. "YB, what are you doin'?"

"Ssshhhhh," YB gestured with his finger to his lips.

He tenderly embraced her from the back. Chaos began to cringe, feeling his broad chest against her back and his arms around her. It was the closest she had ever been to YB, and the feeling was somewhat strange to her.

"We made it this far so let me take you further," YB whispered in her ear.

Chaos tried to let herself go. She wasn't used to a man's love. Sex with her was always paid for and fast. When YB gently ran his tongue across the back of her neck, she closed her eyes and bit down on her bottom lip. She felt YB hardening behind her. His dick felt long and thick and she knew he was a blessed man.

YB continued to hold Chaos under the hot shower and licked every inch of her until her body shuddered with pleasure. He cupped her breasts and massaged her wet nipples with care.

Chaos began to pant, loving the sexual encounter. Both their bodies were dripping wet with lust and passion for one another. Chaos turned to face YB and stared into his dark face. She loved what he did for her. Because of him, Crown was dead.

Chaos pressed her moist tits against YB's naked chest and ran her tongue across the deep scar that lined his cheek. YB palmed her phat ass firmly as Chaos's tongue moved toward his fleshy lips. She kissed him intently, feeling his tongue swimming around her throat. Her pussy was throbbing and wet.

"Fuck me, YB," Chaos cried into his ear.

YB was so hard that it hurt. Chaos's body was in perfect form. He moved his hand up and down her wet thighs and then across her shaven pussy. He picked her up and she wrapped her thick, smooth thighs around him. Chaos held onto him tightly, preparing herself for the ride that he was about to give her.

YB slowly pushed himself into her. Chaos held him closer and let out a loud yell that echoed through the bathroom. She felt herself opening up from below with YB thrusting in and out with one arm secured around her and the other clutching the safety bar in the tub for support. She had her back against the wall, the hot water still cascading off them.

They fucked hard. YB tore into her pussy like a beast, sucking on her neck and nipples, feeling heaven within her. For Chaos, it was the first piece of dick in a long while that that wasn't paying or forced upon her, and she was enjoying every moment of it.

They didn't care about condoms; they just wanted to feel each other raw. YB exploded inside Chaos and trembled a little as he pulled out and took a breather.

It was an encounter that the two would always remember. On that night, Chaos fell in love with YB and knew that he was the man she wanted to spend the rest of her life with. For once, she wanted her life to end like a fairytale, even if the idea was farfetched. For once, being back in New York, she finally felt free.

# 27

Harlem walked into Delaware County Memorial Hospital with his usual scowl. He heard that Crown was still alive and he needed to get a word with him. He moved through Security and the nurses' station with a concealed Glock and dared anybody to stop him.

"Sir, excuse me, sir. You just can't go through there," a nurse called out, trying to stop him.

Her pleas fell on deaf ears. Harlem pushed through the doors to the emergency room and scanned the room quickly. The only things he saw were doctors, patients, and all kinds of other shit that he didn't need to see.

Harlem stood out in the emergency room like Al Sharpton at a Klan gathering. He wore a long, dark parka that was wet from the rain, dark jeans and black Timberlands. Everyone in the ER quickly took notice of the harrowing figure among them and grew wary.

Harlem was about to start searching room to room for Crown but stopped in his tracks when he noticed two Philadelphia cops in the distance, talking to a patient. He knew it would be stupid to act a fool. Soon, the nurse who tried to stop him earlier appeared in the emergency room with two security guards who gave Harlem contemptuous looks.

"You got a pass to be in here, sir?" one of the guards asked.

Harlem returned the man's hardened gaze with his own, knowing that if they were in another place, at another time, the two toy cops would be dead where they stood.

"I'm lookin' for a friend," Harlem said.

"Well, you need to sign your name at the front desk and give us your friends first and last name. You just can't be charging past us like that. We got rules here, sir, so c'mon, let's go," the second security guard said to him sternly.

Harlem smirked at the two toy cops and wished he could kill them both but he let his murderous temper subside. "A'ight. Whatever!" The two uniformed cops were now paying attention to Harlem and watched him closely.

Harlem followed behind the guards to the front desk. Harlem hated to wait, but he did. He took a seat in the waiting area and eyed the two security guards like they were prey to him, making one of them kind of nervous by the look he was giving them. He wanted to kill both of them for coming at him disrespectfully, but he knew their deaths would have to wait. He had to see about Crown. He wanted the west side of Philly to run red with his vengeance. Harlem knew in his gut that YB and Rufus were behind the shooting, but he needed to get Crown's approval and assurance before he could strike back.

Unfortunately, Harlem he got word that Crown fell into a coma and the doctors were doing everything that they could to save his life.

Harlem hated to hear the news and knew when Crown awoke Philly would not be the same for a lot of people. Harlem was a killer, and he knew not to strike at those responsible for Crown's shooting until he personally got the word from his boss's lips that YB and Rufus were the ones involved. Fortunately for Rufus and his peoples, Harlem left town for a while and vowed to come back to settle the score with his enemies.

# 28

As the weeks went by in New York, YB and Chaos got settled in and became used to the Bronx and its way of life. For YB, the setting was much faster and nosier than Philly, but it quickly became home to him and he thought about his options in New York. They stayed at the Howard Johnson for two weeks. They bought new clothes for themselves and toured Harlem, Brooklyn, and even Queens.

YB wanted to become familiar with the city and see how things operated. He took the subway. He drove around in his truck. He walked around the Bronx alone some nights with his Glock on him. He wanted to get familiar with faces and streets. He wanted to learn the city because he hated being lost. The borough was so different from the west side of Philly but then it was also the same: ghetto, the drugs, some areas unkempt, and there was crime. New York just seemed like it was more extreme than in Philly.

YB and Chaos now had a life together, and Chaos wanted to forget about her past and start over. With the money they had stashed, she wanted to venture into doing something new for herself. It would have been easy for her to go down to the local strip clubs like Sexy Dancers or the Wedge Hall and get a gig dancing there, but she was tired of that life and told herself there had to be better choices. Chaos was aware that she had no education, no trades, no degrees, or any talent or skills to get paid like that, so she felt really limited with her career choices. YB was just a drug dealer/thug from the streets of Philly. It was hard for them at first to settle in with something.

For three weeks, all they truly did was fuck each other's brains out. If they weren't fucking they were wining and dining in the city, going on shopping sprees and enjoying their cash and youth.

Chaos went back to her old neighborhood over by East 181st Street and Tiebout Avenue. She wanted to see if some of her old friends were still around. She was excited about being back home and wondered how much her hood had changed as she drove YB's truck down the Grand Concourse.

When she reached 181st Street and Ryer Avenue, Chaos parked the truck and stepped out into the warm air and took a deep breath. The place still looked the same in her eyes; the same buildings still standing, the streets soiled with trash, cars and trucks of all brands lined down the street, making it hard to find parking. The block was filled mostly with Hispanic people going about their business, some lounging around and playing their reggaeton loudly.

Chaos smiled again and looked up at the building she had called home for three years of her life. She had lived there with her foster mother Ms. Joseph and her wild grandson J.K. before she ran away to Philly.

Ms. Joseph was one of the very few who actually loved and cared for Chaos. She was put into Ms. Joseph's care when she was fifteen, and by that time, Chaos was already seasoned to the street life and was a hard young woman to deal with. Ms. Joseph put her all into trying to help Chaos with her life and wanted to raise her right. It was difficult since she was in her mid-sixties and her own grandson was on the verge of destroying himself with drugs and the streets.

Chaos would put her foster mother through hell stealing, fighting, drug use, and sleeping around. Even behind her foster mother's back, she fucked J.K. a few times in her own home. Ms. Joseph was unaware of her grandson and Chaos's sexual encounters but she wasn't naïve to the destructive behavior going on in Chaos.

As the years passed, Ms. Joseph's health began to fail her and J.K. was doing city time at Rikers Island. When it was just getting good with Chaos and Ms. Joseph, her foster mother was diagnosed with a terminal illness and two months later her best friend Rachael was killed on the streets. Three months shy of her eighteenth birthday and before the city could take her away again and place her into another shitty foster home, Chaos ran away to Philly and met Crown.

Chaos stared up at the building she once called home and reminisced about the good and bad times she had. She wondered if Ms. Joseph was still around. She took a deep breath and walked toward the building.

She moved through the lobby and when she reached the eighth floor of the building her heart began to race. Moving down the narrow project corridor, Chaos recalled some crazy nights when her boyfriends would fondle her in the hallways and when she would suck dick in the staircases. She thought about the fights she had with jealous girls who hated on her because of her looks and body.

Chaos stopped in front of her old apartment door and knocked three times. She waited patiently for a response.

"Who is it?" she heard a woman ask.

"Hello, my name is Chaos—I mean, Danielle. I'm lookin' for a Ms. Joseph," Chaos spoke loudly through the door.

The door opened and, hoping that it was Ms. Joseph, Chaos smiled. Her smiled faded when a younger woman in her early forties appeared instead.

"Ms. Joseph? I haven't heard that name in a while," the lady said.

"Is she here?" Chaos asked eagerly.

The woman looked at Chaos with a saddened gaze. "I'm sorry, young lady, but Ms. Joseph passed away two years ago. I'm her daughter, Wendy."

"Oh, I'm sorry. I just thought . . . never mind," Chaos stuttered. "Your mother was my foster parent."

Chaos began to leave but Wendy asked, "Would you like to come in for a while?"

Chaos thought about it for a quick moment. "Sure."

Wendy welcomed Chaos into her home with open arms. When Chaos walked in she had flashbacks of her previous life with Ms. Joseph. Some things were the same, like the furniture, but many things had changed inside.

She noticed a few pictures of Ms. Joseph hanging around the apartment and knew it was definitely her daughter who was maintaining the place.

"So you're one of the children that my mother took into foster care," Wendy said.

"Yeah, I'm Chaos—I mean, Danielle. I just got back into town and, you know, I wanted to say hi. Your mother was one of the nicer ones that I had come into my life. I respected her 'cause she treated me right. I'm sorry for your loss," Chaos stated.

Wendy smiled. "She lived a happy life. She loved children and was a teacher for over thirty years. But I remember you. My mother would call me and always had something to say about you. She said that you were one of the promising kids who were smart and had potential to do something with their life. You weren't perfect, but who was?" She smiled again. "But my mother did like you."

Chaos smiled at the news. "I miss her," she admitted.

"I miss her too. She was a good mother and a friend. But she was loved and is in a better place now."

Chaos glanced around and stared at a few photos of Ms. Joseph.

"So, what are you doing for yourself, Danielle?" Wendy asked.

"Um, right now, I don't really know. I'm staying wit' my boyfriend and I'm also lookin' for a job. I was in Philly for two years and things didn't go to well out there for me so I came back here to stay."

"I see. Well, you're a beautiful young woman. You could have a lot going for yourself."

"I'm trying. Your mother used to tell me that I was too beautiful to give myself away for cheap. She tried to teach me how to be a young lady but, to be honest, I was young then. Naïve, selfish, and did what I wanted to do. Now I see what she was trying to say to me," Chaos said.

Wendy smiled. "So, what are you looking to do? What skills do you have? Maybe I can help you with something."

Chaos shrugged. "Shit, to be honest, most of my life all I ever did was run the streets and do dumb shit. I slept around and used to fight a lot. I mean, I never took school seriously or really contemplated my future. Shit, the only thing that I did that had some skills to it was maybe doing my best friend's hair at times."

"I see. So, there's a start."

"What? Doin' hair?"

"God is a blessing, Danielle, because it so happens that I own a hair salon on Fordham Road and I probably could use a young, vibrant girl like you around in my shop. I mean, if you're willing to take it seriously."

"Are you kidding me?"

"I can get you into a cosmetology school in the city and get you started with obtaining your license to do hair."

"Oh my God, is you serious?" Chaos cried out.

Wendy nodded and said, "I know my mother wouldn't have given up on you, so I'm here to help you make a better life for yourself. So, you're ready to take this seriously?"

"What? Hell's yeah! Oh my God, thank you!" Chaos jumped up and hugged Wendy. "You don't understand how much I needed this."

"You know, it was a blessing for you to come to my door when you did. We'll put together a plan, see what schools are the best, and set you up with financial aid if you need help with money."

Chaos was flabbergasted. She didn't know what to do with herself. She cried tears of joy and thanked Wendy again for the help. God knew that she needed it and she felt that this was the perfect opportunity to do something with herself.

Chaos knew how to do hair, just not professionally. With a little training, she felt she would be the best in her class. She hugged Wendy and thanked her once again. They talked for a while, getting to know each other better and then Chaos left the apartment, gleaming brightly like the sun itself. She couldn't wait to tell YB the great news. It was a start for her, and she knew that with the push and break she was getting, she could finally turn her life around. She finally felt that she could leave her past behind and move on to better things.

Chaos jumped into the truck and started singing to herself. It was a great and gorgeous day and she wanted to be with her man.

# 29

Chaos enrolled into the Empire Beauty School in Midtown Manhattan that same month. She was excited about the program and YB was very supportive of her goals. The tuition wasn't a problem for them because they still had $60,000 left of the money from Philly. I addition to their shopping and dining, some of the money went to getting a two-bedroom apartment in the Tremont section of the Bronx.

The area was okay and not shabby. Chaos was finally happy, and everything seemed to be going well for her. YB was another matter, though. He missed Philly and he was worried about his mom and thought about his cousin and Magic often. He would call his mom from time to time on her cell phone. She was in Barbados and enjoying herself. YB was happy that his mother was out of Philly for a while.

The thing that bothered YB was that he wasn't a nine-to-five dude. He had only worked for himself his whole life by selling drugs, and knew a job couldn't happen for him. He was happy for Chaos, but his situation was a bit different. He knew it would be only a matter of time before the sixty grand that they had left would start to dwindle. Between paying rent, the tuition for her school, and food, they needed a steady flow of income.

As a side hustle, YB got in good with a few other hustlers around the way and started to sell weed. Niggas from the block liked YB's swagger and took him in like he was family. YB played his position, knowing that he was in the Bronx and was on someone's home turf. But he was vulnerable on the streets. He had no real muscle, and his Glock could only do so much. He kept a low profile and did business discreetly. Even Chaos was unaware of YB's side hustle since he was in the drug game again at a slow crawl. She was wrapped up in finishing school and trying to distance herself from the street life.

Months passed and everything seemed to be on the up and up for the couple. Cosmetology school for Chaos was going well, and she kept in constant contact with Wendy. By the fall, Chaos would finally have her license to do hair and she already had a job waiting for her at Wendy's shop on Fordham Road.

YB's future in trying to go straight didn't look so bright. He found a connect in Yonkers and began to mess with the dope game again. Weed money was good but for him, but it was too slow. He was used to moving bricks in his hood while making tons of cash. You could take a man out of the ghetto, but it was hard to take the ghetto out of YB. He only knew one thing, and that was hustling.

With the connect YB had met in Yonkers and the prices he could get for his dope, he knew that he could flip the bricks quickly and kill the game on a whole new level in Philly. He was careful not to cross the wrong niggas in the Bronx, knowing to never shit where you ate. The money was good, though. He knew that in due time, he would have to drive back down to Philly to handle his business.

# 30

Chaos was a week away from obtaining her license to do hair. She was so happy that she was on Cloud Nine for the entire week. She had a job waiting, had her own place, and her own bank account. Thanks to Wendy's guidance she knew that she was going places.

Chaos was also pregnant. She'd been nauseous for the week and went to the clinic one morning to get a test. The doctor informed her that she was six weeks pregnant. Chaos smiled at the news, but when she walked outside, a feeling of guilt hit her. She thought about Sweet and how her life and pregnancy were cut short so quickly. It happened months ago, but it was still fresh in Chaos's mind. She knew that she was going to have the baby and thought about giving her baby—if it was a girl—the nickname "Sweet" to honor her friend.

Chaos sighed and thought about how she was going to tell YB that he was going to be a father. She didn't know if he was going to be ecstatic like she was or just nonchalant about it.

Chaos got into the truck and raced home to see YB.

When she walked into her well-furnished apartment—which had a luxurious décor with the high-end sound system, sixty-inch plasma

TV, rich leather furniture, and the round glass dining table set. YB was on the couch, talking on the phone and smoking weed.

She placed her bag on the table and walked over to him. He was heavily engrossed in his phone conversation and didn't pay any attention to Chaos.

Chaos sighed and said, "I'll be in the kitchen tryin' to get dinner ready."

YB kept on talking and Chaos caught a slight attitude. She thought about the news she had to tell him and it brought a smile to her face.

Chaos walked into the kitchen and kicked off her shoes. She began to put together a few things for dinner when YB said, "We need to talk after you finish cooking."

Chaos looked at him and didn't like the expression on his face.

"I got some news to tell you," Chaos said in a more upbeat tone.

"A'ight, but I gotta make a run real quick; go handle sumthin," YB replied.

Chaos sighed, wishing he would stay with her for the night but before she could get a word out, YB was through the front door and already out in the hallway.

She rushed to the door and shouted, "YB, how long are you gonna be?"

YB waited by the elevator. "Like, an hour."

Chaos didn't want him to leave, but she knew YB was going to do what he wanted anyway and figured it wasn't worth arguing over. However, Chaos knew that hustling was in YB's blood and felt that she couldn't counsel him to change his lifestyle. YB needed to do something while she was in school and she figured he would do what he knew best. She also understood that the Bronx was different for YB. He had to learn new faces, get familiar with certain customs, and earn his respect on the streets again.

Hours passed and Chaos cooked dinner, ate, and waited for YB to come home. It was nearing midnight and she began to worry. She called his cell phone numerous times but always got his voicemail. She even thought about going out and looking for her man, but the Bronx was a big borough and she didn't know where to start. She remained home and continued to worry. She began to wonder if coming to the Bronx was the right move for them even though it was the only place she knew besides Philly.

Chaos walked over to the window and stared out into the streets. It was a peaceful but chilly night. The block was quiet and there were no blaring sirens in the distance. It made her nerves a little calmer to hear the street's stillness for once.

She looked at the time once again and sighed. She continued to sit by the window in long white sleeper T-shirt that sagged down to her knees and sipped a hot cup of tea. She rubbed her belly, thinking about the baby and how much her past troubled her. She thought about Crown and the shootout. She thought about the tricks she fucked and felt fortunate that she didn't have an STD. She thought about the other girls in the house and wondered how their lives turned out without Crown around to terrorize them. Then she thought about Harlem and knew he was still out there, probably waiting for her and YB to show up again.

Chaos felt somewhat safe in the Bronx. It was big enough to get lost in, and no one knew about them and their dreadful past. In everyone's eyes, YB and Chaos were just a couple who moved in together and were working hard. YB's involvement in the game did worry Chaos some. She knew if YB started to make a name for himself, like he did in Philly, then word could get out about him—and not just in the city, but across state lines. If the streets were listening and if others knew about them, there would be a chance that Harlem and others would hear. Chaos didn't want Harlem coming after her and her man.

Chaos continued to sit and wait for YB to come home. She moved from sitting near the window to sitting on the snug couch. It was twelve-thirty in the morning and Chaos let out a worried sigh. She was waiting to tell YB the good news and he was out in the streets doing God only knew what.

When she was about to give up and go to bed, she heard the front door open. Chaos perked up, waiting for YB to appear from the foyer. She wasn't really mad, but she was worried about him. He was definitely changing.

YB walked into the apartment and noticed Chaos was still up. He shot her an annoyed look and asked, "Why you still up?"

"You had me so worried, baby. What's wrong?" Chaos asked with concern.

She walked up to YB, wrapped her arms around him, and pressed her head into his chest. YB held her back and said, "I remember you sayin' that you had somethin' important to tell me."

"Yeah, I do, but you need to talk to me first. What is goin' on wit' you?" Chaos pulled away from YB and looked him in the eye.

"Yo, on some real shit, Chaos, I need to get the fuck outta here and head back down to Philly to go handle some business. You need to stay up here and continue doin' you. You got enough money to hold you down for a while and I'll be back up to come check you. You know I got love for you but this shit here, it ain't me," YB stated.

Chaos was shocked. "What? You don't love me?"

"You know I do. And I'm gonna continue to be wit' you. But I'm a hustler, baby. I just established a relationship wit' this connect and I need to make it happen for myself. I can't go to no school for no degree and I ain't no nine-to-five nigga. This shit here is what I do best, and I can't let it go."

"YB, please think about it. You go down to Philly and there's no telling what might happen to you down there. You know the cops might be looking for us. You know Harlem and his peoples are gonna be lookin' for us and no telling who else. We're safe up here, baby. We got a new life together, you and me." Chaos felt tears building in her eyes.

"You got a life up here, Chaos, not me!" YB spat back.

"So you're sayin' I'm not important enough for you to try and change? I'm not important to you to want somethin' better for yourself? You wanna leave me? I love you, baby, and I want this for us. I want us to have somethin' positive in our life for once 'cause all my fuckin' life, I always lived the negative. I always heard the worse like how much of a slut my mother was and how I would turn out to be just like her. Nobody ever had somethin' good to say about me or my family. I was treated like shit since I was born. I was born in an abandoned building around rats and my mother almost left me to die. I heard the stories about my mother from so many people that knew her and they looked down at me like I was a fuckin' abomination.

"And here you are quitting on me just like she did. She left me and never came back for me. I wanted and needed you to be different, because being wit' you gave me hope for myself. You were the only one that cared about me in Philly. You was there for me when I needed help and now you're ready to walk out on me for this drug shit!" Chaos spewed her feelings while tears streamed down her face.

YB looked at her knowing the hurt she endured during her life. But he still loved her. "I'm not leaving you, Chaos. I just gotta handle my business," he said to her calmly.

"Who's to say that you're business ain't gonna get you killed in them streets, especially in fuckin' Philly? We have enemies YB; do you understand that? Niggas that would blow your head off when they see you, no fuckin' questions asked. I need you here wit' me, baby. Please."

Chaos wrapped her arms around YB again. She loved his closeness and she felt his heart beating against her ear. His embrace gave her comfort.

"Remember what I told you back in Philly, when we were talkin' at the bar? I'm ready to be all the woman I can for you, baby, in spite of my past. I'm gonna continue to be real wit' you. You're all I have right now, and I need you to be here for us," Chaos said.

YB held her in his arm tightly and then picked up on what Chaos said. "Us? What you sayin', Chaos?"

Chaos took a deep breath and then stated, "I'm pregnant."

"You serious? How far?"

"Six weeks and the doctors confirmed it this afternoon. We're gonna have a baby, YB."

YB smiled a little as he continued to hold Chaos. "I'm gonna be a father, huh," he said in an excited tone.

"We're gonna have a family together," Chaos said.

YB closed his eyes and thought about it.

Chaos pulled away from YB again and led him to the couch.

"Let's talk, baby. We need to do this together, you and me. I will not abandon my child like my mother did. And I will not lose you to these streets. I will fight for you and my child, baby. You understand me? I will fight for us to have a better life for our baby, somethin' that you and me never had coming up," Chaos stated sternly.

They both sat on the couch and talked until the wee hours of the morning. Chaos told YB how she felt and YB listened intently. He knew that he had to do something with his life, but he was missing his peoples in Philly dearly. However, things had changed now that he had a baby on the way. It was dawning a new day for him.

# 31

It was 6:15 AM on a breezy fall day when Crown finally awoke from his coma, almost four months after he'd been shot. The doctors rushed to aid him in his sudden recovery. They said it was a miracle that he was still alive. He suffered three gunshot wounds to his chest which missed his major arteries and almost crippled him. Crown could barely move, but he was conscious of what was going on around him. His breathing was sparse and his condition was still critical, but he was finally awake.

Weeks passed, and Crown's condition continued to improve rapidly, which impressed the doctors. They did numerous tests on him. Being in a coma for four months didn't make him forget about the betrayal that happened. He was aware that Chaos and YB had set him up. He often wondered what had happened to the rest of his chicks and his peoples. He wanted answers and he wanted them fast.

Harlem soon learned of Crown coming out of his coma and was back in Philly days later. He wore a white lab coat to conceal his gun, wire-rimmed glasses, and a false I.D. No one challenged him as he looked for Crown's room. He found the room, walked in, and gently closed the door behind him. Crown was asleep. Harlem pulled the long, white curtain around his bed, giving them some privacy from the other patient in the room, who was also asleep. He stared down at Crown's sleeping body.

Harlem cleared his throat. Crown shifted and then opened his eyes to see this tall, harrowing figure in a lab coat, looming over him.

When Crown saw that it was Harlem he became alert. He propped himself up against the headboard and said, "What took you so fuckin' long to come?"

"I was out of town, just recently got the news," Harlem replied

"I'm in bad shape, my nigga. It's gonna take me some time to recover from my injuries. But I didn't forget," Crown stated.

"Just give me names," Harlem said in a low, eerie manner.

"My cousin's dead, along wit' Sweet. But that bitch Chaos set me up. They left me for dead, so I think it's time we return the favor," Crown said in a low whisper.

"Like I said, just give me names to go on," Harlem repeated.

"Muthafucka, YB! I want you to put to death everything that muthafucka loves: his cousin, Magic, and if his mother is still alive, kill that bitch. And then I want you to find them for me, Harlem. I want them gutted like fish. I want them to suffer and burn for this shit."

Harlem nodded.

"I want you to turn this city upside down with murder and terror. I want people to know I ain't down and I ain't over. And I want you to find my bitches and I'll deal wit' them when I deal wit' them. But your first priority is puttin' to death everything that nigga YB ever loved." Crown stared intensely at his number-one killer.

"I got you, my nigga," Harlem assured him. "When I find that nigga and that bitch, you'll be the first to know."

"They shoot me down and rob me? Oh, it's comin' back on them. I want them to suffer, muthafuckin' suffer like it's medieval times in this bitch."

Harlem walked out of the room with his mind on his mission. Crown watched his killer leave and smirked. He had set the dogs loose on his attackers and knew that in due time, vengeance would be his.

Harlem's body count was extreme. He had caught his first body when he was only fifteen, and afterward killing came easy to him. His first victim was Black, a man three years his senior. Black and Harlem never liked each other. He always teased Harlem and cracked jokes about him whenever they saw each other. He was a weed dealer around Harlem's way and was trouble wherever he went. He had a loud mouth and thought he was untouchable until one day, he got touched.

Harlem's reputation was growing and he was becoming a badass on the streets of Philly, coming up under the Rocquelle drug crew in the early nineties. Black figured out a way to get to Harlem and decided to start with his woman. Black tried to push up on Harlem's girl, Tammy, in a club one night and she warned him to back off. Black felt disrespected by Tammy's rejection and slapped her openly in front of dozens of people.

"Fuck that bitch-ass nigga Harlem. Skinny-ass, beanpole-lookin' muthafucka!" Black shouted. "You need to get wit' a real nigga like me, bitch, ya hear? What kind of name is Harlem, anyway? Muthafucka, this ain't fuckin' New York! Let me put that faggot nigga Harlem on my knee and spank him, like he my bitch."

Tammy glared at Black with tears streaming down her face.

"Fuck you! You're a dead man," she spat.

"Bitch, you know who the fuck I am? Yeah, tell that bitch-ass nigga of yours that Black slapped the shit outta you and if he comes lookin' for trouble, I'll slap that bitch silly, too!"

Of course, word got around about the incident. Two weeks later, the hype of the incident died down. Everyone thought that Harlem just was going to let it be and figured he probably feared Black. But that wasn't the case.

One night, Black was sitting in his ride on Lancaster Avenue, getting a blowjob from a hooker. He reclined in his seat, closed his eyes, and enjoyed the oral pleasure she was blessing him with.

Black didn't even notice the tall figure in all black approach his car quietly. Harlem came from the back and was crouched down, focusing on Black in the driver seat. He watched the woman's head bob up and down.

"Ummmm . . . shit, suck my dick, bitch," Black moaned. His hand was on the back of her head, urging her on.

Harlem had the element of surprise and suddenly loomed over Black. The woman felt a shadow over her and gasped in shock when she opened her eyes and saw Harlem with the gun aimed at them.

"Why you stop?" Black complained. He opened his eyes and was stunned by the .45 aimed at his head.

"Suck on this, bitch!"

Black didn't have time to react. Boom! Boom! Boom! Boom! Boom! Boom!

Harlem shot him six times in the head, splattering his blood and brain matter all over the front seat, dashboard, and the female passenger. She shrieked loudly, covered in Black's blood.

Harlem looked at her, thought about letting her go free, and said, "Fuck it!" He fired three rounds into her head, making it a double homicide before he ran off.

# 32

Rufus had come up in the past few months, and the dope game for him was growing daily. He controlled several profitable blocks on the west side and making his mark in the city. He also reopened the house on Brown Street. He had soldiers who would kill for him and workers who hustled hard for him. He drove around in a burgundy CTS and a black ESV Escalade. He was ballin' big time.

His pockets were lumped up, but he was missing YB. It had been months since they'd seen each other or spoken, and Rufus hoped YB would return to Philly one day to be by his side in the game again. He was upset that YB had left, but Rufus knew that with YB by his side, they would be much stronger.

Rufus walked out of his four-bedroom brick house with the wraparound porch on Parkside Avenue. He had his cell phone to his ear and was walking to his truck with two armed guards flanking him. He wore a black-and-white velour sweat suit and was armed with a .380. He glanced around quickly and moved down the stairs.

"Yeah, I'm 'bout to head that way now . . . I got you. Yeah, but you got that for me, right? I don't ask twice," Rufus said into the phone.

Rufus quickly got into the backseat of the ESV that sat on 24-inch chrome rims with tinted windows and bulletproof plating. He was aware that he had enemies, and he wasn't taking any chances.

The driver got in and soon the truck pulled off. The occupants of the truck were unaware that they were being watched closely.

Harlem sat parked down the street, keeping a keen eye on Rufus as he moved out of his crib. He observed how tight Rufus's security had gotten over the months since YB's departure. He also knew that the Escalade had a bulletproof covering. Despite the security measures, the guards and bulletproof truck wouldn't keep Rufus from being slaughtered by Harlem's hands.

Harlem gripped his 9 mm with the silencer at the tip. Rufus is going to die, but not today, Harlem thought. As he watched the truck turn the corner, he got out of the blue Chevy and approached the house cautiously. The gun was in a holster under his jacket and the block was quiet. He walked toward the house and quickly took in everything—the windows, the doors, the porch, the driveway. Harlem made a mental note to himself and then walked back to his car.

"Bars on the windows, armed security, and bulletproof cars won't keep your fate from happening, Rufus. You will die for your actions against my boss. You will die," Harlem said aloud.

He drove off. There were others to deal with.

# 33

Magic puffed his cigar and leaned back in his plush leather chair. He was trying to relax in his office and get some work done. He heard the bass from the music upstairs and knew his club was packed. He looked at the clock and saw that it was 11 PM.

Magic was reading a book about black enterprises and thought about investing his money into more progressive things like franchises. He was already into mutual funds, bonds, and black-owned businesses and wanted to move from Philly and retire from the club scene within a year. He thought about moving to Virginia to be with his only daughter, Shannon, and be a grandfather to his granddaughter. He was getting old; dealing with the strippers and their problems, the young crowd, and trying to handle the constant drama was tiring for a man his age. He still was a gangster on the outside and kept in good shape, but his heart wasn't into the urban lifestyle anymore.

The streets of Philly were getting more violent and deadlier every year. Young men were killing each other for senseless shit they called disrespect.

Magic saw that these young people today were shooting each other senselessly with MAC-10s and Tec-9s. Sometimes they missed the person they wanted to hit and killed innocent people instead. When an innocent bystander who had nothing to do with the game was killed, it only brought down more heat from the police.

Magic was tired of watching the news about children being killed in crossfire or innocent families killed over a senseless twenty-dollar debt. Philly wasn't the same anymore. The youth were more stupid and more heartless than his generation, and snitches were everywhere.

Magic sighed and placed the book on his desk. He stood and stretched, still clutching the cigar. He took another pull and thought about YB. It had been months since his departure, and Magic had to admit to himself that he did miss the boy. He hoped that his young friend was getting his life right.

Magic heard about Crown being shot down and being in a coma. He knew that it was inevitable that YB and Crown would soon clash and one of them would end up dead.

Magic knew that it was good that YB left town for a long while. Cops were investigating the shooting and asking questions everywhere. The streets were definitely talking, and that talk linked the robbery and murders back to YB. Harlem would be looking for vengeance, so Magic always stayed alert and carried his .38 special. He moved through the city with caution and tried not to be too predictable with his actions.

Upstairs, the club roared with "Big Pimpin'" by Jay-Z and the stage was crowded with the beautiful strippers. It was a peaceful night. The ladies were getting money and the fellows were drinking and enjoying themselves.

Angel was content and kept busy by the bar, mixing drinks and talking to the ladies. Even though the club had been peaceful, he did miss Chaos. She was his friend and was always good to talk to. Angel wished her the best, wherever she was. He smiled at the thought about her being happy for once. He made a rum and Coke for a customer and did a little dance to the song that blared throughout the club. Angel was happy and had a new boyfriend. When he heard the rumors of Crown's murder, a smile appeared on his face. Good riddance, he said to himself.

Magic emerged from the basement with the cigar still in his hand. He observed the place for a few moments, making sure everything was in order and going well. He walked over to the bar and said a few words to Angel, poured himself a drink, and had a few words with a stripper. His mind was at ease because Crown wasn't around any longer. Even though he brought good business to his club, it had come with drama that Magic didn't need.

Magic lingered upstairs for about a half hour and went back to his office to chill for the night with the company of Candy, one of the strippers.

Candy was a tall, caramel-skinned beauty who stood erect in six inch wedge heels. She wore her hair in two long pigtails and had smooth, flawless skin.

Candy strutted happily downstairs with Magic. Magic locked the door behind him, making sure that they wouldn't be disturbed. Candy giggled and was ready for Magic to work his charm and sweet daddy moves on her. She had fucked him before and loved the dick. He was able to take Candy places that no other man could.

Candy sat gracefully on his desk and pulled up her skirt. Magic moved closer as he unbuttoned his black silk shirt. Candy smiled, unhooked her bikini top, and let it fall to the floor. Her dark, round, nickel-sized nipples stood erect.

"It's been a minute since you fucked me, Magic," Candy said eagerly.

"I've been busy with all kinds of shit," Magic replied.

He moved his broad body between her open thighs and placed his hands against her hips. He pressed gently against her as he maneuvered his tongue into her mouth. While they kissed, Magic ran his hands across her breasts and palmed her ass, squeezing her thick cheeks.

Candy's body began to tingle as Magic's touch enticed her from head to toe. He sucked on her neck and nipples, while Candy reached into his pants and stroked his thick dick. Magic moaned at Candy's soft touch. She stroked him till he grew hard in her hand and she felt all nine inches of him ready to enter her.

"Um, I love the feel of your big dick," Candy whispered to him.

Magic pulled off her skirt and panties and then removed his slacks and boxers. He positioned Candy in the doggy-style position, parted her ass cheeks, and thrust himself into her. Candy gasped and gripped the desk tightly. Magic fucked her hard, causing ripples in her ass cheeks. He cupped her tits and thrust himself into her harder, causing Candy to cry out.

The bass from the speakers could still be heard from upstairs but the two were making music of their own, drowning out every other sound around them. Candy felt Magic's rock-hard dick opening her up like a canyon and her legs quivered.

They fucked for a while, ignoring everything else around them. Candy was spent after an hour of wild, sweaty sex with Magic. She lay on his leather couch, trying to take a breather. Her clothes were still in a heap on the floor and she was very well satisfied with the dick action that had gone down. She was thirty years younger than Magic, and she thought she loved him.

Magic pulled out another cigar from his desk, quickly lit it up, and took a deep drag. He smiled at Candy and stood naked in front of her.

"Nice," Candy uttered, staring at his well-muscled physique and limp but thick dick.

Magic looked at the time and saw that it was two in the morning. He told Candy to get dressed and he did the same. The two talked as they dressed.

When it neared three, Magic knew that it was time to go back upstairs and manage his club. Candy followed. She went to the bar and ordered a Sex on the Beach. Angel smiled knowingly.

As dawn approached, the crowd began to dwindle. Soon it was five in the morning and the place was almost empty. The staff remained behind to clean up and some escorted the dancers into cabs or home.

Magic was going over the take by the bar while Angel wiped down and put the liquor bottles away. Candy remained behind so that she could leave with Magic and continue their sexual encounter at his place.

When he was done, Angel said his goodbyes to Magic and Candy, got into a cab, and rushed home to be with his lover. Magic was the last to leave since he liked to close up the club.

It was finally just the two of them in the club. Candy went to change into more decent attire and Magic cleaned up the mess his employees had missed. He began sweeping behind the bar. Some nights, Magic wouldn't leave for home till noon. He spent much of his time at his club going over paperwork, rearranging furniture, cleaning up, or just relaxing and enjoying his solitude. Tonight was no different.

With Candy in the dressing room getting herself ready, Magic listened to James Brown that played from the small portable radio that was placed on the bar countertop.

Magic was almost finished cleaning behind the bar and Candy had just walked back in when he heard a sudden noise come from the back. Magic stood still behind the bar and wished he hadn't left his gun in his office. He had a feeling that something wasn't right.

"What's wrong, baby?" Candy asked.

"Be quiet," Magic said.

"Magic, what's wrong? You got me worried," Candy replied edgily.

Harlem emerged from the darkness with his silenced 9 mm pointed in their direction.

Candy eyes widened with fear and shock. Magic remained still as he glared at Harlem.

"What the fuck do you want?" Magic asked in a stern voice. He never took his eyes of Harlem.

"I told you I would be back to check you soon, nigga," Harlem said.

"If it's YB you're lookin' for, I haven't seen him in months."

Harlem chuckled. "Oh, I will find that nigga in due time, but that nigga is the least of your worries now. I'm here on other business."

"Nigga, you kill me and that's the end of your life," Magic warned.

"You think I'm worried? You know my reputation, muthafucka!"

He looked over at Candy, who stood rigid with fear. He aimed his gun at her head and asked, "You know who I am, bitch?"

Candy was too scared to speak, but she nodded. Harlem smiled.

"You know, you need to be fuckin' wit' niggas your own age. Fuck wit' a nigga that can do that pussy right and protect you from dangerous niggas like me. Magic is just old; his time done came and gone. You agree?"

Candy slowly turned to look at Magic with tears streaming down her face. Magic remained detached and alert.

"You love him, bitch?" Harlem asked Candy.

Candy nodded.

"I wanna hear you say it," Harlem said loudly.

"I love him," Candy said choking on her tears.

"That's all I needed to hear." He shot her in the forehead. Candy's body dropped to the floor.

"What the fuck is wrong with you, nigga? She ain't had shit to do with you and me!" Magic screamed.

He was about to charge at Harlem but stopped when Harlem pointed the gun at his head.

"Yeah, nigga! Leap and see how far you'll get," Harlem gloated.

Magic wanted to rip Harlem's chest open, but Harlem had the upper hand.

Both men stared at each other with hate and anger. Harlem kept his finger slightly on the trigger of his gun and toyed with Magic.

"You think you're a big and badass nigga. A tough muthafucka wit' all the bitches lovin' him," Harlem teased.

"I don't think," Magic retorted.

Harlem smiled. In a way, he had some respect for Magic. He was one man that you heard about in the streets and took shit from no one. Harlem was just as ruthless, but came up in a different generation. In a way, he felt bad that he had to kill the old man but it was his job and nothing personal.

"You know, I did have some respect for you. Even now, standing tall when you know you're about to die. Do you fear death?" Harlem asked.

"Nigga, my soul died years ago and soon you'll know what it will feel like to be on the other end of the gun," Magic said.

Harlem didn't pay attention to Magic's words. "You will die the way you lived, old man."

"As we all will do." Magic continued to look death in the face.

Poot!

Harlem fired once into Magic's head and watched the body collapse to the floor. He stared down at Magic's lifeless corpse and fired another shot into his head.

The blood spilled from the back of Magic's head onto the tiled floors. He died with his eyes open.

Harlem crouched over the body and dug through his pockets. He removed Magic's cell phone, a set of keys, and a little notepad. He went down into the office and ransacked the place, looking for anything that would link back to YB or someone he loved. His efforts paid off: Harlem found the phone number and address of YB's mother, Monica Toma. He'd done some internet research on YB earlier and found out that YB and this lady had the same last name: Toma was an uncommon last name for a black man or woman in Philly.

Harlem collected all the information he needed and left the office. He walked past the dead bodies without looking. One or two down, a lot more to go.

It would be a shock for everyone to find out that Magic had been killed. He was such a strong urban figure in the city of Philadelphia and his name did ring out. It would ring out even louder when word got out that he was murdered in his own club.

Harlem got into his truck and drove to Mrs. Toma's address. She would be his next victim of revenge. He wanted to save Rufus for last.

# 34

YB was very supportive of Chaos's pregnancy. He went down to the clinic with her and they both talked to the doctor. She was in her second trimester and they found out that they were having a baby girl.

"Oh a girl. Damn!" YB was at a loss for words.

Chaos smiled. She hugged and kissed her man. She was finally happy. Day by day, she forgot about her past life in Philly. She had somehow convinced YB to stay in New York and they still had a life together. YB was still in the drug game but had decided to slow it down.

Chaos was making good money, doing hair at Wendy's salon. Within two months, she had established a decent clientele and her career as a beautician was looking prosperous.

One night, the two were snuggled up on the couch and watching TV. Chaos said to YB, "You know what, baby? From now on, call me by my real name, Danielle."

"What?" YB said in surprise.

"Chaos was that bitch in Philly who did what she had to do to survive and get paid. I wanna forget about them days and focus on us and our baby. I know our future is gonna get better and I don't wanna continue to live in the Bronx with people callin' me Chaos. I want to be called Danielle," she proclaimed.

YB smiled. "Danielle. It's got a ring to it. But you know I'm used to sayin' Chaos."

Chaos sucked her teeth and said, "Danielle. I'm gonna be a mother now and I wanna start acting like one. Chaos was my middle name, but my name life is no longer suitable for my life, and I want to change that. So from now on, baby, please try to call me Danielle and especially around other people."

"Danielle, look, I promise I'll try. But you know that other name is the one that I'm used to rollin' off my tongue."

"That's all I need to hear. Just try for me, baby."

YB nodded and Chaos hugged him tightly.

"My fairytale." Chaos smiled.

"What?"

"I'm living my fairytale," Chaos repeated.

"What fairytale?" YB asked.

"With you, being my prince and rescuing me from danger." Chaos laughed and so did YB.

"So I'm your prince now?" YB asked humorously.

"Yup. My knight in shining armor."

"Well, I ain't got no armor, but I got a sword that is deadly," YB joked.

Chaos playfully pushed YB for his sexual innuendo. "You nasty."

"Yell, well the nastier the better," YB smirked.

He held Chaos tenderly. He kissed her on her neck and whispered, "I love you."

For Chaos, it felt like time had stopped. She thought that she was hearing shit. Maybe I heard him wrong, she thought. Did he say, "I love you?" It was the first time that she ever heard those three words said to her. Her heart fluttered and she felt a tingly sensation throughout her body. "Baby, what did you say to me?"

YB chuckled. "You gonna make me say it again?"

"I liked hearing it," Chaos said with a big smile.

YB smiled and said, "Nah, once is enough for me. I can't believe you got me to say it once to you."

"But you mean it though, right?"

"Yeah, I do."

"I got a thug in love," Chaos said in a teasing tone.

"Nah, you know I'm still a hardcore nigga. Don't let the smile fool you."

"I know, baby, but you're my own personal thug. Promise that you'll never let me go," Chaos said.

YB hugged his boo tightly and whispered in her ear, "You know, Magic once said to me that we started somethin' together and that we need to finish it together. No matter what your past was about, you're still all woman. And that's what I love about you, Cha—I mean, Danielle."

Chaos felt tears in her eyes after YB's words. She looked at him and knew that she wanted to love him for the rest of her life. He was so rough in the streets, but with her, she felt his compassion and his love. She went through hell to meet her soul mate and knew that it was worth the trip.

With tears trickling down her smooth, beautiful, brown face, Chaos looked at her wonderful man and said to him, "I love you so much, baby." She kissed him passionately. It felt as if they were one and couldn't be separated. Chaos lay on her back and YB rested between her thighs.

Gradually, they undressed each other as they continued to kiss. YB pushed slowly into Danielle and felt her gasp. She pulled him closer and wrapped her arms around him. YB panted at the sensation of her pussy contracting as he thrust into her.

"Oh God, baby! You feel so good," YB cried out.

Danielle's tears of love and joy continued to flow as she felt YB move within her.

"I'm gonna love you, baby. Please, hold me forever . . . please, never let me go," she cried out, feeling loved for the first time in her life.

# 35

Harlem stayed parked on Overbrook Avenue in the Wynnefield section of Philly. He watched the house carefully for two days straight and observed the single female occupant coming and going. Her Benz truck was parked in the driveway. Harlem wanted to make sure nothing was a setup and that the kill went smoothly. He couldn't afford any mistakes.

He wore all black and his loaded, silenced gun rested beside him on the passenger seat, ready for action. He watched the unobservant residents of the street who had walked past him for forty-eight hours without noticing anything amiss.

Tonight, I'll go in and fuck the bitch up, he said to himself.

It was midnight when Harlem decided to make his move. The block was quiet and the traffic was light. The area felt still. The only sounds he heard were cars driving by in the distance. The house was dark, so Harlem assumed that his victim was asleep. He stepped out of his ride, the gun concealed underneath his jacket. He strode toward the house quietly, keeping an eye for any unwanted attention or observers.

He quickly walked to the backyard and when he reached the back door, he pulled on a pair of latex gloves and skillfully picked the lock. He'd cut the main source to the alarm outside with tools and made sure there wouldn't be any police coming around to interrupt his business. Once inside, he closed the door behind him and removed his gun.

The house was dark and Harlem carefully proceeded, making sure not to bump into anything and awaken Mrs. Toma. He used a pen light and browsed through the place carefully. He knew that he was in the right house when he saw pictures of YB and his mother.

He slowly crept up the stairs, looking around, and reached the main bedroom door. Everything was motionlessness around him and the dark gave him comfort. The bedroom door was ajar and Harlem slowly peered inside to see Mrs. Toma asleep.

Harlem stared at the woman as she slept on her side, facing the window. He had the gun gripped in his hand and watched YB's mother sleep for a short moment, admiring her form in the darkened room.

Her digital clock read 12:13 AM in bright red numbers.

Harlem stood outside her bedroom door for ten minutes. At 12:23 AM, he reentered the bedroom and tugged at the sheets, waking Monica.

"What the fuck?" she cried out, startled by the man in her bedroom. She sat up, wearing a white night shirt.

"We can make this quick or we can make this painful. Your son, where is he?" Harlem asked, with the gun aimed at her head.

"What? Get the fuck out my bedroom! Is you fuckin' crazy!" she screamed.

Harlem shook his head. "Wrong answer."

He fired a shot that missed her head by mere inches, striking the wall behind her.

"Next time, it goes into your skull. Now, your son, where is he?" he asked again.

Monica was shaken and frozen with fear. She stared at Harlem, knowing that he meant business. She clutched the bed sheets tightly and said, "I haven't spoken to my son in months."

"Bitch, don't fuckin' lie to me! Where the fuck is your son?" Harlem shouted.

Monica was quiet. She refused to give up her only child. She was old and he was still young and finally getting his life in order. She was scared, but she was willing to sacrifice her own life for her beloved son.

"Bitch, you need to speak up. Where is he?"

"Fuck you!" she yelled.

Harlem was somewhat taken aback by her boldness. He smiled and admired that boldness in her. "You got balls, bitch. You love your son so much that you're willing to die for him tonight?"

"You'll kill me anyway. I know your kind. I grew up around muthafuckas like you, ruthless and having no respect for human life. You should have known my husband Smoke—" Her hand slowly moved underneath her pillow to where she kept her .22.

"Bitch, you don't fuckin' know me! I ain't nuthin' like these niggas on the streets. I'm a different breed," Harlem stated.

"You niggas are all alike! Mindless and stupid and your time with death will soon come, like all the others," she said.

She felt the .22 in her hand and carefully gripped it. She placed her finger on the trigger and waited for the right moment to strike. She never broke eye contact with Harlem.

Harlem was getting fed up with the talk. He came there for answers, not to be lectured about his life and the demons he dealt with. He stepped closer to her.

"I've been patient wit' you, bitch, but I'm gonna ask you one more time: Where is your fuckin' son?"

"Go to hell!" she screamed. In one swift motion, she pulled out the gun and fired a shot at Harlem, striking him in the shoulder.

"Ah shit!" Harlem screamed in surprise.

Monica raced out of bed, knowing he was momentarily in shock. She aimed the .22 at Harlem, going for the kill, but Harlem spun around and, with pure accuracy, shot her point blank between the eyes before her gun went off a second time.

Monica collapsed and her blood spilled out onto the plush carpet in a thick, red puddle.

Harlem was furious. It was the first time that anyone had ever caught him off guard like that. He was even more furious that it was a bitch in her forties who nicked him in the shoulder with a bullshit .22.

He took a deep breath and went over to the body. He glared down at Monica's lifeless expression.

"You lucky bitch!" he cursed.

He crouched down beside her, placed his gun to her head and unloaded his clip into her skull. Her being dead didn't just do it for him; he had to disfigure the bitch also, ensuring a closed-casket funeral.

He left the body there and went through all her personal items, searching for any information that would help locate her son. He dumped out her purse, found her cell phone, and then went through all the numbers in her phone. In the phone history, he found a few incoming numbers that started with the 718 area code. Harlem knew that was the area code for New York and he knew that he finally had a good lead on YB's location.

Harlem searched through the whole house, wrecking it as he went. He nursed his wound in the bathroom by cleaning it with alcohol and bandaging it the best he could. Harlem also wiped down the crime scene of any evidence that would implicate him. He quickly got back to his ride and made a phone call to a doctor he knew he could trust. They set up a meeting place where the doctor could look at his wound in private.

Harlem sighed and then cursed the bitch one more time for causing his injuries. He crossed victim number two off his list. Next was Rufus. Rufus would be a challenge and was the one man he had a hard-on for.

# 36

Thanks to Harlem, the streets of Philly ran red with blood of revenge and disorder.

Meanwhile, YB and Danielle were making do in the Bronx with a new way of living. Every day, Danielle's belly grew and she was excited about becoming a mother. She often went shopping on Fordham Road for baby clothes. She made some friends from her job and had a few from the school.

YB was cool with the BX, but he couldn't stop thinking about his family and Magic. He tried calling his mother but there was no answer. He tried Magic and it was the same thing. He began to worry. He knew something was wrong, and he knew that something was probably Harlem.

He needed to get in contact with his cousin but Rufus's number had changed. YB only had one resort and that was to drive to Philly to see what was going on. He knew Danielle would be against it, but he wasn't going to tell her directly. His plan was to skip out when she wasn't around, leaving her a note to explain his whereabouts. He wanted to do it that way because he couldn't stand seeing her upset, and he couldn't take the chance that she would talk him out of the trip back to his hometown.

While Danielle was at work, he packed a few things into a duffel bag. He left her some cash, a note, and the keys to the truck. He felt wrong about leaving her a note on the kitchen table but knew she wouldn't understand his predicament.

He caught a cab to the Port Authority bus station in midtown Manhattan for the next available bus to Philly. When YB reached the bus station, he felt guilty about leaving Danielle alone in the Bronx while she was pregnant. But she was only six months, and he'd be back in plenty of time for her to give birth. YB knew he had time to handle his business two hours away.

Or so he told himself.

He got the evening bus into Philly that would arrive around nine that night. He tossed his duffel bag in the overhead storage above and then took a seat. The bus wasn't crowded so YB had two seats to himself. He leaned against the window, propped his legs up in the second chair, and took a quick nap as the bus drove through the streets of New York and onto the New Jersey Turnpike.

It was after seven PM when Danielle made it home, expecting to see her man there chilling. She walked into the apartment with a smile on her face, ready to tell YB about her day.

"Baby, you home?" Danielle called out.

She moved throughout the apartment and saw that he wasn't home. She went into the bedroom to change clothes and then into the kitchen to get dinner started. Before she stepped completely into the room, she saw the note on the kitchen table.

She picked it up and read it. Her jaw dropped in shock. A few tears streamed down her face as she began to worry. Her boo went to Philly regardless of how she felt about it. Her first instinct was to pack a bag herself and go to Philly too, but in her condition, she wouldn't get far alone.

Danielle didn't know what to do. She called YB's cell phone several times but it only went straight to voicemail. She left him a few upset messages. She looked at the time and thought that he was probably in Philly already. There was a chance that he could lose his life there and it pained her that the father of her unborn daughter might not be around for their daughter's birth.

Trying not to become frantic, Danielle didn't know who to call or what to do. Her eyes were red from crying and her body was tense with worry. She reached for her phone and decided to call a friend whom she knew she could trust and would probably help out. Wendy picked up after the third ring.

"Hello?" Wendy answered.

"He's gone, Wendy! He's gonna get himself killed out there. He left me and he's gonna get himself killed," Danielle cried into the phone.

"Danielle, calm down. What's goin' on?" Wendy asked. "Talk to me, slowly."

"YB left for Philly sometime today. He left me a note on the table. I told him not to go! I got a bad feeling," Danielle answered.

"Danielle, I'll be there in a half hour. Just stay calm and we'll talk."

Danielle hung up and didn't know what to do with herself but to worry. She dialed YB's number a few more times, but to no avail. She sighed heavily and plopped down on the couch, her eyes filled with tears. She kept the phone in her hand and was determined to get through to her boo somehow.

Forty minutes had passed before Wendy finally arrived. Danielle hugged her tightly and began to cry on her shoulder.

"I need him back, Wendy. I need him here wit' me. We're having a baby," Danielle sobbed.

Wendy comforted her friend and walked her over to the couch. Wendy sat next to Danielle and held her hand while the young girl cried. Danielle told her about the danger YB would be in if he went back to Philly. Danielle was honest with Wendy and told her about Sweet's death. She described how she used to turn tricks for a gorilla pimp named Crown, under the stage name of Chaos. She disclosed more information about her former life in Philly. Even after she could talk no more, Wendy still didn't judge her. She was still a friend and let her know it would be okay.

Wendy prayed for Danielle and prayed for YB to have a safe return home. Danielle appreciated the prayers but wanted Wendy to help her drive to Philly to find her boo. Wendy was against it. She told Danielle that it would be foolish, since she was six months pregnant and Wendy had to open her shop tomorrow. The best they could do was pray, wait for his return, and continue to try YB on his cell phone.

It wasn't what Danielle wanted to hear, but after about an hour, Wendy finally calmed her down and made her some hot tea to soothe her nerves. Wendy spent almost the entire night at Danielle's apartment. She was a friend and wanted to be there for the young girl, knowing that she'd been through a lot. She needed a strong friend by her side.

# 37

Word about Magic being murdered at his place of business spread quickly throughout the city and everyone suspected that Harlem was the killer. Still, no one would speak to the cops about it. They feared Harlem and didn't want to be next on his list. Many took Magic's death really hard—including Angel, who had grown close to him over the years he'd worked at the club. He was the one who found the body when he went to work that afternoon. Angel was emotionally distraught at the sight of his dead boss but he immediately called police.

When Rufus heard the news, he knew it was time to step up his gunplay and security on the streets. He had a gut feeling that Harlem would be coming for him soon and didn't want to take any chances.

Rufus put out a $10,000 contract on Harlem's head and hoped someone would bite at the chance to put that nigga in the ground. He started to carry two guns plus a shotgun for extra fire power just in case he got into a heated gun battle with his enemies.

However, the threat of Harlem didn't deter Rufus from doing

business. He still ran his organization with an iron fist and wouldn't hesitate to shoot a man or woman down if they fucked with him or his money.

When Rufus heard the news about his Aunt Monica's execution, including nine shots to the face, he was furious. He knew it was Harlem's doing and vowed to hunt the madman down and murder him for what he did to his family.

He put extra soldiers out on the streets to hunt Harlem down. He upped the bounty to $60,000 and made sure security around him was tight. He also tried not to be too predictable in his movements around town. Rufus's wrath would be felt throughout the city, and he wanted people to know that he was the man in charge.

The news of Monica Toma's murder made the evening news. Many viewers were appalled by the gruesome death she suffered in her home. Police were all over the scene and declared that they would find the persons responsible for her death.

The homicide rate in the city was high, and the mayor wanted the violent murders to stop. He made an on-air statement in front of the city of viewers about forming a task force for the drugs and gangs that plagued his city. He seemed highly upset about the death of Monica Toma, as if he took her death personally.

With the police stepping up their investigations and patrols, Harlem decided to take a time-out from his killing spree and rethink his plans on exacting revenge. Rufus was his number-one target and he wanted the man's head on a silver platter to serve up to his boss.

Everyone thought that Crown was dead when, in fact, he was alive and well. He wanted to keep his condition a secret and had Harlem pay off the doctors and staff to keep their mouths shut or else there would be hell to pay. When Harlem came to see Crown to report the murders, Crown smiled wickedly and said, "You are one cold muthafucka! I heard the news about YB's mom. You shot the bitch nine times!"

"The bitch pissed me off," Harlem replied.

Crown laughed. "I want YB and Rufus's deaths to be even more gruesome. I want them two niggas to feel pain, and I want that bitch Chaos brought to me. Fuck her up in the process if you have to."

"I'm on it. They're in New York," Harlem informed Crown.

"New York?"

"I checked the mother's phone and noticed a few incoming calls from a 718 area code. I figured it had to be from her son."

Crown smiled. "The fuckin' Bronx."

"What about the Bronx?" Harlem questioned.

"That's where that bitch is from, the Bronx. Them two fled there for safety because it's the only borough that bitch knows and calls home. So far yet so close," Crown stated.

"You ready to take a trip out there and deal wit' them bitches?" Harlem asked.

"Fuck yeah, but before we leave here, I want Rufus dead and in the dirt. And we need to pay Chaos's cousin Bubbles a little visit. I'm sure she can give us some personal information about that bitch."

"It's already done," Harlem smirked.

Crown smiled. Day by day, he was becoming his old self again. He'd been out of the game for a long moment now and planned to return to the streets of Philly. He would redeem his throne again and make those responsible for his fall suffer a wicked death by his right-hand man. Crown wanted to come out stronger and fiercer. Once his enemies were dead and gone, he would run the west side with hoes and drugs and have his name ring out once again.

# 38

YB walked out of the bus station on Filbert and 10th Street with his duffel bag slung over his shoulder. He caught the nearest cab into the hood and was wary about being back in Philly after being gone for so many months. It was eating away at him that he had to run away from his troubles in the first place. He had unfinished business in Philly.

YB gave the cab driver his mother's address. He peered at the streets of Philly from the backseat window. He knew he risked running into some serious danger, but he had his gun stashed in his duffel bag and the confidence that he could handle whatever came his way.

He was changing with the help of Danielle, but he felt in his gut that his peoples were in trouble. He didn't want them to feel like he abandoned them when they needed him.

Twenty minutes later, the cab driver pulled in front of his mother's address. Instantly, YB knew something was wrong. He noticed the unmarked police car parked in front of his mother's home and bits and pieces of yellow police tape dangled from the house to the sidewalk. YB's heart beat rapidly. He was ready to jump out of the cab without paying but the cab driver quickly shouted, "Where's my fare?"

YB reached into his pocket and peeled off a fifty-dollar bill from a small knot of fifties and twenties. "Keep the change," he said as he dashed out of the cab.

He rushed toward the house in a panic, knowing something terrible had to happen for police to be parked outside his mother's crib.

"YB," a young neighbor called out to him.

YB turned to see Shelly, a twenty-year-old friend who cared for Monica as a neighbor. They were like best friends despite their age difference. YB's mother even wanted her son to hook up with Shelly, but YB felt guilty, knowing that he and Rufus murdered her boyfriend three years earlier over a drug corner. The murder was still being investigated and Shelly had no idea that the son of a neighbor and close friend had done the dirty deed.

Shelly walked across the manicured grass in a pair of denim shorts and a black tank top. "Shelly, what the fuck happened here?" YB asked apprehensively.

A sad look crossed Shelly's smooth, caramel face. "You don't know? Oh my God, you haven't heard, have you?" Shelly asked softly.

"Where's my mom?"

Shelly began to tear up again, knowing that she had to be the one to break the disturbing news to YB.

"YB, we need to talk," she said.

"Nah, fuck that! I'm goin' inside and lookin' for my mom," he shouted.

"YB, not here!" Shelly looked over at the police car. "Come over to my house."

"Shelly, what the fuck is goin' on?"

"They might be lookin' for you and if you act out here, what the hell you gonna do when they lock your ass up? Just come wit' me," she said in low tone.

YB choked back tears. He knew that he wasn't ready for the news she was about to tell him, but he followed Shelly to her place.

The cop looked up from reading his paper and glanced at the man following the young woman. He shrugged it off and went back to his paper.

Once inside Shelly's home, she closed the door behind him and stared at YB. She hated to be the one to inform him about his mom.

"YB, I got somethin' to tell you and you ain't gonna like it," she said.

"Shelly, don't bullshit me or sugarcoat it. Just say what the fuck you gotta say."

Shelly took a deep breath. "Your mother was murdered the other night. Some monster broke into her home and shot her in the head nine times."

YB's dark face tightened with anger but he couldn't keep the hard image after hearing the news about his mother. Tears of grief flowed from his eyes and then he let out a loud scream that caught the attention of the cop parked outside. His knees buckled and he grabbed onto Shelly for support.

"What the fuck, yo? What the fuck?" he cried out.

Shelly fell down with him to the floor, holding onto the man that she once thought would be hers. She let his grief pour out onto her shoulders.

"I'm sorry, YB. You know she was like a mother to me too," Shelly stated.

YB cried for a long time and Shelly tried to ease his grief the best she knew how. She asked him questions to take his mind off of his mother's death. She inquired about his whereabouts over the past few months. He told Shelly that he was out of town with a woman, trying to stay cool and out of sight. He left out the name of the city and state because he didn't trust anyone, especially after his mother's murder. Shelly wasn't happy with the news of him being with another woman since she'd loved him from the age of fourteen. Shelly offered to cook him something to eat, but YB wasn't hungry. The only thing he was hungry for was revenge. She also told YB about Magic being murdered in his own club and YB knew that it was Harlem's revenge for murdering Crown.

YB wanted to tear Harlem apart with his bare hands. For Harlem to do his mother that way made him sick to his stomach, and YB knew he would go medieval on him once he saw that murderer again.

YB remained with Shelly for a few hours because he needed to get his mind right. After he mourned for his mother, the killer in him came back out. He needed to get in contact with Rufus, knowing Rufus would be next on Harlem's list. However, Rufus could handle himself.

YB wasn't afraid that Harlem was looking for him. He wanted Harlem to find him and he wanted to destroy that muthafucka. It was war, and now it was personal.

He asked Shelly if he could borrow her car. He needed to get around the city and paying for cabs just wouldn't do for him. She agreed but only if she could come along too. YB didn't want her along, but it was her car and on her terms, so reluctantly he agreed. The two got into her dark blue Maxima and hit the streets of Philly.

YB eyes were bloodshot from crying and filled with hatred. Revenge was in his heart. He checked his gun and knew he needed more firepower to come at Harlem. He was ready to hit the street and hear who was saying what about the murders committed by Harlem.

He soon forgot about Danielle and her pregnancy, because his mind was wrapped up in revenge of the deaths of his mother and Magic. Somebody needed to pay, and someone had to die.

# 39

Rufus was unaware that YB was back in town. He was partying and taking care of business, making the city his personal playground with drugs, women, murder, and cars. He didn't consider Harlem a threat. He walked out of a strip club with his arm around a stripper and went to his truck. Two armed guards flanked him closely. Rufus was laughing and smiling and seemed to have quickly gotten over his aunt's murder.

"Yo, you ready for me, bitch? I'm ready to fuck the dog shit outta you, ya hear? Early, bitch," Rufus said to the girl. He grabbed her ass and fondled her tits as soon as she got into the backseat of the truck. Rufus followed behind and waited for the door to shut behind him before he slid his hand up her skirt and groped her bare pussy. He felt his erection growing and couldn't wait to get to it.

His two soldiers got into the car and waited for instructions.

"Yo, pull away from this bitch and take us somewhere private so I can blow this bitch's back out," Rufus said, rubbing her thigh and staring at his men.

His driver nodded and pulled out the parking spot. The truck was teeming with weed smoke, as the spliff was passed from the driver and guard in the front and then to Rufus. Rufus took a long pull and passed it to his female companion.

"Here, blaze this shit, shorty; get your mind right for tonight." Rufus grinned.

The girl took the weed and put it to her sweet, full lips. She took a long drag, just like the fellows did. She exhaled the smoke from her nostrils and then took another long puff, falling back against the seat and letting her high take control. She took one last pull and passed the burning spliff back to Rufus. He took a few more hits and rotated it back to the driver.

Rufus felt antsy and focused his attention on the girl. She had her legs crossed and her short skirt rode up her meaty thighs. Her eyes closed as she savored her high.

Rufus eyed her long, thick legs and licked his lips. He ran his hand up her thighs and then under her shirt, groping her round, succulent breast.

"I know you feel like suckin' some dick right now."

He had already unfastened his jeans. The girl looked at him and smiled, her eyes hazy from the weed. Rufus cupped his hand around the back of her head and forced her face down into his lap. The young girl pulled his dick out of his boxers and engulfed it in her mouth. Rufus moaned as she went to work. He had his hand knotted in her hair and watched her bob up and down, deep-throating him like a porn-star.

"Yeah, bitch, you know what you're doin'! Shit, that feels good . . . damn, that shit feels good! Aaaaaaaahhhhh!" Rufus let out a long groan, throwing his head back and feeling like royalty as she licked his balls too.

His soldiers were driving and smiling at the sounds their boss made. Both of them wished that they had next with the ho. The driver quickly glanced behind him and saw the young girl sucking Rufus off like she truly loved her work.

"Damn, wish I had me some of that, yo," the driver said.

"Yeah, well, I might pass the bitch off to you when I'm done," Rufus said.

"I hear that, my nigga," he replied.

The young girl continued to suck Rufus's dick and ignored what was being said about her. The truck continued down Market Street as the driver looked for a secluded parking space so that Rufus could fuck the girl.

"Yeah, my niggas, find a spot soon. I'm ready to put a nut in this bitch," Rufus stated.

His driver chuckled. "I got you, boss."

Rufus's cell phone rang and he hesitated in answering the call. He was caught up in his blowjob and didn't want anything disturbing him at the moment. Then he thought that it might be one of his soldiers with something important, like having information on Harlem's whereabouts.

He answered, "Yo, hurry up and talk to me."

"Nigga, where the fuck you at?" he heard his cousin YB say.

"Nigga, I know this ain't YB! Oh shit, cuz, good to hear from you again! How the fuck did you get this number, anyway?" Despite how they'd left things when YB left, Rufus was still happy to hear from his cousin.

"Shelly gave it to me. We need to talk, nigga." YB sounded none too pleased.

"You back in town, cuz?"

"Yeah."

"Yo, I'm sorry about Aunt Monica, but you got my word that I'm on it. I got a large bounty on that nigga's head and I'm turning over every fuckin' rock to find that faggot."

"You need to meet up wit' me, Rufus, ASAP."

Rufus smirked. "A'ight cuz, we'll link up, but a nigga kinda busy right now." He looked down at the girl blowing him. "You've been gone for months now. I stepped up, money is good now, ya hear? And right now, I got shit on lock."

"Good for you, cuz," YB replied nonchalantly. "But my fuckin' mother and Magic are dead and this nigga Harlem is still breathing. I don't give a fuck about business right now, you hear me, Rufus? I need guns and I need plenty of them."

"A'ight, YB. I got you, cuz. I'll link up wit' you tonight, after this session. Meet me at my spot on Brown Street in an hour," Rufus said.

"A'ight, and don't keep me waiting." YB hung up.

Rufus hung up as well. "This nigga home no less than twenty-four hours and still an arrogant bastard! I'm the boss now and it's not like I gotta rush for this nigga."

"Damn, YB back now? That's what's up," the guard in the passenger seat said.

"And, nigga, don't forget who you work for," Rufus quickly reminded him.

The young stripper never missed a beat with the dick. Rufus focused his attention on the girl and ran his hand down her back. He pulled up her skirt to stare at her bare ass which was phat and juicy like buttermilk biscuits.

Rufus was definitely turned on. "Yo, y'all niggas hurry up and find me a nice spot so I can fuck this bitch."

The driver replied, "We got you, boss."

# 40

A dark blue Benz had been on the truck's tail since it left the club. The windows to the Benz were tinted and the driver kept a sharp eye on everything 'cause tonight was the night Rufus would get got.

Harlem had a MAC-10 on the seat next to him, fully loaded with .45 ACP rounds that would cut a man into bloody pieces. He was also armed with his 9 mm with the silencer and a Glock 17 in the glove compartment. He was ready for anything with his arsenal, even a small war.

It was difficult to come at Rufus because he always had security around. His flashy and flamboyant lifestyle prevented him from being alone. He moved around with a large entourage or a few killers who watched over him when he was in public. Rufus had stepped up his game since YB had left town and managed to obtain a small legion for himself.

Harlem knew that just like himself, Rufus was a cruel and ruthless man who would be ready to kill at the drop of a hat. He knew that when coming at Rufus, he needed to be careful and alert. His revenge was so close that he was determined not to fuck it up.

Harlem followed the truck down Market Street. He was two cars behind the truck and noticed that the truck turned left on 32nd Street and drove up to Mantua Avenue, where it parked near the railroad tracks. The street was one-way going north and the traffic was light, with the left side of the avenue lined with dilapidated row houses and littered alleys. The dark street was a good spot for kinky activity and a little privacy. Harlem crept down the block slowly and saw the truck park by the thick cluster of trees and bushes that blocked most of the view of the train tracks.

Harlem parked a few cars down from his victims. He shut off his lights and saw both of Rufus's security guards step out the truck and move a few feet away, giving their boss some privacy to fuck his female companion. Harlem had a plan to move in for the kill and make it quick, painful, and easy. He knew that he only had a few moments and hoped that Rufus wasn't a minute man with the ladies.

He reached into the glove compartment and pulled on a pair of gloves, picked up his 9 mm, and stuffed it into the waistband of his jeans. He watched the men move about the dark street aimlessly, waiting patiently for their boss to finish fucking and keeping an eye out for any trouble that might come their way.

Harlem was a professional and had been in situations like that many times. The two armed men didn't pose a threat for him; they were just mere obstacles in his way to the kill. He knew that the guards were alert and had parked in an open area where it was easy for them to see what could come at them from a distance. The nearest parked car was about thirty feet away, and the bushes were too thick to get through.

Harlem wanted the kill to be neat and quick, but he knew that there was a chance that it could get ugly. He couldn't wait any longer and he had been patient long enough. He looked at the time and five minutes had passed. He started the ignition and slowly drove back the opposite way.

Rufus's men noticed the dark blue Benz pulling out of a parking space some distance away and immediately placed their hands near their weapons. They never took their eyes off the car. When they saw that it made a U-turn and leave, they relaxed a little and kept watch around the vicinity.

# 41

Rufus gripped the girl's booty as she rode him like a stallion. She felt him thrust into her wildly as he palmed her phat ass and sucked on her nipples. They both were sweating profusely in the warm truck, and with their warm breath and body heat started fogging up the windows. It became difficult to see in or out of the truck.

The young girl gyrated her thick hips into Rufus's lap, her back arched as she sat perched on the dick. She moaned and bit down on her bottom lip as Rufus fucked her like the thug he was. Her pussy almost had Rufus speaking in tongues.

"Fuck me!" she panted, her naked tits pressed against his chest.

Rufus felt himself about to cum and fucked her harder. He sucked on her nipples as if he were breastfeeding.

The truck wobbled from the intense sex inside. The guards laughed.

"Damn, Rufus is workin' that ass," one of them said.

"Lucky muthafucka right now," the other replied.

The street was quiet and it seemed like everything was cool—so it seemed.

# 42

Harlem drove the Benz up 32nd street, which was one-way. He had the headlights off and the gun ready. Since the truck was parked on the corner, near the intersection of Mantua Avenue and Wallace Street, the vehicle was wide open for the kind of attack Harlem had planned. He had measured the distance and thought about the amount of time it would take the two guards to react when they saw him coming. He had to be quick and precise. It was a one-shot thing with no second chances.

He slowed the car near the corner of Wallace Street until the truck was in his peripheral vision. The street was dark and kept him from being spotted. He turned the corner, took a deep breath, and revved the engine. With the Escalade in his sights, he peeled off, doing fifty miles per hour. The Benz sped down Wallace Street and charged the truck, which was directly in his path since 32nd Street was perpendicular to Wallace Street.

Rufus's men heard the car racing toward them and reached for their guns. By the time they had their weapons ready to aim and shoot, the Benz barreled down on them, crashing into the Escalade and crushing one of Rufus's men between both vehicles. His legs were broken and he was fatally wounded.

The crash hurled Rufus and his girl into the back passenger door. The girl shattered the glass with her head. Rufus landed on top of her in a bloody human pile of cracked bones and lacerations to the face.

Harlem kept the element of surprise and rushed from the Benz with the MAC-10 in his hand. He aimed it at the one man still alive and gunned the soldier down in a hail of bullets, ripping him to shreds.

With both of Rufus's soldiers dead, Harlem ran toward the truck and opened the back door. Rufus was paralyzed by his injuries and his lady friend was bloody and unconscious. Rufus seemed to be disoriented, his face was covered in blood and his legs twisted under the wrecked seats.

"What the . . . fuck," Rufus stammered, looking down the barrel of the MAC-10 pointed in his face.

"Payback, muthafucka!" Harlem opened fire on Rufus.

The machine gun fire tore Rufus's face to pieces, spilling blood and brain matter all over the backseats, leaving his face looking inhuman. The ho caught it too, receiving multiple gunshot wounds to her face, chest, and neck. Her thick figure was twisted up into a human pretzel.

With his job done, Harlem went back to his car, took what he needed, and left no evidence behind. He tossed everything into a duffel bag and fled down the block toward Fairmount Avenue.

He quickly stole a car and drove off, hearing sirens approaching in the distance. As he drove down 34th Street, he saw three police cars race down Spring Garden Street, heading toward the vicious crime scene he just created. He chuckled as he left them a real mess to clean up.

When the last cop car went by, he drove in the opposite direction. When he was a few blocks away, he got on his cell phone and called Crown.

When Crown answered, Harlem said, "Shit is done."

"Good. Now we go for the main prize," Crown said.

Harlem hung up and was ready to take a trip up to New York. Besides, he needed a break from Philly. The crime rate was too high.

# 43

When YB and Shelly arrived on Brown Street, he knew something was wrong. Cops flooded the area and a helicopter hovered over the neighborhood to film everything from a bird's eye view. It was like a scene from a movie.

YB rushed out the car and went the house on Brown Street, where everyone had already heard the news about Rufus. When Rufus's crew saw YB approaching them, they were all taken aback.

"Oh shit, nigga! You back?" Ray-Lo asked.

Ignoring the question and having one of his own, YB asked Ray-Lo, "Yo, what the fuck happened?"

Ray-Lo's face became curled with anger. He looked away from YB for a quick moment, hating to break the bad news about his cousin.

"Muthafucka, answer me! Where's Rufus?" YB glared at Ray-Lo.

"He dead, man, a few blocks down near Wallace Street. It ain't pretty, YB. Niggas did him dirty," Ray-Lo informed.

Hearing the news made YB even more furious. He lowered his head in grief. Everyone he knew and loved was already wiped out by Harlem.

Without saying a word to anyone else, he rushed back to the car and got in on the driver's side. Shelly scooted over to the passenger side with a sad gaze.

"Where you goin'?" Shelly asked.

"To see what's up," he replied and peeled out.

Within moments, YB pulled up near Wallace Street, where the block was swamped with police activity. Yellow police tape outlined the horrifying crime scene, with dozens of cops investigating the area and combing it for evidence or any DNA that may have been left behind.

The media had their cameras rolling. Reporters had their microphones, pens and notepads out, asking questions to any available officer about the victims and the crime. It was a zoo.

YB got out of the car and got as close as he could. The looky-loos were out, talking among themselves and speculating about what went down. The name "Harlem" floated around but no one dared speak out the name openly—especially to police.

YB stared at the scene. Shelly stood behind him, tense with fear. He saw the Benz that had slammed into the Escalade and about four bodies sprawled out on Mantua Avenue. Bloody sheets covered their remains.

It was a hectic sight, but no one could look away as they were all stunned at the tragic event that took place only a few hours ago.

"Damn, I'm so sorry, YB," Shelly said in consolation.

"He's a fuckin' dead man," was the only thing YB could say. He couldn't look anymore. His cousin was already dead so there was no use for him to see the body on the ground. They got back into the car where YB sat for a moment to think about things.

"I need to take your car," YB said.

"I'm ready, let's go," she replied.

"Alone. I'll pay you for your troubles."

"YB, you're upset now and you don't need to be alone. I can help you," Shelly said with concern.

"This ain't got shit to do wit' you, Shelly. It's my beef, and it's gonna get really ugly. So I just need you to step off and let me handle this shit!"

Shelly sighed. She was reluctant to give him her car in order to chase a killer and maybe end up getting himself killed. She had known YB since they were young and knew how stubborn he could be. There would be no talking him out of it; with his family dead, she knew that he was on the borderline of insanity.

YB reached into his pocket and handed Shelly a wad of cash.

"That's ten thousand right here, more than enough for your car."

Shelly took the cash and stared at YB with a look of apprehension. She sighed again and said, "You be careful, YB. I know you're upset, but just think about—"

"Just get out," he ordered.

Shelly looked at YB one last time. She wanted to hug and kiss him and make things better for him. He was a thug who ran with the most notorious of gangsters, though, and she knew that his way of handling a situation was murder.

YB had the Maxima in drive when Shelly slowly stepped out with $10,000 clutched in her hand. Without so much as a goodbye, YB sped off in the opposite direction, leaving her stranded a few miles away from her home.

YB went back to Brown Street, looking for Ray-Lo. People got out of his way as he rushed into the unfurnished, dilapidated stash house. "Where Ray-Lo at?" he asked a young man.

"He in the back," the teen, no older than fifteen, replied.

YB went to the back with his mind trained on two things: revenge and murder.

Ray-Lo was a lieutenant in the organization who YB trusted to have his back on the streets. He did seven years for a drug charge and assault with a deadly weapon and came home just around time when Rufus and YB were moving H in the streets. Ray-Lo was a ride-or-die type of guy who stood only 5'9" and weighed 160 pounds, but he had the heart of a giant and the skills of a killer.

With Rufus dead and YB off in New York—so everyone thought—Ray-Lo was next in line to run the shop in West Philly. But with YB back in town, Ray-Lo was cool with being second in charge, even though he was older than Rufus and YB by five years.

As YB rushed into the supply room, he thought it was stupid for Rufus to re-open the stash house on Brown Street after the murders on the block by Harlem; but that problem was the least on his mind.

YB entered the room to see a half-dozen teenage girls packaging the H for street distribution by stamping "Devil's Play" on the glassine envelopes that flooded the production table. They were in their underwear and were focused on the product, while Ray-Lo talked on his cell phone a short distance away.

He turned to see YB in the room and said to the caller, "Yo, let me call you back. Somethin' important came up."

He hung up his call and approached YB with an uneasy stare. "Yo, YB! Nigga, you know I'm down for whatever. Rufus was like family to me. You know who did it? Probably those niggas from Diamond Avenue, still beefing over Shyfe Lyfe gettin' killed over here a while back."

"Nigga, I know who's responsible," YB said.

"Who, nigga?" Ray-Lo was eager to know.

"Harlem."

"That nigga? I'm tired of hearing 'bout this faggot-ass nigga! You think he got to Rufus like that? One man?"

"I need guns," YB said.

Ray-Lo smiled. "So we on the hunt now? A'ight, you know I'm down, my nigga."

YB nodded and they both gave each other dap and then embraced in a manly hug. The team was dying out and both men knew that they only had each other left. Ray-Lo was tired of hearing about Harlem having Philly locked down with fear. He wanted his reputation to ring out like that and he knew that taking out Harlem—one of the most notorious killers in Philly—would definitely step his reputation up in the streets.

For YB, it was more personal than having a reputation in the streets. Harlem murdered his cousin, his mentor, and did his mom dirty with nine shots to the head. A man like that had to be put under, even if meant sending himself to the grave.

What worried YB was if Harlem could get close to his mom like that then there was no telling what other information he had on his personal life. Then he thought about Danielle and her being alone in New York. It made sense for Harlem to track his shorty down in NY for revenge—but to do that, he would need to find someone who may have known where she was.

He and Ray-Lo packed some guns in the trunk of the car and raced off toward Delaware, with YB praying that they'd make it in time.

# 44

Wilmington is at the north end of Delaware and about a forty-minute drive from Philadelphia. Wilmington is a prime location because it's geographically centered between Philly and Baltimore. It's where people go to settle down when they're tired of the city life.

It was a temperate, serene morning and the suburban, tree-lined street, West Lea Boulevard was the new home for Bubbles, Danielle's cousin. She'd been living in Delaware for about a year and loved her new life, which included her new house and her new job as a nurse at a nearby hospital. She always wished that her younger cousin could have obtained the life that she now had, but Bubbles knew that Danielle had to change certain things about herself first.

Bubbles, whose real name was Karen Little, hadn't spoken to Chaos in almost a year. Bubbles did miss her cousin, but she had her own life to live and her own worries to deal with. She didn't miss Philly much, especially with the crime being up. Plus, there were things about her past that she wanted to forget. So she moved to Delaware, where she met a guy, fell in love, and was planning to have a family. Her life had definitely changed for the better.

A dark blue Yukon was parked discreetly under a giant oak tree, a few feet from Bubbles's home. Harlem and Crown were inside the truck.

Crown was in top shape again and trying to get back on track with his pimping and running shit in the streets again. He had his bottom bitch Cherish by his side along with Casper, but Midnight had flown the coop. She moved back to her hometown in Kentucky a few weeks after the shooting.

Crown had to restock his hoes again and get that money right. After he was finished dealing with YB and Chaos, he would be back out there once more on the streets, pimping his chicks even harder this time. He was full of rage and clenched his teeth and fists every time he thought about that bitch Chaos and YB.

He sat in the passenger seat of the Yukon with a .380. He wore a black and white tracksuit and had his head shaved bald, which was a different look for him. Losing the braids and the perm made his image look harder, more thugged out. He'd lost a little weight but was slowly regaining it. He had scars on his chest from where the doctors performed surgery and some nights, it was hard for him to sleep. But Crown felt satisfied to know that Harlem took care of the majority of his troubles. He watched the news about Rufus's murder. The media said it was one of the most gruesome killings that the city had ever seen, next to that of YB's mother. It gave Crown some satisfaction to know that they were close to wiping out everyone who was involved with or connected to YB.

Morning crept gradually over the neighborhood. The information that the two men had was viable—money got you whatever you wanted, and knowing the right people in the game allowed them to find where Bubbles was living her new life.

Crown definitely remembered Bubbles since her thick, curvy figure and voluptuous tits could make a nigga cum just on sight alone. Bubbles was a beautiful woman and three years ago, Crown had her working a corner for him. Like Chaos, she had been fresh out of New York, looking for a chance to make some serious money for herself. Crown was there to talk her young ass into the game. She sold crack and pussy for Crown in the early days and at night she was Crown's personal play thing. Her pussy was so good that it was on the same level with Cherish.

Bubbles had two miscarriages by Crown because he beat the babies out of her when he found out that she was pregnant. When Crown got locked up, she found a way to escape his grip and restart her own life. She was one of the fortunate ones to escape from Crown.

Crown smiled at the thought of seeing Bubbles again.

"It's been a long time," he said to Harlem. "She was definitely one of the baddest bitches that I had on the block."

Harlem nodded. "Word."

"Yeah, her body was ridiculous. Shit, it's hard to find a good ho like that today. Bitch always had my money right, ya know? And that pussy was like muthafuckin' platinum baby! Shit, put that bitch on a street corner and moments later, it would be paved wit' gold; that's how lucrative that pussy was on the block. Bubbles had niggas lined up for blocks just to get wit' her. The bitch was somethin' else," Crown proclaimed with a smirk on his face. "Now I see this bitch is wannabe Suzie muthafuckin' Homemaker . . . tryin' to live like the Brady Bunch."

Harlem just sat patiently and listened. He looked at the time and saw that it was five-thirty in the morning. "Yo, you ready to do this? The sun is comin' up all the way soon," Harlem said.

"Yeah, it's time that me and her have this reunion. It's been too long since I've seen the bitch."

Crown and Harlem picked up their guns. They both looked around for a quick moment and then got out the truck. They walked coolly to the four-bedroom split colonial house with a manicured lawn and silver Benz truck parked in the driveway.

Harlem was dressed in all black, holding his gun to his side as he looked around and moved toward the backyard. Crown was right behind him.

The driveway was lined with thick bushes that restricted view from the street, and was a plus for both men. Harlem twisted on the silencer, ready to go inside. He examined the back lock when, suddenly, the motion light came on and they heard movement inside the house.

Harlem and Crown both took cover in the shadows. A clean-shaven white man left the house in a dark gray suit, carrying a black leather briefcase. They watched him lock the door behind him and walk to the Benz.

Too easy, Harlem thought. He leaped from the shadows with his gun aimed at the man's head, startling him. A look of terror crossed his face.

"Shut the fuck up, white boy or I'll kill you now," Harlem threatened. He pressed the .45 to the man's temple and asked, "Who else inside?"

"Just me," the man lied.

Crown appeared behind the man and said, "Why the fuck you lying for, white boy? We know about Bubbles."

"Who?"

Harlem quickly hit him upside his head with the .380. The white man cried out and took a few steps back, bumping into Crown.

"Get the fuck off me, cracker!" Crown said.

The man looked terrified. He didn't know the name Bubbles.

"Bubbles, she in there?" Crown asked.

"Listen, I got money. Take whatever you want, but please, just leave my family alone. I'm not a threat," the man pleaded.

"I know you're not." Harlem was insulted at the very thought.

Knowing that they had to get out of public view, Harlem and Crown forced the man to open the back door of the house. They shoved him back inside the house and closed the door behind them. The kitchen was dark and the sunrise seeped through the kitchen shades. The man watched Harlem and Crown, terrified, as he figured he would try to negotiate with them. "Look, I have $500 on me right now and you can have the truck. Just take what you want and I promise that the cops will not get involved."

Crown chuckled. "Nigga, we ain't here for your fuckin' money or your truck. We here for Bubbles. Where she at?"

"I don't know any Bubbles," the man repeated. He was unaware of his wife's past with Crown. He only knew her as Karen.

"Man, fuck talkin' to this muthafucka! He ain't no use, anyway." Harlem pointed the gun at the man's head and shot him. He fell to the floor and blood oozed from the back of his head.

"You a ruthless muthafucka," Crown stated.

"I just know how to get shit done. Let's just go talk to this bitch and see what she knows," Harlem replied.

Crown nodded and they both moved farther into the house. They heard the shower running upstairs, indicating that Bubbles was probably in the bathroom. They assumed that she probably hadn't heard a thing that had gone on downstairs.

Bubbles was in the shower listening to the news on the portable radio she kept on a shelf over the toilet. As she let the steaming warm water cascade off her brown skin, she listened to the reports of crime in Philly. She sighed after she heard about the killing of four people on Mantua Avenue and said to herself, "Damn, I'm so glad to be out of that city! People are so fuckin' crazy today."

She checked the time from behind the shower curtain and saw that it was a quarter to six. She was getting ready to start her seven-AM shift at the hospital and saw that she had enough time. Her job was only fifteen minutes away and all she needed to do was change into her scrubs, make herself a cup of hot tea, and be on her way to work.

She figured that her husband would be on I-95 already, on his way to a business meeting in Baltimore. They had only been married for six months, but, for her, it felt like a lifetime. She was in love and happy and knew that Jason was the man for her. She hated keeping her past from him, especially about what she been through in Philly, but Bubbles knew that Jason loved her no matter what. She wanted to leave her past like yesterday—her past was history.

She finished showering then brushed her teeth, combed her hair, and wrapped a towel around her shapely figure. She walked toward the bedroom, leaving the radio on so she could hear the news from her bedroom.

The house was quiet and still. Bubbles loved living in Delaware and wished that she had moved there earlier. She felt that it was about time that she had something to call her own in life. Bubbles walked into her bedroom, smiling, and was devastated to see Crown lying on her bed. She immediately noticed the .380 next to him.

"You miss me, bitch?" Crown mocked.

"Oh my God! How the fuck did you find me? And what the fuck are you doin' in my fuckin' bedroom, Crown?" Bubbles shouted.

"Damn, you was always sexy when you got angry, bitch."

Bubbles tried to turn and leave but Harlem got in her way. He seemed to come out of nowhere. "You need to chill and relax, shorty. We're just here for some information," Harlem said to her.

Bubbles stood helpless in her own bedroom, her body wrapped in a towel, unsure of what these two Philly thugs had in store for her.

Crown rose from the bed and approached her with a smile. He loved the way she looked wrapped in a towel and thought about that pussy again. He brushed his hand against her shoulder and said, "Damn, you still look good, baby. Really good."

Bubbles jerked her shoulder away from his touch and glared at Crown.

"Why are you here?" she asked heatedly, feeling her heart beat faster.

Crown stared at her for a moment admiring everything he missed about her.

"I'm just here to talk, that's all. Now we can make this really simple and I can be on my way or I can get into some wicked shit and make it fun for me and my friend here. Oh, I'm sorry, you never met Harlem. Well, let me officially introduce the two of you. Bubbles, this is Harlem and Harlem, Bubbles. See, Harlem here used to be a very hostile dude, but I've helped to calm him down."

Bubbles looked at Harlem. Harlem looked back at her with a grim look. He didn't say a word, but his dreadful presence spoke loudly for him. His face was stone and his eyes were cold and distant.

"So far, he's behaving himself but if anything was to piss him off, well—shit, I don't know what the nigga might do in this room if I left him alone with you," Crown warned.

Bubbles was really nervous. Knowing Crown's dangerous and deadly temper, she feared that she might not leave the room alive. She then thought about Jason. "Where's my husband?"

"Oh, that white boy? He a'ight. We put the iron to his head and knocked that faggot out cold," Crown said.

Bubbles gasped.

"You was always fond of them light-skinned niggas, but, damn, you wit' a white boy? Who would have thought? But then again, you was always that kind of bitch who thought white was right," Crown joked. "But yo, we can leave out here with everyone in one piece and still breathing. Or, if you act up, I can guarantee you it will get ugly in here. We got all day to stay and think of all kinds of enjoyable shit we can do to you."

Bubbles tried to keep her composure. She stared Crown directly in the eye and asked, "What do you want from me?"

"Now that's what I'm talkin' about," Crown replied.

Harlem took a step back, keeping his eyes on Bubbles's shapely, semi-nude figure, and felt his dick getting hard. He definitely liked what he saw and hoped that Crown gave him the go-ahead to have his way with her—because he was dying to.

Crown brushed his hand across her breasts and ran his fingers under her towel. "I need a line on where your cousin Chaos might be staying in New York. The Bronx, I think."

"Chaos? What do you want with her?" Bubbles asked.

"Look, she's your cousin, but that's my bitch and I need to get up wit' her."

"I haven't spoken to Chaos in a year, maybe more. You should know that, Crown."

"Bitch, just give me her last known location, address, or somethin' that can link me up wit' the bitch!"

"Why should I help you, Crown? If my cousin is free from you, then so be it. But—"

Crown cut her off by saying, "Harlem, I see she wanna act up now. Go see about her husband. If he's awake, shoot that muthafucka."

Harlem began to leave the room. Bubbles, not knowing that it was a bluff, said, "Okay, okay. I'll try and help."

Crown smiled and said, "See? When you open your mouth just make sure you're sayin' the right thing to me. You dig?"

Bubbles nodded.

"Now, I need a line on your cousin. If she's in New York, where do you think she might be? I know you know. Y'all been family long enough and I remember you used to write that bitch letters when you was turning tricks for me."

Bubbles took a deep sigh and thought about her options and her life. She hated to give up her cousin but it was something that she was being forced to do. "If I'll tell you, do you promise that you won't kill her or me?"

"Look, Bubbles. I don't care about you. If you wanna live like Mrs. Brady and be a dumb bitch for that white boy, that's you. I'm only here for your cousin. She took somethin' from me and I want it back."

"Money?" Bubbles asked.

"Look, bitch, my patience is wearing thin wit' you! I ain't got time for games. I want information and no more questions from you. You talk out of turn again and we gonna reminisce about the good ol' days, wit' my goon hand coming across your fuckin' face!" Crown exclaimed.

Bubbles knew he was serious. She took another deep breath and said, "She used to stay with this lady, I think her name was Mrs. Joseph. She lived over by the Grand Concourse and East 181$^{st}$ Street," reluctantly informed him.

Crown smiled. "You still got them fuckin' letters she used to write you?" he asked.

Bubbles thought for a moment. "I only have one."

"Let me get that letter."

Bubbles didn't want to give it up, but she knew that Crown wasn't taking no for an answer. She slowly opened her dresser and dug through a few clothes. She pulled out a white envelope that was addressed to her from three years ago. It had the address that Crown needed.

Bubbles passed it to Crown who snatched it from her hands.

*Dirty Little Angel*

"You did good, girl," Crown said.

Hearing those words from Crown made Bubbles feel like shit. She didn't trust him and felt in her heart that something was wrong.

"You happy?" Bubbles asked with attitude.

"Bitch, don't get cute," Crown warned.

Bubbles was terrified. The look that Crown gave sent chills of uneasiness down her spine. "I wanna see Jason," she cried out.

"I told you, bitch, he a'ight," Crown lied.

"I wanna see him!" she screamed.

"Look at you, gettin' all loud and shit, caring for that white boy. He be fuckin' you as good as I did?" Crown asked. "He be deep up in that pussy, like I used to do?"

Bubbles began to cry, knowing that her fate was in their hands. Crown and Harlem hesitated to leave after they got what they wanted. She thought that they still wanted much more from her—something that she saved only for her husband.

"You know, you still look good, Bubbles. How about I get a quick peep at that body for old time's sake? Let me see if you kept that body in good shape." Crown leered. He looked over at Harlem and saw that he wore a devilish grin.

Bubbles tied the towel around her tightly and took a step back from Crown. Her body language said "no," but Crown was unkind and harsh. He approached Bubbles, licking his lips and pulling at her towel.

"C'mon, Bubbles, let me get that peek. Your husband, he probably didn't appreciate what he was fuckin'. I know that white boy couldn't handle you 'cause you definitely did like to get buck wild on a nigga."

Crown tried to wrap his arms around Bubbles, ready to get a taste of her goodies, but Bubbles bolted from his grip and smacked him hard. "Get the fuck off me, Crown! I ain't wit' that shit anymore!"

Crown became angry. "Bitch, you must be fuckin' crazy to put your fuckin' hands on me! I'm gonna kill you like I did your fuckin' husband downstairs."

Bubbles's face flushed with both anger and resentment. She charged at Crown, swinging and screaming, "You heartless bastard! Why you do that? We ain't do shit to you!"

Harlem quickly picked Bubbles up in his strong grip. Crown walked up to Bubbles and punched her in the face.

Bubbles glared back in defiance and spit in Crown's face. "Fuck you!" she cried as tears streamed down her face. "I hate you! Go to fuckin' hell, you callous muthafucka!"

"Bitch, I had love for you and you do me like this? What I told you, Bubbles? Ain't never no escaping me. But yet, y'all bitches always try and then we end up where I gotta fuck y'all bitches up and teach y'all a fuckin' lesson, even if it means death."

Bubbles stared at Crown, knowing that the worst was about to come. All she could do at that point was curse and spit at Crown.

"Now, where were we?" Crown said in a calmer tone. He ran his hand up Bubbles's thigh and positioned it underneath her towel. He grabbed her shaved snatch and fondled her while Harlem smiled.

Bubbles squirmed and tried to free herself, but Harlem wasn't haven't it and clutched her tighter. "Yeah! Damn, Bubbles, I still see that you take very good care of yourself down there." Crown pushed his index finger and middle fingers into her pussy.

Bubbles begged him to stop but Crown kept on stroking.

"Yo, before we leave here tonight, you gonna remember what it felt like to have a true nigga in you," Crown said, unzipping his jeans.

They tore the towel off Bubbles and forced her on the bed as she fought and screamed. Her resistance was useless. Harlem punched her in the head repeatedly, trying to shut her up and held her down as Crown climbed in between her legs getting ready to rape her.

Crown gripped his dick in his fist and told her, "It ain't gonna hurt much, bitch. Shit, if you shut the fuck up, close your eyes, and relax, you just might enjoy it again the way you used to."

Crown showed her no remorse. He thrust into her like an animal while Harlem stood by and watched. Bubbles just stopped fighting and let her ex-pimp have his way with her. When he was done and came in her, he pulled out, and zipped up his jeans.

Bubbles just lay in a fetal position, crying. The pain was unbearable and she grieved for her dead husband.

Crown stood over her. "Yeah, your pussy still good, bitch. You missed me, huh?" He looked over at Harlem and nodded.

Harlem walked up to Bubbles and raised the gun to her head. She turned to stare death in the face and pleaded, "Please, no! Please, I don't wanna die! Let me bury my husband. Please, give me that."

Harlem looked into her eyes and watched the tears flow down her bruised and beaten face. He wished that he had a chance to get with that. He hesitated and then looked back at Crown.

Crown said to him, "Hurry up and kill the bitch!"

Harlem fired three shots into Bubbles's head at such close range that her forehead exploded. Blood and brain matter decorated her sheets and pillows.

Crown nodded. "Stupid bitch. C'mon, we gotta make a trip to the Bronx, my nigga."

Harlem followed Crown, leaving Bubbles a twisted mess on her bloody sheets. Crown couldn't wait to see the look on Chaos's face when he came knocking on her front door, his guns cocked and ready to murder everyone. It got his dick hard just thinking about it.

# 45

Danielle was back and forth between her place and Wendy's apartment. She didn't want to be alone so Wendy kept her company. They often spent the night at each other's places and talked all night. However, despite Wendy's presence, it didn't take Danielle's mind off YB. She was still worried sick about him and couldn't believe she hadn't heard a word from him since he left.

She began to fear the worst and constantly thought about YB's body lying in a morgue somewhere. So many times, she thought about going down to Philly to go look for her man, but Wendy advised her against it.

Danielle would go from being so angry at YB for just leaving unexpectedly, to being worried to the point where she couldn't stop crying over him. The rollercoaster of emotions wasn't helping her pregnancy.

"He'll call, Danielle," Wendy said every time she cried.

"What if somethin' happened to him? I need to see him, Wendy. I need to know if he's okay," Danielle would cry out.

If it wasn't for Wendy, Danielle would have been a wreck. She continued to do hair at the shop and made her doctor's appointment. The doctor ensured her that the baby was fine and told her not to stress herself too much.

Wendy prayed for Chaos and YB. They even went to church one evening where Danielle met Wendy's pastor Mitchell Moore.

Danielle had a long talk with Pastor Moore in his office and she told him everything about her life. She broke down and confessed to him about her former way of life—about her turning tricks on a daily basis, the money that she made, and the beatings she endured at the hands of Crown. She even spoke about the death of her best friend, Sweet. For Danielle, it felt like therapy. For some reason, she was able to open up to him easily and express her concerns and fears.

"My life has always been a mess, Pastor Moore," Danielle admitted. "I know death is comin' for me."

"Why do you feel that death is coming for you?" He began to listen intently.

"The shit I've done. Oh, I'm so sorry for cursing," she said, feeling ashamed.

"It's okay, feel free to go on."

"I mean, I always heard in life that someday your past would catch up to you. It's somethin' that you can't run from. I was happy for a moment, pastor. I'm 'bout to have a baby, but the father of my child left for Philly. I feel he might get himself killed out there."

"And why is that?"

Danielle hesitated. She didn't know what to say to him. She asked, "Everything I say here is private, right? Like between only me and you? You can't tell anyone what we've discussed?"

"I'm here to only counsel, not judge," he assured her.

She looked him in the eye and admitted, "Before I came back to the Bronx, I was involved in a double murder back in Philly. And my friend,

Sweet, got caught up in the crossfire and lost her life. My pimp and his sleazy cousin ended up dead in the basement of his home." Danielle was in tears. "What can I do? I mean, I'm scared, Pastor Moore. I'm scared for my life and my baby's. And I'm lost without YB. I don't even know if he's alive or dead."

Danielle looked upset and it worried Pastor Moore. He placed his hands on her shoulder and tried to console her. "Look to God, my child, because we are all lost without Him. But you confess your sins to Him and let it go. I know you're scared. We all get scared, but your mistakes can be washed away and your worries will no longer trouble you."

"But we're talkin' about murder," Danielle said, trying to watch her language around the pastor. "Should I go to the police and let them know what happened? I don't wanna go to jail. It happened so many months ago that I just wanna forget about everything and live a new life. I also keep having these dreams that one day it will all come to a violent end for me and that my baby is going to suffer. My mother was never there for me so I wanna be there for my child."

Pastor Moore sighed heavily. The situation that Danielle was in was not an easy one to just walk away from. It was much deeper than he alone could handle.

"Do you fear that someone will come after you?" he asked.

"I know they will sooner or later. We took a lot of money from them," she admitted.

Pastor Moore looked Danielle straight in the eyes and said, "I need you to continue to be truthful with me. No lies, just be honest with me."

Danielle nodded.

"Now when you say that you were involved, do you mean that you murdered a man yourself or were you only there to witness the killing?" he asked.

"I, I had the gun in my hand and was with my two friends. We were down in the basement holding my pimp hostage at gunpoint. He was so evil to us that I wanted to see him dead so we set him up to get robbed. I wanted my revenge 'cause he used to hurt me so bad when he got upset. Suddenly, his younger cousin came busting into the room shooting. I quickly shot back and so did everyone else. I don't know who hit him, but he died. Everything happened so fast that it's hard to remember.

"I remember YB's cousin, Rufus, shot my pimp dead after he tried to kill YB. I just stood and watched it all unfold in front of my eyes. Then Sweet just got hit by a stray bullet and I hate myself for her death every day," Danielle wailed.

Pastor Moore bowed his head and quickly prayed for Sweet's soul as well as Danielle's. "There's not much I can do for you, Danielle, except pray for you and continue to talk with you. I'm here for you and I will not abandon you, nor will this church. But you need to contact the proper authorities and let them know your side of the story. They need to start an investigation into your allegations."

"But there's a chance that I might go to jail! And then who's gonna look after my baby? No, I can't abandon her like my mother did me. What kind of life is she goin' to have wit' me being locked up? Huh, Pastor? I mean, Crown was an asshole, the things he did to me was wrong and some nights, I still feel afraid. I still cry and cringe when I think about the horror I endured. But my baby is innocent. She's goin' to need her mother in her life and you want me to turn myself in?" Danielle was horrified.

"You need to do something, Danielle. I understand that you're scared and have a profound concern for your baby's well-being, but a crime has been committed. And as a pastor of the church, I must advise you to confess to the proper authorities and put your sins into God's hand and have Him take care of your worries," Pastor Moore stated with deep concern.

Danielle's eyes were filled with tears. She didn't know what to say or what to do.

"Why it gotta be so hard, Pastor Moore? Huh? Why can't life be fair to me, just once? It ain't right! I wanna be happy. Ever since I was five years old, my family treated me like an outcast because of who my mother was and what she was about. That judgment was passed down to me and they teased me. Nobody was there to protect me or love me.

"And then I meet YB and he was the only one who cared. He was the only one who saw me for who I was and took the time to get to know me. He was the only one in my life who tried to protect me. And I love him. But now, it seems that he cares more about the streets in Philly than he does for me and his unborn child. Why does everyone keep leaving me, Pastor Moore?" Danielle sobbed. "Why can't I live a regular life like everyone else? I will not leave my child. I refuse to give my baby up to the streets like my mother did me."

Pastor Moore knew that Danielle had suffered so much in her short life and was in pain. He knew that one of her fears in life was abandonment by the one she loved.

"You know, God will never abandon you. Once you believe in the Almighty and what He's capable of and accept Jesus Christ as your savior, then you are born again. But you must confess to Him and let go of the life you live now. The worries that you have, pass on to Him and you will be delivered from the wickedness of the world. But you must stay strong, Danielle. You must do what's right," Pastor Moore stated with passion.

Danielle looked at the pastor with uncertainty. The abandonment of her child, along with the possibility of going to jail was still rooted in her head. Even though she found some comfort in the Pastor's words, she knew that she wasn't going to turn herself in. "I need to think about it. I need to go home and rest." Danielle stood slowly and dried the tears from her face. Her belly was growing and so were her worries about her life with YB.

Pastor Moore gave Danielle the church phone number, his cell phone number, and his home number. He wanted to keep in contact and make sure that if she needed him that he would be there. She was so young but he saw strength in her. He also saw a change in her and knew that motherhood was bringing something wonderful out of her.

Pastor Moore was concerned about Danielle and knew that she would not give up on her young child. She wanted to feel loved and appreciated, and in God's house, she was already and loved. He just had to get her to see it.

Danielle hugged Pastor Moore tightly and thanked him for listening. He walked her to the door and once again encouraged her to think about her options and to make the right choice. He also guaranteed her that his door was always open when she needed to talk or needed help with anything. He told Danielle not to hesitate if she needed something. Danielle promised that she would be back but she wasn't so sure that she would keep the promise. Maybe it was a start for her, but the only thing she cared strongly about were her pregnancy and her man, YB. Her life was already crazy and she didn't want it to get even crazier by turning herself in to the police and taking a chance of not being a mother to her baby or, if given the chance, a wife to YB.

# 46

YB and Ray-Lo were ten miles from Delaware, on their way to see Bubbles at her hospital job. YB's gut was telling him not to go there. He felt something in him that told him to head back to New York. Dusk was settling over the road and Ray-Lo was doing seventy-five down the long stretch of highway.

YB had his mind on Danielle and knew it was wrong for him to keep her out of the loop for the four days he'd been gone. He had been so focused on revenge and chasing Harlem that he literally forgot all about her and now guilt ate at him for failing to call. She was six months pregnant and he knew she loved him very much.

He stared out the passenger window, watching cars and trucks fly by on the highway as "Be Without You" by Mary J. Blige played on the radio.

Danielle was heavy in YB's thoughts and he knew that it would probably be best to be with her—especially after everything that had happened in Philly with his mother and Rufus's murders. She was in danger too since Harlem was still out there and killing everyone close to YB. Everyone he loved was being put to death.

YB turned to look at Ray-Lo, who looked to be in his own deep thoughts. "Yo, don't get off I-95. We goin' to New York."

"What? New York? You serious?" Ray-Lo questioned.

"I need to be in the Bronx right now. I need to be wit' my shorty."

"What about Harlem? He need to be got," Ray-Lo said.

"We'll hit that nigga in New York. I know he's on his way out there now."

"You sure?"

"Nigga, trust me. He knows where we at. So let him hunt us and we'll be waiting for that nigga when he shows up."

"A'ight, my nigga. I'm wit' it," Ray-Lo replied.

They continued on I-95 toward New York City with a car full of guns and ammunition. They were ready for war and eager to set a trap for Harlem and whoever he brought with him.

YB wanted to take his time when killing Harlem. He wanted to make that nigga suffer for a long time. It was the only way he saw to make things right. The only way he could be at peace was to kill the man who had done so much harm to his family. An eye for an eye, he thought.

# 47

The dark blue Yukon raced across the George Washington Bridge, doing sixty miles per hour. The sky was turning to dusk as the city lights became illuminated from a distance and the traffic on the G.W. Bridge was starting to thicken with cars and trucks.

Crown was reclined in the passenger seat as he looked at the city with a deadpan stare. Jamaica, Queens was his hometown and he hadn't been back there since the early nineties. He still had enemies in the city, but that thought didn't put fear in his heart.

It would be worth the trip just to see his bitch Chaos and YB one last time. He had so much he wanted to do with the loving couple that he didn't even want his money back. It was now personal. Crown just wanted to hear the bitch scream while his hands were around her neck, squeezing the life out of her.

The Yukon was filled with guns and the men were ready to spill blood on the Bronx streets. It was Harlem's first trip to the Big Apple and he wasn't impressed.

"Fuck New York," he uttered in a vile tone, as he cruised across the Cross Bronx Expressway.

Crown chuckled. "Bad experience?"

Harlem just gave Crown a "whatever" look.

The two made it into the Bronx that night, just as the city's nightlife was about to jump off. The streets were buzzing with traffic and people and the city became electrified with lights and noise.

Crown looked at the address on the envelope and guided Harlem in the direction. They drove toward the Grand Concourse and looked for 181$^{st}$ street.

When they drove up the block, it was filled with people, mostly Hispanic, who were enjoying the balmy warm night. They lingered outside their buildings seated or standing and playing their reggaeton music or just talking to neighbors.

Harlem parked the car and looked around, taking in the layout of the crowded street. He prepared himself for anything. He was already irritated with New York with the heavy traffic and loud music. He turned to Crown and asked, "What now?"

"Now, we look for the place," Crown said.

Both men crossed the one-way street. Some of the residents on the block took notice of them but minded their own business. They looked like they were from out of town—probably drug dealers or just here for trouble, neighbors whispered amongst themselves.

Harlem and Crown stood in front of the tall building and Crown compared the address with the one on the envelope. He nodded to Harlem.

"Yeah, this is it," he said.

"Yo, I ain't come here to sightsee," Harlem said.

Crown walked off and Harlem followed. Crown always hated the Bronx. There were too many Puerto Ricans and Dominicans blasting music, crowding the streets, and speaking a language he didn't understand. Back in the days when he had business that involved being in the Bronx, he was always in and out.

Both men entered the lobby and headed to the elevators. They could hear music blaring from behind an apartment door.

"Damn, don't these people ever stop wit' the music?" Harlem complained.

The elevator came down to the lobby and both men stepped in. It reeked of urine and Harlem twisted his face from the smell. Crown pushed for floor number eight and soon they emerged from the elevator and stepped into the narrow hallway. Harlem had his hand near his weapon and looked out for any trouble they might stumble upon.

They reached the end of the hallway and found the apartment they were looking for. Harlem cocked his gun subtly. Both men were quiet as they stood outside the apartment as they didn't know what was behind the door.

Crown knocked on the door politely. Harlem stood off to the side, trying to stay out of sight. They didn't want to scare whoever was inside by having the occupants see two thugs outside the door.

Crown continued to knock, but no one answered and he was becoming upset.

"The bitch ain't home," Harlem said.

"She's somewhere close. I know. I can feel that bitch," Crown stated.

Crown knocked again, this time a bit harder in case the occupant didn't hear the last couple of knocks. He turned to look at Harlem, who looked like the Angel of Death standing across from him.

"We'll just come back," Harlem said.

Crown was quiet. He hated to leave without knowing something more accurate about Chaos or YB. He wasn't even sure that the address he had was their exact location. Bubbles did say to him that the letter was three years old. The Bronx was a big borough, but somehow Crown knew that Chaos was close by. It had been her home for so many years.

As they were about to leave, a young woman walked out of a neighboring apartment. Crown saw this as an opportunity to elicit viable information.

The young Puerto Rican girl looked as if she was in her late teens. She was dressed like she was about to go to the club in a short mini-skirt, high heels, a halter top under a butter-soft leather jacket and long, black hair falling gracefully down to her shoulders. She was beautiful. Crown admired her and thought that if he hadn't been there looking for Chaos, he would have talked her into working a track.

Crown hurried to the young girl before she could disappear.

"Excuse me, beautiful. I need a minute of your time," Crown said politely.

The girl turned and looked at Crown. She stopped in the middle of the hallway and waited for him to approach her.

"What you want?" she said with some attitude.

Crown smiled. "Nice tone of voice."

"Nigga, I'm in a fuckin' rush. I gotta cab waiting downstairs."

"I'm not gonna take up too much of your time, but I need to know somethin'," Crown said.

"Like what?"

"Who stays in that apartment right there?" Crown pointed to the apartment where he'd been knocking.

She sucked her teeth. "Why is it your business?"

Harlem was becoming fed up with the girl's attitude and was ready to make her talk with a gun in her mouth and a fist across her face.

"Look, I'll make it worth your time," Crown said. He reached into his pocket and pulled out a knot of hundred-dollar bills.

The young girl's face lit up and suddenly her nasty attitude changed.

Crown peeled off two C-notes but before he gave her any cash, he said, "You need to talk, first, before I pass this."

The girl smiled . "Oh, that's Wendy Joseph's apartment."

She wasn't telling him shit. "And?" Crown asked. He needed more to go on.

"And look, if she ain't home, then she's probably at her shop, doin' hair. And if she ain't at her shop, then she's probably at church 'cause that lady got more religion in her than Christ himself. And look, if she ain't at church, then I don't know what the fuck to tell you. 'Cause she ain't gotta man and she always home if she ain't workin' or at church. You happy?"

"Nah, not yet," Crown said. "I need more."

"More? Nigga, I done told you everything about the bitch! What else do you want to know?" she snapped. She looked at her watch and added, "You know I gotta cab waiting downstairs."

"Where's this shop you mentioned?"

"It's called New Style Hair near Fordham and Jerome Avenue."

"And the church?"

"Look, what is this, a fuckin' census or sumthin?" The girl was getting irritated by the questions.

Crown peeled off another hundred from his wad to cool her attitude. "And the church?"

"I don't know. I think it's on Third Avenue somewhere. I never been to her church," she stated.

"One last question," Crown said.

The young teen sucked her teeth loudly and stared at Crown rudely. "What?"

"Is she alone? I mean, have you seen another young girl around her lately?"

"Nah, not really. The only girl I see her with is, like, this pregnant girl sometimes. But she don't come around here hardly."

"Pregnant?"

"Yeah, pregnant. You know, somebody fucked her and dropped that seed in her. What, your peoples never told you about the birds and the bees?" the young teen joked.

Crown nodded and smiled. Instinct told him that the pregnant girl was Chaos. He was very happy with the news he just heard. Chaos was pregnant, which made the hunt for her even more thrilling. He looked at the young girl and passed her the three hundred dollars but warned her to keep quiet about their talk. She agreed and quickly snatched the money from his hand. "Thank you!" she said as she prepared to board the elevator.

Before the doors could close, Crown shouted to her, "Beautiful, what's your name?"

"They call me Fly around here," she stated.

"Well, Fly, if you ever want a lot more where that came from, you need to come see me. I can make you a rich woman," he boasted.

Fly smiled. "It's whatever. Thanks for the cab fare and the club money."

The elevator doors closed. Crown and Harlem stood in the hallway and pondered their next move.

"Why you pay that bitch three hundred? We could have gotten shit from her with my gun in her face," Harlem said.

Crown looked at Harlem. "Sometimes, it pays to be subtle. I don't wanna tip anyone off that we're out here lookin' for Chaos. Let it be a surprise."

Harlem didn't say a word. He came to New York for a reason and he didn't want a two-hour road trip to go to waste.

# 48

Danielle was making herself a snack in her kitchen while Wendy was in the bathroom. She listened to the radio and cried silently. She took a deep breath and thought about YB and her options. She thought about her unborn child and she thought about Sweet. It seemed like everything was coming down on her all at once.

The butter knife shook in her hand as tears streamed down her soft olive-colored cheek. She didn't want to cry. She wanted to be strong, but being strong was hard. She didn't know what her future looked like anymore. The talk that she had with the pastor was refreshing but it had made her nervous. He wanted her to confess to her sins and talk to the cops.

In a few months, she would hold her baby in her arms, but if she went to prison that wouldn't be possible. She wanted to see a bright future with YB beside her and them becoming a loving family.

Thoughts of Crown still haunted her, though, and Sweet's death still bothered her. She looked at the phone, hoping that YB would call. She walked over to the window, hoping to see YB strutting into the lobby to see her again. When she peered down and saw nothing but litter blowing in the wind and dusk descending over the streets, she sighed heavily and began to rub her stomach, soothing her unborn child.

"Danielle, you okay?" Wendy asked as she exited the bathroom while drying her hands.

Danielle turned to look at Wendy. She looked so angelic with her friendly smile and soft eyes.

"I'm just thinking," Danielle responded.

"How did your talk with Pastor Moore go?"

"It went good. He's a nice guy."

"Yes, he is. But you need to do what's right, Danielle. I know you love YB, but do not let him upset you. If he wants to leave and do wrong in his life, then that's on him, but you have to care about yourself. You need to think about your baby and consider the advice Pastor Moore gave you. You are not alone, Danielle. I'm here and the church is here for you," Wendy proclaimed.

Danielle nodded.

Wendy continued to talk and Danielle listened intently. Wendy was just like her mother, Mrs. Joseph—loving, caring, and full of wisdom. It felt like Danielle had a second chance in life when God replaced Mrs. Joseph with her daughter, Wendy. She was such a blessing for Danielle.

"Look, I want you to come down to the shop tomorrow morning. I'll braid your hair for you and we can continue this talk. But get some rest and think about it." Wendy gave Danielle a kiss and a hug.

Danielle smiled.

She walked Wendy to the door and watched her walk into the elevator. When she was gone, Danielle let out another deep sigh and decided to get some sleep for the night.

The building was quiet and the radio was playing Mary J. Blige.

She listened to Mary sing her heart out while she put the dishes away.

She rubbed her belly again and walked back over to the window to peer down at the streets again. She imagined seeing YB walking inside with flowers and candy in his hands, hurrying up to the apartment to apologize to her for his sudden departure. Then she chuckled to herself 'cause YB wasn't that type of dude to bring flowers and candy.

Danielle finished and then went to get some much-needed sleep. Then, maybe she'd go to the police. Maybe she did need to let go and involve the police in her situation. She knew Harlem was still out there, and she kept having visions about Crown. She had a deep concern that maybe he wasn't dead—and she knew that he had men who wouldn't stop hunting her until they found her. She wouldn't be any good to her baby if she and YB were both dead.

Danielle kept having these recurring dreams about Crown coming and she was scared. She was taking a chance at doing the unthinkable by going to the police, but in her mind, she had to. She had to do something different with her life. She couldn't keep running and worrying about Harlem or whoever coming after her. She sighed, hoping that she wouldn't regret her decision.

She needed to come clean with herself. It was hard to do, but she knew that in order for her to truly start out in a new life—one without conflict and deception—she had to come clean with her past.

# 49

It was two in the morning when YB and Ray-Lo drove across the G.W. Bridge. There was no traffic, and even from a distance the city was so bright and alive with movement.

YB had no time to sleep. He tried to call the apartment but got no answer. That worried him. He told Ray-Lo to hurry, fearing that they might be too late. He feared that Danielle could already be dead.

YB checked the ammunition in his gun quickly and was satisfied that everything was in working order. He knew that he hadn't been gone for too long, only a day or two. But those four days had been enough time for Harlem to destroy his whole family starting with Magic.

The car raced down the Major Deegan Expressway doing eighty miles per hour. YB kept calling his home, hoping that Danielle would pick up the phone. Unfortunately, there was still no answer and that made him furious.

"Hurry this shit up, Ray-Lo," YB exclaimed.

"Nigga, I'm trying! Shit, it ain't like we in a Porsche," Ray-Lo shot back.

YB stared out the window, trying to keep tears from escaping and trying to be strong. Now was not the time for him start tearing up and getting emotional. In the past year, he had developed a profound love for Danielle. She gave him some insight on what happiness could be, and he wanted to be there for her. He wanted a family away from the streets with a caring woman under his arms, a child to love and raise, and a life away from the drugs and gunplay. He was gradually changing and maturing. YB remembered the advice that Magic once gave to him, and now it was beginning to take root in his heart.

He wanted his life with Danielle to continue and prayed that Harlem didn't snatch her and the baby away from him. YB gripped the deadly steel in his hand, feeling his heart race. He couldn't help but shed tears for the lost of his mom, Magic, and his cousin over the past four days. There was a deep fear in him that it would be all over soon. He also feared that he would be too late and Danielle and his unborn daughter would be dead.

YB continued to clutch the fully loaded steel of death and his breathing became heavy. The more he thought about Harlem murdering Danielle he knew he was going to kill Harlem when he got the chance.

"We gonna catch this muthafucka," Ray-Lo assured YB as they got off at the exit closest to his home.

YB didn't respond. He continued to stare out the window, crying in silence, missing his family and praying that it wasn't too late.

# 50

Crown and Harlem decided to pay Ms. Wendy Joseph a second visit, figuring that in the wee hours of the morning she'd be home.

The dark blue Yukon was parked on the congested block with other vehicles. They returned to the building. The hood was quiet as the cold winter days were nearing, Crown and Harlem got off again on the eighth floor and walked down the hallway to the apartment. They assumed that this woman Wendy had an idea where Chaos was, and they were going to find out by any means necessary.

When they stood in front of the door, they pulled their guns and cocked them back. Crown hoped that Chaos was inside because it would be such a sweet revenge. He looked at Harlem and said, "Do your thang."

Harlem passed Crown his gun, crouched near the doorknob, and picked the locks in a couple minutes, so as not alarm the occupants inside. He slowly pushed open the door and walked into the dark apartment. Crown followed and closed the door quietly, trying not to alert any of the neighbors of their presence.

Harlem removed his pen light and looked around the neat and modestly furnished apartment.

They crept toward the bedroom, trying to be as quiet as possible. Crown's heart raced; he was so close to feeling vindicated. The hallway to the bedrooms was long, with pictures of family and friends lining each the wall.

It was a two-bedroom apartment and when Crown entered the master bedroom, he saw Wendy lying in bed, sound asleep. Harlem walked in and startled a woman waking up in the middle of the night. He smiled, ready to get to work.

# 51

When Ray-Lo finally pulled up to YB's building, he didn't give Ray-Lo a chance to put the car in park. He jumped out and raced through the lobby and up the stairs, fearing the worse. Ray-Lo quickly followed.

When YB got to his floor, he pulled out his gun and rushed toward the apartment. His heart beat faster and faster with every passing second. He gripped the steel in his hand tighter and tried to prepare himself for anything.

He unlocked the door and pushed it open. The apartment was dark and quiet and he assumed that Danielle was in the bedroom, asleep. Then he was scared that he might be walking into a trap. Could Harlem and Crown already be here? He carefully searched each room and saw that she wasn't home.

"Shit," he muttered, dropping his gun to his side and plopping down on the bed.

Ray-Lo burst into the bedroom and YB quickly raised his gun and almost fired. Lucky for him, he didn't have an itchy trigger finger. Ray-Lo was startled.

"What the fuck, Ray-Lo?" YB exclaimed.

"Damn nigga!" Ray-Lo shouted. "She ain't here?"

"What the fuck you think?"

YB looked around the apartment, trying to find any indication of foul play but the apartment was clean. He checked the closet and saw that Danielle's clothes were still there. Everything seemed normal.

"What now?" Ray-Lo asked.

YB began to think. Where would she go? Where would she be? He remembered her friend Wendy. If Danielle wasn't home, then surely she was spending the night over there. They had to hurry and find Danielle, because there was a good chance that Harlem and his peoples were already in New York.

"C'mon," YB said, rushing out of the apartment.

Ray-Lo just shrugged and followed his friend. They hopped back into the car and raced toward Wendy's place.

# 52

"**B**itch, you ain't gotta make this shit so fuckin' hard! Where are they?" Crown yelled as he continued to punch Wendy in the face.

Harlem stood by and watched the show quietly. He let Crown get his hands dirty with the beating. Wendy was stoic. The beating was painful, but she refused to give up her friend. She kept praying and telling herself that the nightmare would end because she was in God's hands.

Crown stood over Wendy's beaten body. "C'mon, bitch! We can end this now. She stole somethin' from me and I want it back. This don't have to be your beef. I just want an address."

"May God have mercy on your poor, miserable soul," Wendy said to them.

"Shit, this bitch and her fuckin' religion is pissin' me off!" Crown said. "Bitch, right now, your life is in *my* hands. *I* am God!"

Wendy looked up at him with disgust. Both her eyes were blackened, her face was bruised, and her bedroom was in shambles. Harlem and Crown had ransacked everything.

"This bitch ain't tryin' to talk, Crown. Shit, she would have done so by now," Harlem said. "You want me to handle her?"

Crown scowled at Harlem and then turned his attention back to Wendy. "Listen, bitch," he threatened, "it ain't a game right now. We will fuck your shit up right now if you continue to be stupid. Now, I wanna know where the fuck is Chaos and YB?"

Wendy just stared at Crown. Her spirit was far from broken and the fight in her was strong. "I will pray for your soul," she replied calmly.

Crown wanted information on Chaos and was angered that he couldn't get it out of this woman. He hit Wendy in the head with the butt of his gun, spraying her blood against walls, the bed sheets, and the carpet.

"It hurt, don't it, bitch!" Crown gloated.

Wendy lay in the corner of her bedroom, beaten and bloody. Her body was broken, but her soul and spirit were stronger than ever. She had always known that Danielle's dangerous past would probably catch up to her and that she might have serious trouble coming her way. But God was talking to her and He told her that if it came down to it, then she might have to die for her sister, in order for Danielle to live. Crown had no idea what he was getting himself into. There were forces at work that Crown wouldn't understand since he didn't believe in God. Crown only believed in power and himself.

Crown beat and tortured Wendy more but she still didn't talk. They had the TV volume up to block out the screams from her. They were confused when Wendy didn't scream at all. She took the beating like a warrior and Crown couldn't understand it.

"Bitch, why don't you fuckin' talk?" he shouted. "It ain't that hard. This shit can be over with, just give her up! What the fuck is she to you, anyway?"

"My sister in need," Wendy stated.

*Dirty Little Angel*

"Your what?"

Wendy tried to get up from the floor, but Crown smacked her back down.

"You get up when I tell you to get up," he shouted.

"Crown, let me get a go at the bitch. I'll make her talk," Harlem suggested.

"She's mine," Crown retorted.

"Fuck this bitch!" Crown exclaimed.

Crown pressed his gun to the center of Wendy's forehead.

"I'll send you to meet your God sooner than you think if you don't talk to me right now and tell me what I need to know," Crown threatened.

Wendy just closed her eyes and began to pray. She waited for death to come to her but understood that she would continue on to live an eternal life.

Crown wanted to pull the trigger so badly but he knew that she was the link to finding Chaos and YB in the Bronx. He needed Wendy to talk but she was a tough bitch. He almost had to respect her loyalty.

Harlem stood to the side and waited for the shot to go off. He also knew that Wendy was more vital to them alive than dead. They needed another tactic to get her to talk.

Harlem stepped up to Wendy. He was getting tired of the bullshit. He glared down at her and said, "You believe in life after death, huh? Well how about this? You won't see Heaven anytime soon, 'cause we'll tie you up and take you out of here and drive you off somewhere far, where we can really have our fun torturing you. You'd be miles away from everything and then the real torture would begin. I'd keep you alive for days, maybe weeks if I had to and then you'd see what Hell on Earth would truly feel like. You want that? 'Cause we got nuthin' but time, and I guarantee that it will be more fun for me that it will be for you."

Crown smiled. He loved the way Harlem brought intimidation and fear to the table.

Wendy didn't look scared. She was still silent and that displeased Harlem. He lived off the fear of others and wanted to see the horror on her face. But she showed none at all.

Suddenly both men heard a slight noise coming from outside the bedroom. They became alert and kept quiet.

"You stay here wit' her, I'll check it out," Harlem said.

He slowly crept out into the hallway with his gun raised. It was still dark and hard for Harlem to see anything helpful without his pen light. He narrowed his eyes and searched the apartment as best he could. The apartment became quiet again and that bothered Harlem. He knew something was wrong. He felt someone was there.

He moved into the kitchen but it was also dark and empty. He slowly walked back into the living room but found nothing. He began to think that it was probably his imagination finally getting to him. Crown imagined the ghosts of the many men he murdered over the years, fuckin' with his mind.

When he was satisfied that it was nothing, Harlem walked back to the bedroom to finish what he started with Wendy. He took four steps down the hallway before he felt a presence that made him uneasy. He knew he'd fucked up somehow, overlooked something, somewhere or was just slipping on his game.

Before he could react, he felt a large, double-barreled shotgun pressed hard against the side of his head.

"Finally gotcha, bitch!" YB whispered with satisfaction.

"Fuck me!" Harlem cursed, as he closed his eyes and braced himself for impact.

*BOOM!*

The shotgun made Harlem's head explode into little pieces and splattered his brain and blood all over the hallway. Harlem's body dropped to YB's feet and he finally felt vindicated.

The blast almost woke up the entire building. YB still had the smoking shotgun in his hand and knew Harlem didn't come alone. He and Ray-Lo walked toward the bedroom, not knowing what kind of carnage they would find inside. YB's heart began to beat fast again. He was hoping that he didn't find the body of his girl in the bedroom, but he prepared himself for the worst.

Ray-Lo followed behind YB cautiously. YB still held onto the shotgun and then took a deep breath and burst into the room. He was immediately greeted with intense gunfire.

YB got hit in the shoulder and dropped. Ray-Lo charged in behind YB and fired the gun, aiming for the head. Crown was relentless and continued busting off rounds at his attackers. He hit Ray-Lo in the abdomen. Ray-Lo dropped and scurried for cover as he bled from his gut.

YB was shocked when he saw Crown's face. He screamed from the hallway, "How's your bitch ass still fuckin' alive? We killed you, nigga!"

"Karma, muthafucka! I don't die. I don't fuckin' die!" Crown screamed back. "I'm Crown and I came for you and that bitch!"

Wendy managed to take cover by the bed as the gunshots rang out. She was breathing heavily and was in pretty bad shape. YB dropped the shotgun and pulled out the 9 mm. Ray-Lo was in bad shape also, but he was ready to bang out. He was breathing heavily and bleeding when he looked at YB from across the room and saw him nod.

Simultaneously they stood and let off a barrage of rounds at Crown. Crown returned fire as he escaped out a nearby window and climbed up the fire escape.

YB gave chase. He quickly followed Crown up the fire escape. He wanted Crown's head on a silver platter.

As YB gave chase, Ray-Lo lay on his back dying. Wendy came over to him and tried to nurse his wound the best she knew how. The night just kept getting crazier and crazier for everyone.

"Hold still, while I put pressure on the bleeding," she told him.

Ray-Lo continued to be still on the floor, trying not to die.

Out on the rooftop, twelve stories up, YB still chased Crown. They continued to fire rounds at each other until Crown's gun was empty. He had nowhere to run and was trapped as YB approaching him.

"You started this, nigga!" Crown yelled out.

YB stood a short distance from Crown. He knew Crown was helpless. YB still had a few shots left.

"You should have stayed dead, nigga! You fucked wit' my family! You fucked wit' my family!" YB screamed in rage.

"You fucked wit' mine first! Chaos was mine. I had that bitch in pocket until you came along and wanted to save a fuckin' ho."

"Niggas like you are a fuckin' disgrace to the game. Where's Chaos?"

"Fuck that bitch! When I see her again, I got somethin' for that ass. I'm gonna rape her somethin' lovely, then put that bitch out on the track twenty-four seven and there ain't shit you gonna do about it."

Down below, they could hear many police sirens blaring in the distance. They knew that dozens of police cars would soon surround the building and lock it down.

Both men glared intensely at each other. YB raised the gun to Crown's head. He hated that man with all his heart. A bullet was too good for Crown. He wanted that muthafucka to hurt and feel some serious pain, but there was no time.

"Nigga, you too pussy to pull the trigger. I'll fuck you like I do my bitches. This ain't over, nigga. This ain't over—"

*Blam!*

YB watched Crown drop on the rooftop. He walked up to the body and stared down at the dead man. He still wasn't satisfied with his death.

"Fuck this!" he muttered.

He dropped the gun, grabbed Crown's body and dragged it to the edge of the rooftop. He then looked down the twelve stories and felt butterflies in his stomach.

He tossed the body off the rooftop and watched it fall to the hard ground. Crown landed in the alleyway face first. It wasn't a pretty sight.

YB stared down at the body and heard the sirens out front. He looked around for his escape and thought about Ray-Lo and Wendy. He needed to see Danielle but knew that jail was not an option right now. He picked up his gun and made a run for it, hoping Ray-Lo and Wendy would be all right.

# 53

Danielle rode silently in the backseat of the cab, feeling somewhat relieved, but couldn't stop crying. The guilt she felt bothered her, but Pastor Moore's words did give her guidance. She wanted to change her life completely and live a life completely free from her past. In order for her to do that, she had to confess.

The cab pulled up in front of her building and she slowly stepped out. Her belly was growing and so was her conscience. This was a chance that she decided to take. The night felt still around her. Danielle took a deep breath and looked around. She was determined to be a mother to her unborn child, no matter what happened in her life.

"I'll be right back," she told the driver.

She walked toward the lobby but stopped in her tracks. Her jaw dropped when she saw YB standing just a few feet ahead of her with blood on his shirt and jacket.

"YB?" Danielle said in shock.

YB smiled and said, "I'm back, baby."

"Oh my God!" Danielle ran to her man, threw her arms around

him and hugged him tightly. Tears of joy and relief flowed down her cheeks.

"I didn't know if you were dead or alive! But you're here. You came back!" Then she remembered the blood on his shirt and pulled away from him. "Baby, what happened?"

"We're good, baby. We're good. I took care of everything. Harlem and Crown are dead," he informed her.

"What . . . what you mean?"

"They can't touch us anymore, I made sure of that," YB said proudly.

Danielle didn't know what to think. She looked into his eyes and saw the love she'd been looking for all her life.

Dawn was soon breaking and Danielle held onto her man in confusion. He had gone to war with dangerous men from Philly just to protect her and the baby. She loved him but knew something was wrong.

YB hugged his girl as the sun began to rise. He cried as he held Danielle in his arms. He cried, thinking about family members he'd loss. He missed his people from Philly and wished that he could bring them back but he knew a new life awaited him in New York.

Danielle felt safe in his arms. She grabbed his T-shirt, not caring about the blood on it. "I'm so sorry, baby. I'm so sorry. But I think it needed to be done."

"What needed to be done?" YB asked.

She hesitated and continued to hug him a little bit longer. Then she said, "I called the cops and confessed to everything that went on in Philly. They know about the murders and the money," she admitted.

YB's heart stopped. "Baby, you did what?"

"I told them about the murders. I was scared and didn't know if you were coming back home so I talked to a detective and gave up everything."

For some reason, YB wasn't mad at her, though. He had just escaped a shootout, killed two men, and his boy, Ray-Lo, was probably dead. A jail sentence was inevitable.

"We gonna be a'ight, baby. We gonna be a'ight," YB said.

As the sun continued to rise, YB heard the sirens piercing the morning air. He knew that they were coming for him. He knew his time with Danielle was over and it was time to pay for his sins.

He continued to hug Danielle, blocking out the sounds of his fate. He closed his eyes and shed a few tears while the police came nearer.

"I love you, Danielle," he proclaimed.

"Baby, I love you too," she replied.

Two police cars raced up the block and stopped abruptly in front of the loving couple, holding each other as the sun rose above them.

Officers jumped from their cars with their guns drawn and shouted, "Get down on the ground now! Get down!"

They had their weapons aimed at every part of YB and Danielle and were ready for anything. YB ignored them for a short moment, holding his woman in his arms. He knew it would probably be a long while before he would be with Danielle again.

The cops continued to shout out their commands and kept their guns trained on the couple. YB squeezed Danielle and said to her, "I'm glad that I took that chance with you. You gave me hope and a future. Whatever happens, I will always love you."

Danielle didn't want to let him go, but knew it was safer to do so. She could hear the chaos going on around her and knew that a normal life sometimes felt impossible. At this point, her life felt like a movie playing in her head.

YB gently released Danielle, raised his arms in the air, and slowly got down on his knees. By now the block was flooded with cops and the sirens woke most of the neighbors as they observed the arrests from a short distance.

YB was quickly subdued and put into handcuffs, while Danielle was detained for questioning. For Danielle it felt like since the day she was born, the nightmare would never end for her. Her life was chaotic; her mother definitely gave her the right middle name, because it fit her life so well.

# EPILOGUE

Danielle gave birth to a healthy baby girl and named her daughter Blessing. She wanted to break that cycle of abandonment. She became a wonderful mother to her baby girl and continued to do hair in the shop with Wendy.

Wendy's wounds eventually healed. She was never upset with Danielle due to the beating by Crown and Harlem. They were still best friends and loved each other like mother and daughter. Wendy became the godmother to Blessing and treated her goddaughter like her very own.

Danielle's life gradually became normal. She went to church with Wendy, got baptized, and became a Christian. She also became a motivational speaker to young teenage girls.

Unfortunately, her life with YB wasn't so happily ever after. Even though Danielle wasn't charged with the murders in Philly because YB took responsibility for the crimes, they hit YB with eight counts, including first degree murder in both New York and Philly, resisting arrest, and gun possession. He copped a plea and got twenty-five to life in an upstate prison. They wanted to give him the death penalty, but his lawyers bargained for a lesser sentence.

Even though YB's future looked bleak, he felt a sense of peace. Danielle brought their daughter to see him a month after she gave birth and YB got to finally hold his baby girl in his arms. He knew that Danielle was going to provide Blessing the life that Danielle herself never had, and he was content with that.

He was saddened by the loss of another good friend. Ray-Lo died of his injuries right after the shooting. YB had to learn to live with the murders and pain he had caused throughout his life.

Danielle convinced YB to repent for his sins and accept Christ into his life. He changed his ways and became a better man for hisAnout the Autyhor family. He knew that with good behavior, anything was possible—even parole.

It was a new beginning for the couple and they wanted love and a family for Blessing. It was a new day for everyone.

# ABOUT THE AUTHOR

Who is Erica Hilton? Writing under a pen name, this prolific writer is an Essence® Magazine bestselling author. She currently resides in New York. Or does she?

# MELODRAMA PUBLISHING ORDER FORM
## WWW.MELODRAMAPUBLISHING.COM

| Title | ISBN | QTY | PRICE | TOTAL |
|---|---|---|---|---|
| Wifey | 0-971702-18-7 | | $15.00 | $ |
| I'm Still Wifey | 0-971702-15-2 | | $15.00 | $ |
| Life After Wifey | 1-934157-04-X | | $15.00 | $ |
| Still Wifey Material | 1-934157-10-4 | | $15.00 | $ |
| Sex, Sin & Brooklyn | 0-971702-16-0 | | $15.00 | $ |
| Histress | 1-934157-03-1 | | $15.00 | $ |
| Den of Sin | 1-934157-08-2 | | $15.00 | $ |
| Eva: First Lady of Sin | 1-934157-01-5 | | $15.00 | $ |
| Eva 2: First Lady of Sin | 1-934157-11-2 | | $15.00 | $ |
| The Madam | 1-934157-05-8 | | $15.00 | $ |
| Shot Glass Diva | 1-934157-14-7 | | $15.00 | $ |
| Dirty Little Angel | 1-934157-19-8 | | $15.00 | $ |
| Cartier Cartel | 1-934157-18-X | | $15.00 | $ |
| In My Hood | 0-971702-19-5 | | $15.00 | $ |
| In My Hood 2 | 1-934157-06-6 | | $15.00 | $ |
| A Deal With Death | 1-934157-12-0 | | $15.00 | $ |
| Tale of a Train Wreck Lifestyle | 1-934157-15-5 | | $15.00 | $ |
| A Sticky Situation | 1-934157-09-0 | | $15.00 | $ |
| Jealousy | 1-934157-07-4 | | $15.00 | $ |
| Life, Love & Lonliness | 0-971702-10-1 | | $15.00 | $ |
| The Criss Cross | 0-971702-12-8 | | $15.00 | $ |
| Stripped | 1-934157-00-7 | | $15.00 | $ |
| The Candy Shop | 1-934157-02-3 | | $15.00 | $ |
| Cross Roads | 0-971702-18-7 | | $15.00 | $ |
| A Twisted Tale of Karma | 0-971702-14-4 | | $15.00 | $ |

(GO TO THE NEXT PAGE)

## MELODRAMA PUBLISHING ORDER FORM
### (CONTINUED)

| Title/Author | ISBN | QTY | PRICE | TOTAL |
|---|---|---|---|---|
| Up, Close & Personal | 0-971702-11-X | | $9.95 | $ |
| Menace II Society | 0-971702-17-9 | | $15.00 | $ |
| | | | | |
| | | | | |
| | | | | |
| | | | | |
| | | | | |
| | | | Subtotal | |
| | | | Shipping** | |
| | | | Tax* | |
| | Total | | | |

Instructions:

*NY residents please add $1.79 Tax per book.

**Shipping costs: $3.00 first book, any additional books please add $1.00 per book.

Incarcerated readers receive a 25% discount. Please pay $11.25 per book and apply the same shipping terms as stated above.

Mail to:

MELODRAMA PUBLISHING

P.O. BOX 522

BELLPORT, NY 11713